The Hotel at the End of Time

Michael James

ALSO BY MICHAEL JAMES

Trapped

For Brady.

Again and always.

Contents

Chapter 1

Vain attempts to rob a bank.

What worried Vain most about robbing a bank wasn't the danger, or the cops, or getting caught. No, it was that it might not work, and then she'd need to consider Roman's insane and unworkable plan to get normal jobs. But jobs, even temporary ones, meant staying in one place. Talking to other people. Trapping yourself. Pass, pass, and pass.

Was it her first bank robbery? No way to tell. She had no memory of anything before the Hotel, so possibly, she'd been an expert. Maybe that had been her past life; going from town to town, robbing banks, making her getaway while clutching dollar-sign inscribed sacks to her chest.

Probably not. More likely this was her first, and something cool to cross off her bucket list. Item number one on her bucket list was to create a bucket list. A problem for later.

Her original plan included dressing up like cowboys and talking in a western drawl because western bank robberies ruled, but Roman pointed out that while entertaining, it would draw more attention. She reluctantly agreed but insisted on wearing a cowboy hat, which made him laugh. Their lives didn't hold enough joy, and the risk was worth it to make him smile.

"It's nearly six." The enormous cowboy hat fell over her eyes and she pushed it back. "Bank-robbing time, y'all."

"I'm not sure an ATM counts as a bank," Roman said. "And stop talking in that horrible accent."

"See here, little lady. An ATM machine counts as a bank."

"I'm not a lady, and ATM stands for 'Automated Teller Machine', so you don't need to add the 'machine' at the end."

"After we rob this ATM machine," she said, emphasizing the last word, "we should have enough cash to keep us going for a while. Yeehaw."

Going where, though? She had no idea, although she'd never admit that to Roman. He counted on her to keep them moving and invent plans to keep them safe. Deal with today and make it to tomorrow. Life, since the Hotel, came in heartbeats.

From their vantage across the street, Vain scouted the ATM nestled into the building's brick exterior. Cars and pedestrians made it easy for them to hide in the open. Downtown Denver buzzed with crowds this time of night and no one paid attention to them, rad cowboy hat notwithstanding. Even if anyone looked, all they'd see is a mild-faced, brown-haired man and a girl with huge eyes and angular features wearing an absurd ten-gallon hat. Two people out for a stroll, staring intently at a bank, talking in cowboy lingo. Standard, everyday stuff.

Vain cracked her knuckles, impatient to get started. The best plans were like wrestling matches; not a detailed list of moves, but rather a series of big spots that led to a finish. Lock up, do a table spot, nail a suplex, done.

"A good plan is a lot like wrestling," she said to Roman so he'd have a chance to acknowledge her clever comparison.

"I've told you before," Roman said, pinching the bridge of his nose. "A good plan is exactly unlike wrestling. A table spot? Like when a wrestler gets thrown through a table? What's the analogous 'table spot' in this specific plan?"

"Shush." She waggled her finger at him. "Should be showtime soon. Y'all."

They had been scoping out that ATM for a few days. Every night at six o'clock, the bank guy came, opened the door, and refilled the money with stacks of bills from his giant money truck. That would be their moment to strike.

"If this were a movie, I'd say something like 'Roman, let's go over the plan one last time' and dump a bunch of exposition." She liked movies.

"Yeah, movies are great. Screenwriters are hacks. The guy is coming. Are you ready?"

"Yes." She pulled a sliver of energy from him. It filled her up; inflated her. He trembled, almost imperceptibly, but she noticed. No matter how he tried to hide his discomfort from her, she always saw. Screw the Hotel for making them like this.

The bank guy opened the ATM and Vain got to work. She concentrated the energy into a circular shape, no bigger than a plum. To anyone watching, it would appear like a girl in a cowboy hat was having a staring contest with a wall. She guided the invisible energy ball past the man's shoulder and into the opening of the machine. It was hard to see that far across the street, but she didn't need to be precise. She only needed to wedge it into the compartment of the ATM.

"Got it." She pushed the ball into place.

"Okay," Roman said. Sweat glistened on his forehead despite the cool night air. "Anchor it."

They'd never tried anything like that, but they were almost out of money and entirely out of options. Roman didn't like stealing, but Vain reminded him that banks weren't people, they were things, and it didn't technically count as stealing. She likened it to removing lint dust from a vacuum cleaner, another kick-ass analogy he seemed to find deeply unsatisfying.

"Come on." She plucked his sleeve. "Time to go."

A tree-filled park across the street provided plenty of nooks and alcoves to hide in. They'd picked out their spot already, a couple yards inside the tall gates and off to the side. A dirt path branched off the main paved strip and led to a wooden bench behind some broad bushes. The bank was no longer visible, but they were close enough for Vain to control the energy ball. No one would bug them.

Eventually, the ATM-guy would finish his work and close up the machine with her invisible energy ball inside. All they needed to do was wait for dark and then she'd detonate it, breaking the door and giving them access to all that sweet, sweet guilt-free money. Money that Roman believed would be destroyed along with the door, but he didn't have any better ideas.

She played with her fingers while she waited and Roman rested his head on his jacket. He closed his eyes, his breath coming out in shallow puffs. Was he greyer? Maybe. Maintaining the energy ball meant pulling from him constantly. Only a little, but it took its toll.

She loved Roman. He was her best and only friend in the entire world. It bothered her when he suffered, even a little, and she wished her ideas didn't require her to suck energy from his body like some kind of horrible leech. For the hundredth time, she promised herself that one day they wouldn't need to do this anymore. She'd stop the Hotel. Somehow.

Plans and strategies whirling through her head, she hardly noticed when someone entered the alcove and sat on the bench between them. Roman groaned and opened his eyes.

Vain bristled, ready to tell this new person to scram when she caught a better look at him. She gasped and her heart did cartwheels. Tall dude. Suspicious eyes and light brown hair. Permanent frown. Cauliflower ears.

A Wyatt.

He'd found them. Vain tried to get to her feet, but the Wyatt gripped her arm, painfully. With his other, he jammed a gun into Roman's side. She froze.

"Sit down, Vain," said the Wyatt.

All thoughts of ATM robberies vanished from her mind. She dropped the link to the energy ball but kept the conduit to Roman open. With the Wyatt holding her in place, her entire body stiffened. Roman recoiled when he realized who had joined them.

"Good girl," said the Wyatt. It took all of her self-control to prevent herself from trembling at the sound of his smooth and greasy voice. He pressed against her; touching her. She wanted to throw up. "We've been following you for days. Appreciate you finding the perfect spot for this chat."

"I appreciate you being a jerk," she stammered. God. What a terrible comeback. The Wyatt's unexpected appearance had her rattled. How did the Hotel find them? They'd been so careful. The Wyatt pressed his gun in Roman's side and her eyes froze on it. A gun. Pointed at Roman. Her Roman.

"I know you have the Padlock on you," the Wyatt said. "Give it to me. Once I have it, we'll talk about what happens next."

"I threw it in the river," she said. Shoot, did Denver even have a river?

"You'd never part with it. We both know that. Listen, Arthur doesn't want to hurt you, okay? He wants his property back. You give me the Padlock and I'll let you go."

The Wyatt was lying. His aw-shucks smile hid the monster underneath. The instant he had the Padlock, he'd kill them both. Roman licked his lips and gave her a terrified glance.

"The Padlock is in my shoe," Vain lied. The Padlock rested in her pocket. Close enough. "I need to stand up to get it. Okay?"

"Don't try anything, Vain. If you so much as breathe funny, I'm shooting your battery. I don't need him. I don't need you, either. No weird stuff. Clear?"

"Clear." Vain rose to her feet. The Wyatt dropped his grin, all business now, and pushed the gun further into Roman's side. "I'm going to bend over and get the Padlock from my shoe."

"I'm serious," said the Wyatt. "A single twitch and I'll kill him. I'm not joking."

"I don't think you're joking," Vain said. Theoretically, she could take him out with an energy blast to the skull. Easy; pull from Roman and attack. But if she looked at the Wyatt while doing it, she'd squint, or her pupils would dilate, or something. Wyatts were tricky, and they knew the signs when a Utility pulled from a Conduit.

She'd need to strike without looking at him. Risky, but she didn't see any other way.

She bent over to fumble at her shoe, eyes on the ground. He wouldn't be able to read any signs from her. All she needed to do was fire off a blind shot and hope it hit him, not Roman. Half a foot separated them. Almost nothing. She might miss. If she missed, she'd kill Roman. Where had the Wyatt's head been? She concentrated to her left, praying she didn't miss. Her mouth flooded with sour bile.

"You're taking too long," the Wyatt said, and she fired an energy blast with her mind. Something wet splatted against her cheek, and she gasped. From the corner of her eye, Roman's worn sneakers pressed against the Wyatt's leather shoes. Neither moved. She couldn't make herself turn her head.

"Holy shit," Roman said.

Vain jumped to her feet. The Wyatt hung over the back of the bench, half his head missing. Blood dripped off Roman's face, and he wiped it with his sleeve. Vain's eyes were suddenly misty. Allergies? Probably allergies. She fanned herself with both hands.

"Roman," she breathed. "Roman." It was all she could say. He was alive. It worked. She didn't kill him. Why were her allergies acting up, though? Strange.

"Vain. I'm okay. I promise." Roman said. He had his frowny face on. He didn't touch her because she didn't like that.

"I know you're okay. I didn't worry for a second." She wiped allergy-based moisture from her cheeks. He was safe. Her stomach unclenched, letting her breathe again.

"How did he find us?" Roman asked.

"Doesn't matter." Now that the danger had passed, her mind revved into overdrive. "We have to go. Now. How much cash do you have on you?"

"Less than a hundred," he said. Vain bit her lip. She had around six hundred bucks. Hardly enough.

"The train station," she said. "We'll take a cab there and get on the first train."

"What about our stuff back at the motel?"

"It's gone. We're leaving it. We have to go. Come on. Use your jacket to wipe off the blood. You look like Carrie at the prom."

Roman nodded and cleaned himself up. He still looked horrible and rust-stained, but it was a marginal improvement. He knew the drill, same as she did. If one Wyatt appeared, there would be more. They hunted in packs.

Her dumb cowboy hat had fallen from her head in the commotion, and she left it in the dirt, feeling stupid. What if the hat led the Wyatt to them? But she knew the truth. It wasn't the hat. It was the Padlock.

She reached into her pocket and removed it, turning it over in her hands, as always struck by how improbably heavy it was for its size. It had a burnished gold base, with the word *SAFE* scratched into the metal. It emitted a faint glow and vibrated ever so slightly in her palm. All their problems traced back to that simple object; that Device; that thing they stole a year ago when they left the Hotel. Such a small thing to cause all that trouble.

"Chin up," she said. Chin up felt like something to say in that kind of situation; something a spy would say, or maybe a war hero. "Stay sharp," she added. She wasn't scared. She wasn't. There were more Wyatts out there, but she would keep her *chin up* and *stay sharp*. What else?

"Keep your head on a swivel," she finished. There. Perfect.

"Come on," Roman said. Without sparing a backward glance for the dead Wyatt, they ran onto the main road. Time to put all of her advice to use. Chin up. Sharp. Swivel head.

There, on the corner. Another Wyatt. Same brown hair, same angry face, same weird bowlegged way of walking that made it seem like he wanted to knock down an invisible wall with his forehead.

"I see one," she said. Her voice sounded small. The fist around her heart squeezed. Hard.

"Me too." Roman pointed to the opposite end of the street. Another Wyatt. That Wyatt signaled and walked towards them, followed by another.

"I think we should run." She tried to sound brave, so Roman wouldn't panic. Her heart thumped, but that was probably because she'd run out of the park.

"I agree," Roman said. He sounded terrified.

Vain picked a direction at random and ran, shoving her way through the crowd. Behind, the Wyatts also picked up speed, realizing that the chase had started.

"Stop them," one of the Wyatt's yelled from thirty feet behind. "They stole my wallet!"

The world being what it was, the Wyatt's plan backfired. Now that the crowds of pedestrians believed her and Roman to be criminals, they parted to either side, giving them a clear path down the sidewalk.

Two could play at that game. "Stop them," she yelled over her shoulder. What was worse than stealing a wallet? "They're chasing us because they want to steal our… tennis rackets." People moved further apart, and she reflected that everyone, generally, sucked.

They sprinted for three blocks, her ragged gasps getting louder and louder in her ears. A one-way street littered with orange pylons and construction vehicles forked off from the main road. She skidded into the turn, and Roman crashed into her back, sending them both tumbling to the ground. Her elbow banged against something hard, and her teeth came together with a painful clack.

"Come on." Roman hoisted her to her feet and wiped his forehead. Rivulets of sweat created jagged tracks through the dried blood on his cheeks.

Vain's breath sawed through her lungs. The Wyatts. Where were the Wyatts?

"There." She pointed between two buildings. "The alley."

"Really?" Roman asked.

She shoved him and got moving.

Only a few feet separated the buildings. She dodged between overflowing dumpsters and discarded cardboard boxes filled with filthy rags. The odor of frying grease clung to everything, and she gagged through the scent, trying to breathe through her mouth. Every breath sent a stitch of misery down her side. At the end of the alley, a rusted chain-link fence with barbed wire at the top blocked their exit.

She slammed her palm into the fence. "Fire escapes. Where?" was all she managed to gasp.

"Wrong city. Not New York." Roman bent over to catch his breath.

The Wyatts appeared at the mouth of the alley, and Vain bit off a moan of fear. The fence was too high to climb. They needed to move.

"Come on."

A sign over the nearest door said, 'deliveries in front'. Vain kicked it open, thinking she probably looked sort of cool when she did that. They stumbled into the middle of a crowded kitchen. Dozens of people carrying sizzling pans of food stopped what they were doing, mouths hanging open.

"Hey!" A man with a stained apron yelled at them. "You can't be in here."

In front of her, a rack covered in pastries made a tempting target. She knocked it over as she ran past, followed by yells of outrage.

"The people chasing us will pay for the cakes." She shouldered through the doors into a noisy restaurant.

"At the back," Roman said. "Stairs."

She ran ahead of Roman, ignoring the cries behind them, ignoring the commotion they were causing, ignoring the intensifying stitch in her side that reminded her she had not prepared for this much running.

They hustled up five flights of stairs before stopping at a fire escape. She pushed the door open and stumbled out onto a gravel-covered roof. They both bent over, sucking in huge gasps of air.

"Did we lose them?" Roman asked.

"I'm positive we did," Vain said as the rooftop door slammed open and three Wyatts burst out.

Everything happened at once. Two Wyatts threw themselves at Roman while one tackled her to the ground. She kicked and scratched, but the Wyatt outweighed her by about a hundred pounds, and he pinned her underneath his body. One hand gripped her throat; his other hand rummaged through her pockets. She choked and struggled. Muffled grunts and the sound of fists hitting flesh came from somewhere to the right.

"Leave him alone," she coughed.

"Leave her alone!" Roman yelled at the same time.

The Wyatts addressed neither of their complaints and instead continued to hammer them both. A huge, meaty Wyatt fist thumped against her head and spots blossomed in front of her eyes. She fought her way out from underneath him, inching towards the building's edge. A three-foot lip circled the roof, and she pressed her back up against it. The two Wyatts threw Roman to the ground beside her and he groaned. Bruises showed on his face. Her lip curled back into a growl.

Maybe it was the end.

She wanted to tell Roman how much she loved him, how much his friendship had meant. Christ, hug him. Why couldn't she hug him? She'd never done any of those things but wanted to. Someday. As long as she drew breath, she'd fight for that.

"Take another step and I'll drop the Padlock." She stood and held her clenched fist over the lip of the building, glaring at the Wyatts. One shrugged.

"Okay."

Vain's chest heaved. Roman spat bright red blood onto the roof and cradled his face in his hands. In the distance, a lone bird let out a solitary cry. One Wyatt scratched his nose. The silence stretched.

"I mean it," she tried again.

"We believe you," the lead Wyatt said. "We will pick up the indestructible magic Padlock from the ground below after you drop it. It's irritating, but whatever."

"You stupid clones." She poured all her contempt into the last word.

"No. We're not clones. Clones would imply we're identical copies."

"It's more accurate to call us instances," the second Wyatt said. "We're each a unique instance of the same person."

"We find the term 'clone' to be offensive," said the third. "After we finish this violent abduction, you owe us an apology."

Vain rubbed her forehead in frustration.

Her bond to Roman allowed her to sense his presence. He was like a permanent resident in her head. She couldn't make out his thoughts or emotions, but the essence of him always existed. He was too beat up to take any more from without rendering him unconscious. But without energy, her powers didn't work. She was defenseless. Option A equaled bad and option B equaled terrible.

But maybe she didn't need a full amount. Maybe a trickle would do.

Okay, so that was a tough spot to be in, but she could be scared and useless, or she could do something.

"Don't kill me." She dropped to her knees, hands in front of her, locked in prayer. "I'll give you anything you want. Sexful things." She tried to make her eyes smouldery and puckered her lips.

One Wyatt sighed and snapped at the other. "Take it from her."

She allowed a bit of Roman's energy to flow into her. It was barely anything; a feather-light kiss. As the Wyatt approached, she held the Padlock in the palms of her hands like an offering. He reached out.

Now.

She pulled the Padlock behind her back with one hand and grabbed him with the other. She bound him to her in an energy ball and pulled with all her strength. It caught the Wyatt off-balance and he lurched forward. She released the energy, and he tripped, going over the edge of the roof.

"Ha!" she said.

Unexpectedly, he pulled her with him.

"Shit!" she said.

The sensation of falling took her by surprise, but less so than the reality of her plan not working.

As the ground rushed up to meet her, her final thoughts were of Roman.

Chapter 2

Roman tries to escape.

Roman looked up as the Wyatt pulled Vain off the roof. He reached out and yelled, "No!" ineffectually before she vanished.

"Holy crap," one of the Wyatts exclaimed. He rushed to the ledge and peered over. The other followed and let out a low whistle. From far below, the sounds of car alarms and people screaming floated to the top of the building.

"The amount of blood in the human body has always surprised me," the Wyatt said. "You think you have a handle on how much eight liters is, but then it's splashed across the pavement and you realize it's quite the amount." He shook his head. "One of life's miracles."

Roman tried to block out what he was hearing. There would be time to mourn later. He suspected grieving over Vain's death would soon become the singular focus of his life, but that was a problem for a different time. For now, he had to escape. With Vain and the Padlock gone, he was useless to the Wyatts, which meant he was disposable.

Both Wyatts stood peering over the edge of the roof with their backs to him. His entire body ached from the beating they'd given him, but he lurched to his feet on drunken legs and dashed for the door that led into the building.

He made it about two feet before falling.

"Oh. Hey," one of the Wyatts said. "We're not done with you. Stop trying to escape."

Roman ignored them and crawled towards the door. Footsteps crunched behind him, and something hit him in the back of the neck with enough force to knock him stupid.

"When I say stop trying to escape, that means stop moving," the Wyatt said. "Just a heads up for next time."

"What an asshole," said the other. "Some people. Get him tied up while I figure out what to do next." Their voices drifted into Roman's consciousness as if from a great distance.

"It was your bright idea to force them into a corner. I told you to wait. We could have come at them as a group."

"I'm not the idiot who threatened her."

"That idiot is now dead in a park with half his head missing, so he got what he deserved."

"What an absolute disaster." For several moments, the only noise perceptible to Roman was the labored sound of his own breathing. The Wyatts continued talking.

"We have to report what happened."

"I hate it when we die. Really makes you think about what it all means, you know?"

"Do we get health insurance?"

"I'm almost positive we don't."

"Well, what if the one on the ground is only mangled, with broken limbs and permanent spinal damage or whatever? That could get awkward."

"That human slurry on the ground seems dead to me."

"What if he's not? I don't want to picture myself being fed through a tube. That's a grim insight into my own mortality that I don't need."

"I'm sure Trick will work something out."

Even through his haze, the name Trick jolted Roman to awareness. He rolled over to better see the Wyatts standing over him, continuing their conversation. Trick was Arthur's second in command, and if he had taken an interest, it meant serious trouble. It was one thing to have the Wyatts after you. It was another to deal with Trick.

"We weren't supposed to kill them," the other Wyatt said. "Trick was perfectly clear on that point. Do not, under any circumstances, kill the girl."

"What if we were never here?"

"You mean, get rid of this one altogether? It won't work. They can't suddenly be off the grid. Trick knows we were on their tail. He'll never buy it."

"Shit. Well, let's grab him and go from there."

"Yeah." The Wyatt looked around. "Man, this is a disaster. No Padlock and two of us dead. Trick will be livid. You know what he'll say? He'll say, 'How is it that four of you couldn't stop a single girl and her walking solar panel?'"

They continued to argue, but Roman forced himself to ignore them and look for a way out. They were going to take him back to Trick. He'd almost rather be dead. He feared the Hotel; Trick terrified him.

What would Vain do? She'd make some obscure movie reference before effortlessly inventing some plan to save them all. She was brilliant and unstoppable, but he was only him; simple, harmless Roman. A battery. That's what the Wyatts called the Conduits, both to their face and behind their backs. Bags of meat that generated energy; energy that provided no value unless the Utility was there to pull it out.

If Vain taught him anything, it was that you didn't stop fighting until you were dead, and he wasn't dead yet. Options always existed. All he needed was a distraction; something to take the Wyatts' focus off him. Then, he would break for the door, maybe hide in a washroom or something.

But what to use? There. That electrical wire dangling above the roof. It looked frayed, and he could-

One of the Wyatts lumbered close, packaged him up, and zip-tied his arms behind his back.

Oh.

"Come on," said the Wyatt. "Pick up the battery and we'll take him to the safe house."

They dragged him to his feet. His ribs groaned in protest, and his knee gave an alarming click. He leaned against the Wyatt, and his face flushed in hot shame. He wrestled himself from the Wyatt's grip and stumbled away. Sadly, also away from the door, but any port in a storm.

"Jesus Christ." The Wyatt sighed behind him. Something struck him on the back of the leg and he dropped to his knees. The Wyatt grabbed him by the hair and pulled his head back, fist cocked to deliver another punch. Roman shut his eyes, bracing himself for the blow.

He waited.

"I think if I punch him again, it'll kill him," the Wyatt said.

Roman peeked through a single eye.

The Wyatt leaned forward. "Buddy, you don't look so good. I think you have a concussion. Can you stop being a douchebag for a second? We've got stuff to deal with here and you're not helping. Why don't you sit there and cling to consciousness while we figure our shit out?"

Roman lashed out with a vicious headbutt. The Wyatt moved away and Roman fell forward onto his face.

"Okay. He's not going to stop. I'm putting him out. We'll carry him downstairs and get out of here. Cops are coming soon, anyway."

Something sharp pinched the back of his leg. A needle. His vision swam and darkened, and the last thing he heard was, "Jesus, what an asshole."

Chapter 3

Emma explains how names work.

Emma wasn't having the best day of her life.

She shouldn't have agreed to this dumb speed-dating event, but her friends convinced her to go. *You need to meet someone,* they said. *You need to get out more,* they said. Funny advice. In her experience, people who had met someone stopped going out because they stayed home with the person they met. You went out to stop going out. Why not skip the middleman and stay home? Case in point, none of her friends had come with her.

She didn't have time for this. Between work and graduate studies, a social life would remain a dim and distant theoretical. Besides, she enjoyed living within her routine. Wake up, study. Work, work, study. Make dinner, study. TV, study, study. Life had so many secrets waiting to be uncovered. Why bother with anything else?

This bar was a little outside the usual college hangouts; the kind of place where a drunk would never get cut off and everybody knew their name. Only here, it was more a horrible commentary on the ruthless indifference of the free market and not a charmingly quaint theme song.

Someone had organized the tables so the women sat with their backs to the wall while the men shuffled around the inside. The overhead lights had their brightness set to 'flattering'. Dim enough to hide flaws, but not so dark that it became creepy. In fairness, most of the people she'd met seemed nice enough, but small talk made her uncomfortable, and she stumbled through conversations struggling to make genuine connections.

While she wasn't unused to attention, she preferred her own company. Some guys seemed attracted to any redheads which made her feel less like a person and more like a middle-age crisis car. Or whatever the equivalent was for guys approaching thirty.

She checked her phone. Eight-thirty. Halfway through the night. The next guy sauntered up to her table, wearing a white tank top under a hoodie, with baggy pants that sagged below his hips. He leaned back in the chair as the buzzer sounded, giving them ten rushed minutes to fall in love. She introduced herself.

"Hey," he said. "I'm Stan." He reached out to shake. "If you don't mind my saying, you're really pretty. I have a thing for redheads."

Strike one.

"Anyway, my friends call me Smoove Dick."

"I'm sorry," she said. "Smooth what?"

"*Smoove*," he corrected. "Not smooth. It's like '*groove*', but even smoother than that, so *smoove*."

She attacked the linguistics of that sentence from several different angles but found it impenetrable. Unsure of how to respond, she nodded.

"Smoove Dick is my rap handle," he said. "I'm a rapper."

"Oh, okay." She knew rap, sort of. "So, you're like a DJ or something?"

"No. DJs spin tracks. I spit rhymes."

She fiddled with her braid, confused.

"They put down beats, and I flow over it."

"Sorry. I don't understand what any of that means."

He opened his mouth to clarify, but she held up a hand and waved him off. "It's fine. You don't need to disambiguate any further. I'm good."

An awkward pause followed, the type that only ensued after you told someone your preferred name was 'Smoove'.

"So, should I call you Stan or Smoove—I'm sorry, you said—Dick?"

"Yeah." He seemed proud.

"Is your middle name Richard?"

"No, it's Jonathan."

Emma squinted. "Hey, do you find it strange that no one ever goes by the common version of their middle name? For instance, my full name is Emma Elizabeth Patterson, but I bet no one would say 'Emma Beth'." She paused and tapped a finger against her chin. "Okay, maybe if I was from Alabama."

He laughed. "You're funny."

She didn't mean to be funny. The oddity of his nickname had her mentally snagged, and she needed more information.

"If Jonathan is your middle name, wouldn't you be Smoove Jon?" She snapped her fingers. "I know. Your rap name could be Rapping Fresh Stan." She was proud of herself for coming up with such a good rap name on the spot. "Why would it be Smoove Dick?"

As soon as she said it out loud, she realized where the second part of his name came from and blushed.

"You know," he said. Unfortunately, she did. "I'm Smoove like butter. With my moves." He gestured vaguely towards his crotch.

She was vaguely nauseated and entirely finished with the conversation.

Strike two.

On the spot, she decided baseball was too lenient on batters. Two strikes were plenty. Three were too many.

Eight minutes left. God help her. She gamely soldiered on.

"That's fascinating," she said, not at all fascinated. "I always wondered how people came up with rap names. Like how did Grandmaster Flash decide to be a grandmaster? And why the Fresh *Prince* of Bel-Air instead of the Fresh *Viscount*? Does a Prince outrank a Grandmaster in rap circles? I'm not sure of the hierarchy. Technically, one would own a Duchy and the other would be a great bridge player, so it's tough to tell."

He tugged at his ear, seemingly unimpressed with her knowledge of rap titles. Her nerves were getting the best of her and she rambled when she was nervous. Speed dating was not her friend. She continued without a pause for breath.

"How does Dr. Dre fit in, given that a Doctor isn't a designation of nobility? Would he be like an adjutant? Also, do you think Sir Mix-a-lot got knighted by the Fresh Prince?"

"Do you want to hear some of my rhymes?" he interrupted, mistaking her panicked rambling for interest.

"God, no," she said, way too fast. He looked hurt, and she tried to recover. "I mean, you understand. The bar. The noise." She attempted to make a gesture that would convey that bars are bad acoustics for freestyle rap, which ended up being a weird double hand wave, but Smoove Dick missed the nuance.

"It's tight," he said. "Check this." He straightened in his chair and tapped out a simple beat on the table, bopping his head to the rhythm. "I crush it when I rhyme, and my flow and beats are sick, your mouth can call me Smoove and your hand can grab my d—"

"Would you look at that," she said. "I bet they'll be calling the buzzer any second now." Despite not wearing a watch, she tapped her wrist so he would know where she kept time. "It was nice meeting you, Mr. Dick, or Smooth Stan. I hope your rapping works out."

"There's still like six minutes left?"

She began to explain that time is variable based on who is perceiving it when a massive charge of electricity slammed into her brain. Her back arched and she tried to scream, but no sound came out. A vibrant pain, unlike anything she'd ever known, coursed through her body. She fell out of her chair, convulsing and grinding her teeth.

In the tiny part of her mind where coherent thoughts still formed, she mused that it might be a better alternative to continuing a conversation with Smoove Dick. As she arched and seized, he jumped to his feet and yelled, "Hey, help! This chick is having a seizure!", then crouched beside her and wrung his hands.

The last thought that filtered through her collapsing brain was that her rap name would be Viscountess Emma Rapsalot.

*

"No, you have to blow, not suck. Give me her mouth."

Before that exact moment, Emma would have been hard-pressed to come up with worse words to regain consciousness to, but there she was with a winner.

She blinked. Hands slid under her neck and someone plugged her nose.

"I'm fi-ormph—"

A mouth clamped over hers and blew hot, vodka-soaked air into her lungs.

She coughed and jerked up, pushing random hands out of the way. Beside her crouched Smoove Dick and the man who had been giving her mouth-to-mouth, who, thankfully, was not Smoove Dick.

"Are you okay, miss? Take it easy." A guy with a chin-beard rubbed her back. She thought she remembered him as one of the event coordinators. "Move away, everyone," he said to the crowd who had gathered around. "Give her some space."

The gaggle of curious bar patrons made concerned cooing noises and many of them had their phones out, filming the whole embarrassing incident. Now that she was conscious and not dying, they were losing interest.

"I'm okay." She waved everyone away. "I just…" She just what, actually? She had no idea what happened. One second she had been unhappily talking to Smoove Dick, and the next she woke up on the floor. Was that her way of getting out of the conversation; the social equivalent of throwing up after you ingest poison? It seemed excessive, and at the same time, an appropriate response to the nightmare of Smoove Dick. It was hardly fair that for the rest of her life she would collapse her way out of awkward social situations. Why couldn't she learn to pretend to get a text?

"Yo, you had a seizure," said Smoove Dick, leaning over with his hands on his knees. "Are you okay? Are you epileptic or something? Do you have an eppy pen?"

"What?" Her disorientation made it challenging to follow what he was saying.

"You know," he clarified. "An eppy-leptic pen. You stab yourself with it when you have a seizure." He pantomimed a helpful and terrifying stabbing gesture.

"That's horrible," she said, receiving only confused looks. She shook her head and staggered to her feet, resting her hand on the table as she got up. Legions of horses galloped through her skull, the brutal pounding leaving her dizzy and breathless.

"Do you want me to call an ambulance or anything?" said the event coordinator.

"No. Thank you, though. How long did that last?"

"I'm not sure. A minute? I heard a commotion and this guy yelling." He hitched a thumb at Smoove Dick. "When I came over you were on the floor, having a seizure. Are you sure you don't want an ambulance?"

"No," she said through gritted teeth. The throbbing in her head intensified. "I'll grab an Uber or something."

"I can drive you home," said Smoove Dick. "It's no problem."

She forced her mouth into the shape of a smile. "Thank you, Stan, but I'm okay."

After a few more minutes of protestations and assurances, she convinced everyone she could get home by herself and didn't need an ambulance. Having an abrupt, violent, minute-long seizure wasn't that big a deal, and so on. Smoove Dick made one last play for her phone number, a gesture that was such a gross combination of irritating, creepy, and flattering that it left her even more discombobulated. She rushed out of the bar and into the fresh night air.

Outside, streetlamps cast shadows onto the sidewalks, and people clustered like leaves, rushing to the next party or heading out to dinner. Pulling out her phone, she tapped messages to her friends, telling them the night didn't go terribly well, leaving out the part about the seizure. She wasn't sure how big a deal to make of what happened. She didn't think she had a history of epilepsy in her family, but then again, she didn't even know if epilepsy was hereditary.

Her mom might have an idea. She could call to ask, but then they would get into a whole thing about her not eating enough, or her eating too much, or her eating at the wrong time. Without fail, the result would be that she ate the wrong thing—hot sauce?—and she needed to eat more of the right thing—avocado?—. Her mom was a firm believer that eating caused every mysterious illness while also solving every mysterious illness. Emma debated going to the hospital to get checked out. Was it possible to have a stress-related seizure? She didn't feel stressed, but it wasn't impossible.

Stress wouldn't be a strange occurrence for her; she pushed herself hard. Her friends joked she didn't understand how relaxing worked because she was always reading something. She spent her happiest moments in the company of books. They were easy to relate to and had simple rules. The expectations from a book were the same every time, perfectly spelled out with no ambiguity. You spent all your moments with them, poured over them, and they would tell you their secrets.

Rather than take a cab, she made a split-second decision to walk the entire way home. The fresh air was rejuvenating, and surprisingly, her headache faded a little. With each step, the negative effects of the seizure drifted away. She remembered reading somewhere that seizures left a person drained and exhausted, but she buzzed with energy; it was almost effervescent. She let herself float down the street in a body lighter than air.

On the crowded sidewalk, she weaved through groups of people, and each person she passed sent a fresh jolt into her. Not like a shock, but like a hit of espresso. It was exhilarating.

What the hell was going on? She had a momentary flash of concern, but everything seemed too pure and too right to be dangerous. Bemused, she floated in the ocean of energy that surrounded her and let the waves carry her back to her apartment.

Chapter 4

Vain hates Arthur, like, so much.

Vain screamed. She clamped both hands over her mouth. Her body trembled and her breath came in short bursts.

"What. The. Fuck," she whispered.

She pulled her knees close to her chest and hugged them. An odor like rotten fruit permeated the filthy alleyway she now found herself in. Where was the Wyatt that tumbled off the roof with her? Was this a different alley? A different building? Why was it now broad daylight? It had been dusk when she fell.

Why wasn't she dead? Although she wasn't an expert in how much it took to liquify a falling human, five stories seemed like the upper limit. Both she and the Wyatt should be sloppy puddles of goo; and yet she felt perfectly healthy, if a little shook up.

She inspected her body, looking for injuries. Nothing. Last night, a hangnail irritated her. Now, no hangnail. She focused on her hangnail-less thumb, trying to puzzle through the implications. Something was wrong.

She stood on shaky legs, using the dumpster beside her for support. A wave of dizziness hit and she leaned against the cold and tacky metal, ignoring the smell of garbage and cat urine.

Where was she? More importantly, where was Roman?

Through the link they shared, she reached out for his presence. It seemed distant. Not top-of-the-roof distant, but hundreds-of-miles-away distant. It was as thin and soft as it had ever been. Nothing about that made sense, but the important thing was that the link still existed. If she sensed him, that meant he was alive.

Her stomach clenched, heavy with guilt. It had been her idea to take them to the roof. Only the Wyatt was supposed to topple over the edge, not both of them.

The Padlock.

She still gripped it in her hand. She hadn't even noticed. Typically, the Padlock hummed. Now, it was only cold metal, devoid of any energy. An ordinary thing.

It was also open.

She shivered. She and Roman had been trying to open the stupid thing for a year. They didn't know what it did, but if Arthur wanted it, that was good enough for them. If they could coax it open, perhaps it would lead them to a cache of powerful items or a secret safe. What else could that word scratched into the side mean?

She sighed. All this power at her fingertips, but barely any understanding of how to use it. Through the years they had spent as prisoners in the Hotel, no one bothered to teach them anything. Arthur only used them as solar panels; things he could draw energy from. Energy that he'd dump into the storage device in the center of the Hotel. He didn't like them using their abilities without his permission, and punishment waited for those who disobeyed.

Focus. Time to regroup.

Pro: She was not dead. A feather in her cap, given that she had plummeted off a five-story building.

Pro: She had escaped the Wyatts and was safe. For the moment.

Pro: Roman, judging by the comforting knot of awareness lodged in her brain, was still alive.

Con: He didn't seem to be anywhere close. Given how faint his presence was, he might very well be on the other side of the world.

Con: The Padlock was possibly broken.

Throughout Vain's life, or what little of it she could recall, people had told her that her plans were 'dangerous' or 'insane' or 'dangerously insane'. That was the point, though. Safe and easy plans had safe and easy results. Enormous risks; big payoffs. It's how she got them out of the Hotel and how she'd kept them away from the Wyatts. She was used to stress.

Honestly, though, a day where she flipped off a roof only to wake up in a pile of garbage in a weird alley with a broken magical object—that was stressful, even by her standards.

Vain shook her head. She had two options. Option one, continue to pointlessly muse over things she didn't understand. Or option two, do something. She picked number two. Action over inaction. Always. She'd figure this out like she figured everything else out.

She sauntered out of the alley onto a broad sidewalk where well-dressed men and women sipped their coffees and navigated the busy streets. Cars honked and yelled helpful tips to each other out their windows like 'move' and 'fucking move'. It was chaos. Rush hour bedlam. A man in a suit passed by, head buried in his phone.

"Hey, buddy." She plucked his sleeve. "Where am I?"

He stopped, maintaining his distance with a sour and guarded expression. "Rough night?"

She probably didn't look great, what with being exploded to a new location and waking up in a pile of trash. She ran her fingers through her short, choppy hair to smooth it, but stopped. Excuse her for not having a tiara, or whatever it was he expected.

"Very rough. Help me out, okay? Where am I?"

"Cooper Street," he said, "about four blocks from City Hall."

She twirled her finger. "I'm not a human map, pal. I don't know Denver that well. How close am I to the ATM machine by the big bank? You know, the one by the park?"

His expression turned from mild irritation to slack-jawed surprise. "This is Boston. You're in Boston. How much partying did you do last night? Do you need help?"

"Boston." Her jaw dropped, and she slumped against the side of the building. No wonder Roman felt so far away. How did she end up there? And if she was in Boston, that meant Roman was by himself, surrounded by Wyatts, without her there to protect him. She swallowed against a hot rush of bile.

"Jesus fuck," she said.

"Uh, okay. Gotta go. Good luck." The man stepped around her but seemed to reconsider and pulled out a crumpled twenty that he thrust at her. "Listen, there's a shelter a couple of blocks from here. I think they work with people like you. This is all I have. I'm sorry I can't help."

She hardly noticed taking the money. Her head spun with the implications of what he'd told her. Panic wouldn't get her anywhere and it wouldn't help Roman, but she had to force herself to relax. So many things didn't make sense.

The priority had to be getting back to Denver and bailing Roman out of whatever mess he had gotten himself into. So typical of him to get into trouble without her. She told him to keep close, and just because she had teleported thousands of miles away—

apparently across both space and time—that didn't give him an excuse to stay behind. Some of her sick fear got shoved aside by irritation, which improved her mood. She'd figure this out and find him; and once she had him back, they'd work on the next steps together.

Noon found her in a small sandwich shop munching on a ham and cheese croissant and sipping a diet coke. All of her clothes and belongings traveled with her, including her cash.

The now-dull Padlock sat on the table in front of her. Stealing it when she'd escaped the Hotel was a last-minute decision. She didn't even know what it did, but it was Arthur's favorite plaything, so what else was she supposed to do? Not steal it? An eye for an eye. He ruined her life, so she ruined his right back.

Arthur called them Devices. Physical objects imbued with power that anyone could use. Whatever the Devices did seemed related to the actual object itself, but it's not like she was an expert in this.

So what did the Padlock do? What made this Device so special that Arthur carried it around with him all the time? Why did someone scratch the word 'safe' into the burnished gold base? Her original theory was that it protected a cache of powerful artifacts or something. But what if the word on the side wasn't a *thing*, but a *description*? What if 'safe' referred to what it made the person holding it? Something for protection. When she fell, it activated, released all the energy, and pushed her away from the danger. It kept her *safe*.

It made sense, sort of, or as much as any of it did. It would explain why Arthur wanted it back and why he always carried it with him. Something that protected the person holding it from mortal harm? He'd be pretty pissed off about losing that.

Except she had it. And now it was broken. Whoops.

She finished her sandwich and dusted crumbs off her jeans. Enough thinking. The next step was to get on a bus and find her way back to Roman. Fretting about the trouble he must be in made her jittery with worry. A small voice in the deep recesses of her mind whispered to her that this was all her fault. If she hadn't taken the Padlock, the Wyatts wouldn't have come after them with such force. But if she followed that thought to its conclusion, it meant she was responsible for Roman's predicament. It meant she was responsible for… other things. Things she didn't want to think about.

Her eyes filled, and she blinked to hold the moisture back. The dumb restaurant must have had a gas leak or something. If they had a comment card, she'd fill it out and give them a frowny face rating. Imagine, making her cry. She never cried. Why would she cry? For sure it wasn't caused by thoughts of Roman being beaten up by Wyatts, or dead in Denver, or any one of the other horrible things that pinged through her brain, making her heart flutter in her chest with enough force she had to take several deep breaths to settle it.

Enough. She had to get moving, get herself closer to wherever Roman was. She threw a few bucks on the table and pushed her chair back with a screech. Muttering to herself about the lack of comment cards, she opened the door. A red SUV sat parked across the street. Her breath hitched and before thought caught up to action, she dove back into the diner and crouched beneath the window. A younger couple stopped eating to gawk at her.

"I think I saw Pat Sajak," Vain said, shrugging at them from her spot on the floor.

The woman sniffed and deliberately turned back to her boyfriend. Vain put them out of her mind.

It was probably a random SUV. Thousands of them drove by every day. Just because it was the same model the Wyatts drove, the same model she'd trained herself to always be on the lookout for, it didn't need to mean anything. It could be a coincidence, but usually, coincidence was cause and effect that hadn't been properly introduced.

The red SUV was parked a few buildings up, facing away from the sandwich shop. It seemed innocuous enough, and she had no reason to assume it was the same Wyatts who attacked her. She didn't know the distance between Boston and Denver, but it was unlikely that they could regroup, drive the whole way, and locate the exact spot she was eating lunch, all in this short a time. Without Roman, she had no energy to draw on, and by herself, she possessed the raw punching potential of a five-foot-two human with no training, meaning none. If they had known she was in there, they would have grabbed her.

Somewhat reassured, she crept out of the diner, trying to look normal. She'd do a quick check, make sure it was a normal car, then leave. Cars honked and tires squealed as she scurried across the street and approached the SUV from the back. She *almost* had herself convinced she was overreacting when the passenger door opened.

A Wyatt.

Every Wyatt stood over six feet tall, all solid muscle, with angry frowns and cauliflower ears that looked like raw gristle from decades of fighting. Sometimes the Wyatt would have a goatee; sometimes a beard. Some preferred to shave their heads; some grew their hair long. She didn't know what passed as fashionable in their circles.

That one had his hair parted to the side and wore beige cargo pants, a checkered dress shirt, and a blue suit jacket that strained against the size of his shoulders. A stylish guy about town, out for a good time. Attractive, if you didn't know what he was; but she knew.

The Wyatts were Arthur's hit squad, and she and Roman spent many nights in the Hotel theorizing about where they originated. The rumor she heard was that Arthur picked them out from one of the many versions of Earth he had access to.

At the back of the Hotel, in a section the Utilities were not allowed anywhere near, stood an elevator. An ordinary, run-of-the-mill elevator, or as ordinary as anything in a time-displaced Hotel could be. From the outside, it looked normal.

Inside, so the rumor went, was a floor-to-ceiling panel covered in buttons. Some had numbers, some had letters, some had incomprehensible symbols. The buttons could be pressed in any order, in any combination. Hit those buttons, close the door, and wait.

The elevator would travel.

Oh boy, would it travel. Sometimes it went up, sometimes down, sometimes sideways, or so she heard. The doors would ding open to a new world, new versions of Earth. Alternate realities, or parallel universes, or whatever. Infinite worlds, infinite times, infinite places. A person could spend endless lives pressing buttons and riding the elevator and never run out of combinations. But Arthur seemed to have many lifetimes, and time worked funny in the Hotel.

People said one button combination opened to a world where the only food was pizza, which was great, but only vegetarian, which was miserable. Allegedly, another was a version of Earth where humans never existed. The Wyatts came from an Earth gone sideways; one ravaged by a virus, where game show hosts and criminals ran the place.

Rumor also had it that a specific sequence of buttons led to a jail cell where Wyatt—the original Wyatt—was being held. Arthur would visit him and have a chat. No one knew what he said, but when he concluded, Wyatt would come back to the Hotel. Arthur would go again. A second Wyatt. And again. A third Wyatt. On it went until Arthur had his own private duplicate army of psychotic murderers, all free from a life of incarceration and all fanatically devoted to Arthur. She heard it got to where Arthur trained Wyatts to recruit other Wyatts, ensuring a never-ending supply of goons. The whole thing made her head hurt.

There looked to be three of them: two in the car and one on the sidewalk. The one outside was looking at something in his hand and facing away from the sandwich shop. He leaned in the window and spoke to the others, pointing up the street.

Arthur used the Wyatts for many things, but their primary function was to go out in the world and find people like Vain and Roman; people with the unique brain composition suitable for conversion into the odd power-and-source relationship that made them valuable to the Hotel. The Wyatts hunted in packs of two or three. He couldn't send them out in larger teams because entire armies of identical psychopaths raised eyebrows.

It was sick, what they did. But today, it meant good news for Vain. Given that they weren't looking at her and weren't orienting on the sandwich shop, it seemed likely they came here for someone else, someone who hadn't been activated yet. Nothing to do with her.

So why was she shaking? Why was she grinding her teeth with enough force to cause her jaw to ache? Did that sandwich give her rickets?

Or was it because those stupid, bow-legged bastards were going to take someone else? They were going to ruin someone else's life, like they ruined hers. Someone else would have their memories ripped away, only to be held prisoner in the Hotel for eternity.

She had plenty of good reasons to run. Roman needed her. She needed to figure out how to fix the Padlock. She needed to get away from the Wyatts, who would take her back to Arthur in the blink of an eye, even if they were after someone else. Without Roman, she had no way of defending herself. She was scared. She was tired. She *still* didn't know how Game of Thrones ended. Lots of great reasons to remain uninvolved.

There was only one reason, really, to involve herself. Whatever the Wyatts were up to, it would piss Arthur off if she disrupted it; and the opportunity to further irritate Arthur was too great to pass up.

Vain decided she'd follow at a distance. Keep an eye on them. If it looked like things were going sour, she'd bolt. No commitment, no fuss. A quick peek.

They got in the car and drove away. She hopped in a cab and told the driver she was renting him for the day, pressed some cash into his hands, and told him to shut up. He seemed irritated but shrugged and did what she wanted.

Vain gazed out the window and rolled the broken Padlock in her hands. A plan was taking shape in her mind. What if she repaired Padlock, somehow? With that kind of power, a lot of schemes she once thought were unrealistic suddenly seemed doable. Schemes with lots of exploding.

Maybe, just maybe, she could stop the Hotel. Forever.

Chapter 5

Emma feels great, but also horrible.

Emma sprang out of bed. Despite hardly sleeping, she felt well-rested. All night she lay awake, pulses of energy flowing into her from everywhere. It was like trying to sleep after chugging a gallon of Red Bull. It both exhilarated and terrified her. At one point, she picked up one of her more boring textbooks—first-year geography—hoping that a few dull chapters about the mountains of Northern Africa would bore her to sleep, but instead became engrossed learning that the Atlas Mountains only facilitated east-to-west air movement. Stupid, fascinating geography.

As she puttered around her apartment, trying to figure out what was going on, the more rational part of her assessed the facts.

Fact one: she had suffered an abrupt and intense seizure.

Fact two: she had an insane amount of energy, manic in its intensity.

Fact three: she was unnaturally happy, as if her body was compensating by releasing a flood of endorphins. It felt like she could throw a dump truck through a brick wall.

It all pointed to a serious medical problem, and she had to get someone to look into it. She should have gotten checked out right after it happened, but Smoove Dick was to blame for that one. There was no universe where a ride to the hospital with him ended in anything other than murder.

She made herself a cup of decaf tea and did some quick Googling: abrupt seizure plus insomnia plus manic energy. The first link lead to a page of potential conditions associated with those symptoms. Lyme disease, sugar withdrawal, restless leg syndrome, hypothyroidism, and, of course, a brain tumor. The decision tree that made up the Internet's self-diagnosis engine always ended up at the same spot; even something as minor as a toe sprain would link back to a brain tumor.

Sighing, she rubbed her temples. It would take forever to go to the hospital. Besides, all they'd do is recommend a bunch of tests. More time and more bother.

Instead of deciding, she opted for some healthy procrastination. She vacuumed her place from top to bottom, flew through a yoga routine, and reorganized her book collection by alphabetical thematic intent, starting with abuse of power and ending at unconditional love. Instead of tiring her out, it made her even more awake and energized. And, in fairness, the book organization game had been fascinating. Was Slaughterhouse Five about the illusion of free will, or the acceptance of inevitability?

It was when she picked up the mail downstairs that she got a new clue. Her neighbor puttered by, a wonderfully sweet woman named Joyce, and they stopped to have a quick, apartment-based chat. Things like, 'I tripped on that pesky bump in the stair' and, 'oh my god that cat last night was so loud'. Energy from Joyce bled into Emma's body.

People. The energy came from people. Impossible as that fact was to reconcile, it seemed incontrovertible. Along with that realization came creeping dread. What if she was hurting them? What if she was making Joyce sick, simply by being around her? With an abrupt squeak about how she left her kettle on, Emma scrambled back up to her apartment to hide and do more thinking.

As she sat in her living room, sipping her third chamomile tea, her phone vibrated. *MissD.* Her friend, Doreen.

how did last night go?

fine, dull

did u meet that special someone :)

ha no, I'll tell you later, but I met a guy calling himself smoove dick

oh god do they use words to mean size now I can't even

doesn't matter. Night was a bust :(

awww

Emma fiddled with her phone. She didn't want Doreen to worry, but she was tired of wrestling with this thing alone.

one thing did happen last night

??

I had a seizure. One minute fine, the next minute pow

OMFG what!!!! Are u ok

ya I'm okay. It was weird, they said I was out for a few minutes

did u go to the hospital?

no

OMFG GO TO THE HOSPITAL

I feel good tho

don't be all Emma about this, go to the hospital. Do u want me to come to take u?

no, I'm fine. Great actually

don't be a dumb bitch, I'm taking you

Now that someone else said it, she realized how foolish she was being. None of what was happening to her was at all normal. She reassured Doreen that she didn't need a ride, but would go to the hospital right away.

It was after one p.m. Enough stalling, time to get it checked out. The hospital was only five miles away, and she figured if she jogged she might burn off some of the energy.

She gave her legs a half-hearted stretch before starting. The crisp and cool fall air invigorated her, and she settled into an easy rhythm. Through her headphones, Adele's singing provided a soothing counterpoint to the steady *thump-thump-thump* of her feet on the pavement, and she picked up the pace. The ground sped by beneath her and she lost herself in the run. Everything fell away; her fears, concerns about being sick, stress about school. She stopped worrying and let light and strength flow into her.

At the end of the street, the hospital loomed, a sleek and reassuring monument to modern-day science. She checked her phone and blinked, not sure if she could believe the display. Twenty-five minutes. That's how long it took her to run there. It meant a five-minute mile. She wasn't even breathing hard or sweating. What was that? What kind of brain tumor gave you super-running powers? What was happening to her?

With a little more urgency, she pushed through the doors.

Chapter 6

Vain discovers the hero life is mostly tedium.

Vain yawned into the back of her hand and attempted to stretch in the confines of the cab. The Wyatts had been following an odd, but regular pattern. Drive, get out, check something they'd hold up over their heads, and get back in the car. She couldn't tell what they were looking at, but she bet it was a Device; something to help them locate people they might activate. Finding one person in a city filled with millions had to be an inexact science, so it made sense that they needed to stop frequently. She didn't even bother to tell the cabbie to keep his distance; they obviously weren't expecting anyone to follow them.

The car turned down a narrow street and slowed to a crawl. A solitary jogger sprinted towards a large hospital, headed for the emergency entrance. A red ponytail bobbed out from behind a baggy grey sweatshirt. Vain was certain; they were after the jogger.

And who jogs to the emergency room? What kind of lunatic were they after?

The Wyatts came to a stop and one got out and lit a cigarette, seemingly content to wait. Whatever kidnapping guidelines the Wyatts followed, grabbing people in broad daylight wasn't part of their process.

She paid the fare and got out of the cab. Now that she knew with absolute certainty they weren't after her, the smart play would be to walk away. She was not going to get involved in that. It had nothing to do with her. She was no hero, and she wasn't trying to save the world. Practical. That's what she was. Practical. And practical, smart people didn't get involved in kidnappings. She was not going to the hospital and warn the woman. The train station just happened to be in the same direction. For sure it was.

An older lady with a small, cat-sized dog walked towards her clutching a purse that cost more than Vain's entire wardrobe. The cloying scent of perfume announced her presence.

"Hey, miss," Vain said, using her friendliest voice. "The train station is that way, right?" She pointed towards the hospital.

"No." The woman adjusted her glasses as she took in Vain's appearance. The dog yapped at her feet, straining against the leash. "It's in the other direction. Are you lost, dear? Do you need some help?"

Why did everyone keep asking her that? "I'm okay, miss, thank you. I've had a long night. You're saying the fastest route to the train station is a beeline towards the hospital?"

"I'm not at all saying that. I'm saying the opposite. Are you sure you're okay?"

Vain wasn't sure why this woman insisted on giving her incorrect directions. She probably didn't even live in Boston. People were the worst. The dog let out a few more high-pitched yaps.

"Alright, thanks very much then." Vain gave the dog a quick scratch under the chin and continued down the street. She heard the woman mutter 'drugs' behind her. Ah, that explained it. The woman was a drug addict and needed some drugs. Of course. Impressive she managed to live that long and that well and own a dog despite being a remorseless meth addict. It really did take all kinds.

Well, look at that, the hospital. Right in front of her.

As long as she was here, and as long as it was on the way to the train station, she might as well pop in and give the jogger a quick warning. That barely counted as getting involved. She'd give some lighting fast advice, and then it was off to Roman. Maybe she could even get better directions. No doubt if she followed the spun-out drug addict's advice, she'd be lost in moments. Or, at the minimum, be directed to a meth den.

Honestly, some people didn't know how to be helpful, that was the real problem.

Vain shoved through the emergency doors, grumbling to herself.

Chapter 7

Emma receives a non-insane warning.

Emma sat in an uncomfortable chair in the emergency room, listlessly flipping through a Field and Stream magazine, although this specific issue contained articles about neither fields nor streams. She filled out a form with her symptoms and was told to take a seat. The admitting nurse seemed concerned about the seizure, but then much less so when Emma mentioned she'd jogged herself to the hospital. It would be a long wait. There were people there in worse shape than her, and she thought they might get in first.

Across from her, a younger man cradled his bloody, bandaged finger close to his chest. Whoever he was talking with on the phone had him more agitated than the horrific damage to his appendage.

"No, don't throw it out," he said. "Most of the blood ended up on the wall and the floor, barely any made it into the pot." He listened. "Right, but it's about four batches of chili." Another pause.

"Why not, though? What do you think I was cutting? I'll tell you what. Steak. Raw steak. And do you know what raw steak is filled with? Blood. So, when you consider it that way, you were ready to eat at least a half-cup of cooked bl—" He cut himself off, his cheeks flushing. "Don't you throw out my goddamn chili!" He looked around, embarrassed, and continued to whisper a series of chili-based threats to the person at the other end of the line.

She tuned out the conversation and tried to focus on the magazine article, but a smoldering wave of energy pulled her attention to a woman coming into the room. She had dark spiky hair; an obvious home-cut, like someone hacked at it with a lawnmower. Underneath, blonde roots poked through the dye job. Her eyes were wide and angry, and all of her features were sharp. The energy coming from her blazed, and Emma shrank into her chair by reflex.

After scanning the room, the woman locked onto Emma and looked straight at her. Despite there being several dozen empty chairs in the waiting area, she walked over and plopped into the seat next to Emma.

"What are you in for?" she asked.

Emma could barely muster an answer and scootched over to the edge of her seat with her jaw hanging open.

"Oh, you know," Emma replied, hoping that would be the end. She flipped through her magazine, landing on an article about the ten best rifles for murdering elk. Everyone knew that with your face in a magazine or book, other people weren't allowed to talk to you.

"I don't know," said the woman. "Are you sick?"

Emma forced a smile. "I'd rather not say. Thanks, though."

"Why not?"

Clearly this woman was crazy, perhaps in the middle of a manic episode. She looked the part. Her clothes were disheveled like she either hadn't slept in a while, or did so on piles of garbage.

"Well, why are *you* here?" Emma countered.

The woman tilted her head. "Syphilis. Full-blown."

Okay, so she was crazy. "It's been nice talking to you," said Emma, putting her magazine down. "I have to use the washroom. Excuse me." She smiled and got up, but the woman grabbed her forearm in an iron grip.

"Listen," she said. "Sometime within the next little while, identical bow-legged men with cauliflower ears will come for you. I don't know what they'll say, but these men are dangerous. You have to run."

Emma's stomach dropped in that way it did when you found out the person you were talking to was dangerous-crazy, instead of ordinary-crazy. This woman was a lunatic. Emma wondered if anyone would help her, but the chili-man still argued on the phone and the nurse wasn't paying any attention.

"I see." Emma pried her arm from the other woman's grip. "Thank you for telling me. I'll make a note of that. Please don't touch me again."

The woman ignored Emma's request and pulled her closer. "I get this sounds nuts, but you have to pay attention. If you ignore everything else, remember this. Duplicate men. Brown hair. Crummy ears. If anyone like that comes near you, run. Got it? Good."

Emma lowered her expectations for this encounter to not getting stabbed. It was a low bar, but under the circumstances, she'd count it as a win.

With a final glare, the crazy woman nodded, dropped Emma's forearm, and walked out of the emergency room, taking her intense, angry energy with her. It was as if someone had turned a light back on.

Well, that was abruptly and weirdly terrifying.

Double men with dark ears? Or did she say angular ears and long legs? Did she mean elves? Elves would kidnap her? How did someone that dog-barking crazy function in everyday society? As she pondered the many vagaries that life presented, the nurse called her name.

*

Hours later, she was relaxing back in her apartment, no closer to figuring out what had happened to her, but feeling better about the whole thing. The doctor seemed concerned about the seizure and less so about the after-effects. She instructed Emma to drink lots of fluids, get plenty of rest, and make a follow-up appointment with a neurologist. Done, done, and done.

With a structured plan in place, Emma was ready to put all of it behind her and move on with her life. It was after six, so she made herself a quick dinner of pasta and poured a glass of wine, settling in to relax for the night.

She cleared a spot at her small kitchen table by shoving textbooks aside.

She should have been famished; aside from a few small bites at breakfast, she hadn't eaten all day; but after the first mouthful, she was done. She had no appetite. It wasn't like being full; more like not needing to eat at all. A sip of wine provoked the same reaction. A sense of panic bubbled up again; the whisper in her brain that said, *this isn't right.*

Even worse, she still buzzed with inexhaustible vitality; the endless, vibrating force that made her feel like an alarm clock tossed into a washing machine. She had sprinted back from the hospital, doing the miles in twenty minutes. When she stopped, she wasn't out of breath; she could have gone all night. She also wasn't tired, despite having not slept in close to thirty-five hours. Nothing the doctor said explained any of that.

Emma found that if she focused, with every muscle flexed and with fierce concentration, the flood of energy slowed to a trickle. But as soon as she relaxed, the rivulets came back, flowing into her. It was everywhere. No matter how she tried to distract herself, the presence of other humans intruded; in the apartment next door, in the hallways, even out in the street. It was the same energy she'd been tingling with all day, except—

Except now there was that furious, unique signature she'd only experienced once. Had that crazy bitch from the hospital followed her home? She wiped her hands on her jeans. That woman was dangerous; there was no doubt.

She picked up her phone, ready to send a text to Doreen. Could Doreen even help? How? Besides, what would Emma say? Oh, hey, Doreen. Listen, I went to the ER and now I'm good at running and a crazy woman with a lawnmower haircut told me to watch out for elves.

A knock from the door made her flinch.

Startled, she let out a small yelp and dropped the phone. Jesus, had the crazy woman walked right up to her door? But no, that energy seemed further away, maybe across the street. The energies by her front door were gray and uncanny. Although there were two of them, they were identical. As she focused more intently, her stomach flipped, and she tasted bile. Whoever they were, they weren't good people. She didn't understand how she knew that, but it was true nonetheless.

After picking up her phone, she walked to the door and tried to ignore the flutter in her stomach.

"Who is it?"

"Hi, ma'am," said a friendly male voice. "We wanted to talk to you about your energy bills. Did you know solar power can reduce your annual costs by as much as three percent?"

The tension drained out of her and she took a deep, calming breath. Salesmen. No wonder she was nauseated. With an embarrassed chuckle, she opened the door, ready to tell them 'no, thank you'.

Two identical men stood on the landing wearing smarmy grins that didn't seem to fit on their faces. One had a shaved head and sunglasses worn turned around, stems poking from behind his ears.

Poking from behind his *cauliflower* ears.

Double men. Twins.

Her eyes darted to where their legs bowed out from the knees.

Their smiles vanished.

Elves. The woman had been right. The elves were here.

Emma tried to close the door, but one of the men blocked it with his foot. Their eyes met and he smiled. This time, it was a real thing, the smile that fit on his face, and it was horrible. Monstrous. A smile devoid of warmth or compassion. Emma groaned, and he punched the door open, knocking her to the floor. What was happening?

Saying nothing, they hauled her off the ground. One pinched her arm, and she yelped in protest. Although she tried to pull away, their grip was too strong. They pulled her out into the hall.

"Hey, stop! What are you doing?" What a dumb thing to ask. She knew very well what they were doing.

Scream. She should scream.

Before she could put her plan into action, one pulled a bag over her head, and everything went dark. Something slammed into her stomach and she exhaled in a rush. Had one of them hit her? She almost couldn't believe it. Never in her entire life had anyone hit her.

She tried to tell them she'd buy whatever they were selling, but before she could, a solid object thudded against her temple, and she staggered. They had punched her. In the head. It dazed her, and they picked her up and pulled her down the stairs.

"You are needlessly aggressive salesmen," she whispered from under her bag.

They dragged her out into the cool night air.

Chapter 8

Vain does nothing like a huge loser.

Vain sat on a wide, three-person bench, eating a bag of barbecue potato chips and considering her next move. It was dusk, and the sun dipped below the skyline. After the hospital encounter, she followed the Wyatts and the jogger, reasoning that Roman would want to know what happened. For narrative closure. Roman, she reflected, was obsessed with narrative closure. So, here she was, in a quiet part of the city with shoulder-to-shoulder, pencil-thin houses that competed for the largest amount of white trim to circle a window. Most of the pedestrians seemed to be students, judging by the backpacks and oversized headphones.

Vain wondered if she had ever gone to school. She had no real memory of anything before Arthur's Hotel. It was as if her life started the day she woke up in that horrible place, scared, alone, and confused.

She and Roman weren't sure of either of their ages, but they estimated she was somewhere in her late twenties and he was somewhere in his early thirties. There was no way to tell for sure, though. Time didn't work right in the Hotel, and aside from eyeballing it, they had nothing else to go on.

She had a small scar on her elbow, about an inch long, that she would play with anytime she was distracted. The scar didn't have stitch marks; it was a raw, ragged line. She thought the lack of stitch marks was a clue and she tugged at that fact, trying to wring it for every piece of data. Whoever she had been in her previous life, she had cut herself badly enough to leave a scar, but she hadn't gotten it stitched. That *meant* something. That had to mean something. Did she not have parents who could care for her? Had she not lived close to a hospital? Did she get the scar going to school, like these naïve, shiny-faced kids who walked by, unaware of the world that existed in the shadows?

Roman was, for sure, educated. He was smart and wise, and Vain imagined that was the temperament you got from going to college. She pictured Roman in a school setting, surrounded by kids, learning important things like how to drive a car and how taxes worked. Would he be smoking a pipe? That felt right.

It was time to get back to him. His absence had become an ache, a persistent stitch in her side. No matter how many breaths she took, it never went away. Plus, there seemed to be a great deal of humidity in the air, given how often her eyes filled up at the thought of him, alone and afraid. Boston was apparently a wet hellscape of airborne moisture.

Following a pack of hunting Wyatts was beyond dangerous. And besides, she'd already done more than could be expected by providing the jogger with a precise warning and concrete next steps. Done and done.

The problem was, Roman's world was exclusively made up of things to protect; the thought of leaving a person defenseless would be an anathema to him. Oh, he'd say that he understood and that he was glad Vain was safe. He'd also get that Roman look on his face; the horrible one that said he still loved you, but he was so, so disappointed in you. Damn it.

She slapped her thigh and stood up. She'd have to live with Roman's displeasure, because there was no way to stop that. Across the street, two Wyatts headed into the brownstone building, while one waited out front, leaning against the passenger side of the vehicle.

Within moments, the two Wyatts came back out, the woman sandwiched between them, her legs not quite touching the ground. The one who had stayed outside opened the back door and they threw her into the car. The whole thing took seconds, and unless you were watching as closely as she was, you would have missed it.

Her legs shook and she couldn't seem to catch her breath. That was it, then. Wyatts one, un-kidnapped women, zero. Now they'd take her to the Hotel, wipe her memory, and keep her captive. Like they'd done to Vain. Another life thrown into the garbage. She rubbed her face, unable to look away.

A cab drove by and she surprised herself by raising her arm and flagging it down. It slowed to a stop, and she hopped in the back seat as the red SUV pulled away from the curb.

"Where to?" said the driver.

"Follow that red SUV," she said, pointing.

He arched his eyebrow. "Are you kidding me?"

"My money says I'm not." She showed him the rest of her cash. He considered her for a few beats before shrugging and pulling away from the curb.

"So, do I keep a distance, or can I follow behind them? Is this a spy thing?"

"Just follow it, man, I don't know. I'm not an expert in car-following techniques. Isn't this something you cover in cab school?"

"I got my license in the mail after filling out a form online. It took eight minutes. Why are you following them?"

She rubbed her temples. "Do you need my life story? Is that a prerequisite for this ride? Stay behind them and keep quiet."

"You're the boss." He smiled and drove in silence for ten seconds before turning back to her. "Are they going somewhere?"

"Jesus Christ. Listen… Pranav," she said, reading the license hanging on the back of the seat. "They stole my wallet, okay? I was sitting there, minding my own business, when they stole my wallet."

"How is it you still have money?" asked Pranav, cheerful now that he had drawn her into a conversation.

"Because I keep my money in my bra. They're getting further away, don't lose them."

"Should we go to the police? Wallet stealing is a serious offense. I can radio it in right now." He picked up his CB and wiggled it.

Shit. The last thing she wanted was the police.

"Actually, it's their wallet," she blurted. "I found it after they dropped it. Like I said, I keep my money in my bra, like a normal person." She emphasized by pointing at her chest. "So now I'm returning a wallet I found. Did I say stole? I often get the words 'found' and 'stole' mixed up. Honest mistake."

"Sure," he said. "But wouldn't it be easier to mail it to them? Is there any identification inside? This seems like the hardest possible way to return a wallet to someone."

Vain gave him an irritated glare. "What the shit, Pranav? Are you a taxi driver or Carey Mahoney?"

"Who is Carey Mahoney? Is he the owner of the wallet?"

"No, he was in 'Police Academy'. Never mind. Keep driving."

"All I'm saying, miss," said Pranav, apparently the nosiest cab driver in the world, "is that your story isn't particularly good and if I'm going to follow another car, I'd like to know the reason. I don't want to get mixed up in anything. Especially not drugs, although you don't look like you're high." He smiled at her through the rear-view mirror.

She exhaled sharply. "Fine, you wanna know why we're following them? They're human monsters from an alternate universe, brought here by a violent, unstable megalomaniac named Arthur. They've kidnapped a woman who they are bringing back to his Hotel—which isn't like a normal Hotel, mind you, it's more of a waypoint between all time and space—that sits on a floating island made of rocks surrounded by red lightning. Once they get there, they'll wipe her memory, connect her mentally to another person, and make her channel energy for some inexplicable, fathomless purpose. Good? Is that enough of an answer? Have I earned the right to this cab ride now?" She flopped back in her seat and crossed her arms. Pranav seemed entertained by the whole thing.

"That's a spectacular story," he laughed. "Very, very good. You tell better stories than most of my passengers. Driving is boring, and I drive for many hours, so stories help the day go faster. What will you do when you catch up to these men, these supposed kidnappers?"

"That's a great question, Pranav. I have no idea. I'm making this up as I go."

He turned on to the highway and Vain thumbed through her stack of cash while eying the meter. Dollars and cents ticked by on the counter with alarming speed.

"I won't be able to follow them indefinitely," said Pranav. "Unless you have a great deal more money."

"When we get to where they're going, I'll give you a thousand dollars. They should go past my, um, Uncle's house. He's rich and owns a moose." That sounded like something a rich person would own. "Don't sweat it Pranav, I'll take care of you."

Pranav gestured to the meter. "The ride is already at twenty dollars, miss…?"

"Vain," she said.

"What?"

"My name is Vain."

"Are you with the circus or something?" Vain shook her head and Pranav continued, "I am not as familiar with American names, but that does not seem like one. Once, I drove a woman who told me her name was Matthew. I pointed out that was a man's name and she called me a misogynist, chained to antiquated notions of fixed gender. I learned a lot that day about how gender is an arbitrary social construct, which was helpful, although I didn't get a tip. I should learn my lesson and stop commenting on people's names, but I can't help it. They're becoming more bizarre. Everyone is named after a state now. Montana, Dakota, Alabama, Iowa."

"Come on, no one is named Iowa."

"Maybe not," Pranav agreed, "but names are strange and hard to remember now. Vain, for example. Is that a new trend, to name people based on personality traits? Are your millennial friends called Entitled and Lazy and Addicted?"

"Your prejudice is showing there, Pranav. Focus. You're all over the map conversationally, and we're losing them. Look, they're pulling off at that exit. Stay close behind."

Vain cracked her knuckles. It was time to continue to not get involved.

Chapter 9

Emma makes a joke about license plates.

Emma's feet skimmed the ground as the salesmen dragged her from her house and threw her into the back seat of their car. The entire process took maybe thirty seconds. They had done this before.

Randomly, she worried that they hadn't locked her door. The blow to her head made it hard to focus. Her mind reeled through the crisis. The rational part of her brain attempted to gain control, but it was impossible. Raw, animal panic had taken over.

The car smelled like stale bagels and pizza. Crumbs on the upholstery stuck to her palms. When the car sped off, she realized that this was an actual thing and it was actually happening to her. She was being kidnapped. The crazy woman from the hospital had been right.

One of them removed the bag from her head and she shrank back against the door. Beside her was a man wearing a blue blazer. The two that grabbed her were in front. She recognized one by his stylish olive-green jacket; the other, with the sunglasses, was driving. Clothes and haircuts aside, they were identical. They all looked distressingly normal; three guys out for a drive, not a care in the world. Shouldn't they have been dressed in black or licking knives? Didn't kidnappers lick knives? She couldn't wrap her head around a world where kidnappers looked identical to ordinary salesmen.

"What do you want with me?" she asked. "Please let me go. I won't tell anyone about this."

None of them even glanced at her. Sunglasses continued driving, looking bored. Blue Blazer laughed at something on his phone.

"Please," she said again. "I don't know what you want."

Blue Blazer grinned with a grotesque, lecherous expression on his face. "We only want one thing, sweetheart." He licked his lips and she almost threw up, a painful cramp shooting through her stomach.

"Give it a rest, Wyatt," said Sunglasses from the front.

Wyatt shrugged and looked back out the window. "She won't remember any of this, anyway."

Everything they said was terrifying, and each individual statement propelled her further into this miserable kidnappee experience.

"Where are you taking me?" she asked.

"Settle down, little bird," replied Sunglasses. "This will all be over soon. Sit there and keep your mouth shut."

"Why are you doing this?" A hitch made its way into her voice.

Green Jacket turned to face the back seats. "Shut her up."

Wyatt shrugged and punched her in the chest.

The blow slammed her against the car door and her head bounced off the window. For what seemed like minutes, her world narrowed to her struggle for breath and the sound of small gasping noises coming from her mouth. Blackness bled into the edges of her vision.

They had now punched her three times. There was still a small part of her brain that didn't believe it was happening, but the animal part yowled in panic. She choked out a sob and huddled up against the side of the car, hugging herself.

"Nothing personal, kiddo," said Green Jacket from the front, "but here's the drill. You shut up nice and quiet. Behave for the whole car ride, and we won't punch you anymore. Good deal?"

She wasn't sure if they wanted her to respond, or if speaking would earn her another punch. The man in the back seat looked at her expectantly. She gave him a small, hesitant nod.

"Great," said Green Jacket. "We'll get along fine." The man beside her winked, and Emma had to close her eyes to press out all the tears that made her vision blurry. They made hot, wet tracks down her cheeks.

They drove in silence, Emma scrunching as much of herself into the door as possible. Sunglasses got on the highway, down the I90 West towards Springfield. He drove responsibly, in the slow lane, and passing cars broke the darkness with flashes from their headlights as they zoomed by. She let her mind go blank. Even through this whole ordeal, power still flowed into her.

"Let's grab a bite," said Sunglasses. "It's a long drive to the Hotel."

The word, with its ominous undertones, jerked Emma out of her reverie. "What's the Hotel? Is this a sex thing? Can I give you money instead? There isn't much, it's only my Mom and me, but maybe we can work out a deal?" The floodgates of her nerves burst open, and she rambled. "My Dad died when I was young. He collected license plates he thought were keen. My mom kept them in the garage, you can have all of them. I'll help you sell them. I bet you'll get a lot, one spells out 'boobs' with numbers. It's not funny, but then again, some people like having body parts on their cars. I wonder if there's an *elbow* license plate? I guess it would be 31604? No. That doesn't seem right."

"You talk a lot," said Wyatt.

"Please don't punch me again. I don't like it. I only wanted to know about this Hotel place and to make sure you understand that there is money in it for you if you let me go. And not any old money, sweet, antique license plate money."

Green Jacket rubbed the bridge of his nose. "Jesus, lady. Even if I told you about the Hotel, it wouldn't make sense."

"Tell me," said Emma. "Why are you kidnapping me?"

Green Jacket reached into his coat pocket and pulled out a small, round compass with a single giant arrow. It pointed at her.

"Do you see this?" he asked. "This points us towards people like you. It went off yesterday, like nothing I've ever seen. Normally, these things give us hints and nudges. It takes us forever to track someone down, but this led us right to you."

"What do you mean, people like me?" Her voice rose. "Redheads? Grad students? Women who watch reruns of Gilmore Girls? There are millions of us, it's a delightful show."

"People with a specific potential that is very important to the person we work for," said Sunglasses.

"What potential? I don't have any potential. I can do a headstand for over a minute, but that's about it, and even then, it's only against a wall. Do you mean my energy thing? That's because I had a seizure. I'm sure it's not permanent. Sure, I can't sleep, which is weird, and I seem to suck the energy out of people, but it's a side effect. I'm sure they'll give me some pills or something and it will go away."

"What do you mean, you can suck energy? Like a Utility?" said Green Jacket. "That's not possible, no one's turned you on."

"You keep saying this isn't a sex thing, but then you continue to use sex terms. I don't understand what any of those words mean in the context you're using them. Ever since I had a seizure the other day, I can, I don't know, absorb energy." An errant, manic giggle tried to escape and she clapped her hand over her mouth. She sounded like the crazy woman from the hospital. "If that's why you thought you should take me, I can assure you I'll have that cleared up in a jiff." She felt like she was making good, logical progress with her violent, irrational kidnappers. Surely, they would realize their mistake. "Here, I'll show you."

Without understanding how she did it, she shifted the focus of the energy absorption and pointed it right at them.

"Wyatt, can you feel that?" The back-seat Wyatt looked at her intensely but spoke to the man in front.

"Yeah," said Green Jacket, also apparently named Wyatt. "You're pulling energy from us, little chickadee. How are you doing that? We're not even Conduits."

"Beats me," she said with artificial cheerfulness. "Are you all named Wyatt? Are you twins, or, I guess, triplets?"

"We're not triplets, we're all the same person, and yes, we're all named Wyatt," said Wyatt in the back seat.

"We're not clones if that's what you're thinking," Sunglasses Wyatt said, in a misguided effort to provide clarity.

"I'm calling Trick. Something isn't right," said Green Jacket Wyatt. He punched a few buttons on his phone and raised it to his ear. "Trick, hi, this is Wyatt. We've got one, but there's something weird about her. She's pulling energy, almost like she's activated already. We can all feel it."

A car pulled up beside them with a young child in the backseat, clutching a stuffed bear. He pressed his little hands and face to the window and they gazed at each other from across the gap. Emma mouthed the words 'help me'. The child laughed and blew a raspberry at her before the car sped off into the distance. Emma exhaled and leaned her forehead against the cold window. She'd never been so alone. The Wyatt continued talking.

"I don't know how, but she's doing it. Said she had a seizure and now she's able to—." The Wyatt listened to the person on the other end and made small nodding gestures. "Yeah, that's what it sounds like to me, too. I didn't think it was possible either." After another moment, he said, "You got it," and hung up.

"Change of plans, everyone. No side trips and no other pick-ups. Trick wants us to lickety-split our way to Nevada. Arthur wants to examine this one himself."

Examine. Emma's stomach clenched and her throat burned as bile climbed up her throat. Would the nightmare never end?

They drove off the highway into the parking lot of a fast-food chain. Apparently, they still wanted a meal before stealing her away forever. They parked at the back of the lot, picking a secluded spot with no other cars around aside from a taxi that pulled in behind them.

"Okay, here's the deal." Green Jacket Wyatt turned around. "We're going to get a quick bite, then we're driving all night until we hit the Hotel. You," he pointed at her, "should use this time to figure out what you can and can't do. Trick would like us to have some idea of what's going on." He looked at the Wyatt in the back seat with her. "He'd like us to be attentive in our efforts to get answers."

All three laughed; a grotesque, sloppy sound that could only be produced by men who were plotting terrible things.

"She'll be good. Won't you?" asked the Wyatt beside her. Before she had time to respond, he grabbed her by the shirt and slapped her. His expression never changed.

Four times. Four times she'd been struck in less than half an hour. She had gone her entire life without ever being hit, and all of a sudden she was an expert at taking a punch.

His hand left a burning mark on her cheek. She was prepared for the pain, but not the immediate shame that followed. It horrified her. It was an order of magnitude worse than the slap itself.

Her Wyatt, as she had now come to think of him, pondered her with a hollow, dead-eyed expression. Another day at work. Kidnap a woman; slap her around. Ho-hum.

They called out burger orders to Sunglasses, who confirmed drinks and fry sizes. He and Green Jacket got out of the car, leaving her in the backseat. The click of a lighter came from outside. One of them lit a cigarette, embers blazing red against the foggy window.

She rubbed goosebumps from her forearms, wondering if she would ever see her mom again. Surely a hidden camera somewhere recorded the situation. Surely it was a joke for a YouTube video. Social influencers were the worst people on the planet, and she wouldn't put a mock-kidnapping past them. Anything for internet points.

Emma rested her forehead on the window and wondered if death would hurt.

Chapter 10

Vain discovers a new use for a tire iron.

Vain kept her eyes focused on the rear lights, two floating red blips in the darkness. The vehicle took an off-ramp onto a side road littered with signs for restaurants and gas stations. It turned towards a crowded strip of stores and pulled into the back of a fast-food parking lot.

"Easy does it," she said, while Pranav pulled into a spot several cars behind them.

The streetlights and giant neon signs bright enough to allow a perfect view into the interior of the car. The two Wyatts up front were laughing. One in the back grabbed the woman by the shirt and slapped her.

Vain recoiled. There was no way she heard the meaty *thwack* of the slap. The distance was too far. But she swore she heard it.

"Your friend looks to be in trouble," said Pranav. He wasn't smiling anymore. "What are you mixed up in? I'm calling the police."

"Don't you dare."

"Get out of my cab," he said, all traces of humor gone. "Get out right now."

Across the parking lot, the Wyatts milled about. They were laughing, swapping jokes; another day at the office. Meanwhile, the woman slumped in the back seat, miserable and huddled up.

The Hotel stripped you of your memories, so Vain didn't remember how they took her. Her first recollection was waking in a small room on a dirty cot. Bruises covered her body, one cheek marked by a welt that took a week to heal. She didn't dwell on that for long, and soon discovered that everyone was in terrible shape when they first woke up.

But now, watching the Wyatts, she wondered about those bruises. Maybe they liked their jobs a little too much. Maybe as long as they brought people in alive, they were free to bang them up to their heart's content.

She rubbed her cheek, her temples throbbing. Pranav's squawking for her to get out became louder. The whole time she had been staring at the red SUV, but now she looked Pranav dead in the eyes. He stopped in mid-sentence.

"Open the trunk."

"Just go. I don't care what you're mixed up in."

"Open the trunk," she repeated. "Then you can get back to your little cab driving world with its funny stories."

Pranav objected, but she continued to glare at him, unblinking. He trailed off and swallowed.

"Are you going to hurt me?"

"You're not the one who needs to worry, Pranav, assuming you *open your fucking trunk.*"

Slightly pale, Pranav reached beside his seat and pressed the release button.

She stepped out of the car, clenching and unclenching her hands. A Wyatt wearing sunglasses chose that moment to amble past. She held her breath, but he didn't so much as glance at her. The throbbing in her temples intensified. She went around to the back of the cab and peered into the trunk. It was littered with crumpled grocery bags, the spare tire hatch visible beneath. She pulled the cover back. A tire iron nestled in the opening.

Perfect.

She grabbed it and walked over to Pranav, holding out a wad of cash.

"Thanks for the ride." She kept her eyes on the SUV. One Wyatt, wearing a green flak jacket, had gotten out of the car to smoke.

"What are you going to do?" he asked.

She put on her sweetest smile. "Pranav, I'm going to have a talk with my friends over there and explain to them how hitting people is wrong." She held up the tire iron. "I'll punctuate several elements of my argument with this."

All thoughts of Roman and the Padlock and running were behind her, replaced by memories of those bruises and that welt on her face. She relived the sheer horror she experienced, waking up in a dark, unfamiliar place with no understanding of who she was. The dull throbbing in her forehead reached a crescendo and everything else washed away.

She walked towards the SUV, her steps synchronized with the beat in her temples. The smoking Wyatt leaned against the vehicle and gave her a lazy look. Not concerned, but curious. She'd never once in her entire life approached a Wyatt on purpose.

"Excuse me," she called out using her most cheerful voice. The redheaded woman peered at her from the backseat, misery painted across her face.

"Beat it," he said, disinterested. "Keep walking."

"No problem." She kept her voice artificially happy and kept the tire iron against her thigh. "I have a question for you, though. Do you know why people find juggling so difficult?"

"What?" The Wyatt looked up.

"There are too many balls!" She kicked him in the nuts as hard as she could.

A Wyatt's skill set presumably included defensive countermeasures. Thankfully, protection against a small woman unexpectedly drop-kicking his genitals like she was trying to hit a field goal was not one of them. He dropped like a stone, gasping for breath.

"You bitch," he gasped.

"Bitch, am I?" She drew back the tire iron. "Would a bitch do this?" Her aim was a little off; instead of hitting his head, she caught him on the shoulder. He dropped with a howl of pain. On reflection, hitting a recently ball-kicked person with a tire iron seemed exactly like something a bitch would do, so maybe her quips needed some work.

She leaned over him. "Nice face you have there. It would be a shame if someone stomped the shit out of it." She emphasized her words by stomping the shit out of his face.

Her body trembled with both excitement and pent up anger. The Wyatt rolled around on the ground, covering his head with his forearms. If the rest of her life consisted of nothing more than this parking lot, this moment, forever stomping on his face, she would be eternally happy. This was goddamn fantastic.

The car door opened, knocking her to the ground. A new Wyatt dove out and landed on top of her, driving the air from her lungs. She lashed out with her tire iron, but he caught her hand and slammed it on the pavement, sending the weapon skittering across the parking lot. He walloped her with a brutal punch to the temple. Adrenaline kept her conscious, albeit barely.

"Help me, you lazy bitch!" she yelled at the lazy bitch who sat in the car doing nothing. "They're going to kill us both!"

The Wyatt punched her again, knocking her silly.

Nothing ever worked out the way you expected. That was her final, pithy thought before the blows rained down on her.

Chapter 11

Emma attacks.

The streetlight in the parking lot threw deep shadows everywhere. They reminded her of spotlights at a concert. The area was so deserted. The only car nearby was the taxi from earlier. A tiny figure got out and talked to the driver. Emma tried not to let her excitement show. If she signaled the person somehow, got them to understand the situation via hand gestures, maybe they'd call the police. What meant "Help, I'm kidnapped"? Maybe a thumbs down?

Emma squinted, not trusting what her eyes were showing her. The person had short, choppy hair and disheveled clothes. It looked like the crazy woman from the hospital. Almost pretty, if not for the permanent grimace of anger. The woman headed straight for the Wyatts.

Maybe she was in on it.

Not three seconds later, crazy hospital woman was jumping up and down on smoking Wyatt's head.

Maybe she wasn't in on it.

The Wyatt beside her saw the commotion and said, "What the hell?" and lunged out of the car. He tackled the woman to the ground and wrestled with her, trying to punch her skull through the concrete.

Emma watched all of this in horrified silence, pushing herself harder against the back of the door. It was all too much. From outside, she heard the woman yell, "Help me, you lazy bitch!" Emma presumed she, herself, was the lazy bitch in question.

The Green Jacket Wyatt struggled to get to his feet while her Wyatt kept battering at the woman. Emma watched dispassionately, like viewing a tv show. Time slowed to molasses. She was supposed to do something. Fight. Run. Something. Her hand formed itself into the shape of a fist without any conscious thought. Energy poured into her. That bored, dead-eyed monster had hit her four times. Rather than concentrate on her fear, she ruthlessly shut down every part of her mind that was non-essential to the task at hand. The number hammered at her. Each time it did, she lost a little more of herself.

Four.

Thud.

Four times.

Thud.

Four fucking times.

Thud.

The Emma that stepped out of the car was no longer scared. Energy had been flowing into her all day, and it stood as a buffer against the fear. Only anger remained; smoldering, ruthless anger.

She focused and the energy responded, leaping to her control. Her Wyatt raised his fist, but Emma caught it in a ball of energy. It was like stopping a baby from moving their arms. So easy. She pinned his other side and expanded the energy to envelop his head, his torso, and his entire body.

The power. God, so much power. She was unstoppable. She was everything.

It ripped through her like the harsh burn of cheap whiskey. Her Wyatt was trapped. She concentrated and lifted him off the crazy hospital woman who rolled onto her stomach and curled up, protecting her head. Emma rotated the Wyatt to face her. He was immobile, shock and fury evident in his expression. He certainly wasn't bored anymore.

"You are not a nice person, Wyatt." She put every ounce of collected energy into throwing him, and he rocketed through the air as if shot from a catapult. After only a few brief seconds, he became a speck in the sky and dropped over the horizon. She sagged against the SUV as all the power drained from her body.

The other Wyatt got to his feet and rubbed his neck, staring in the direction she had tossed her Wyatt. "What did you do, you dumb bitch?"

Emma was tired of people calling her that.

Crazy woman pushed herself off the pavement, nasty bruises blooming on her face. Blood poured from her nose. She picked up a long metal bar—*a tire iron?*—and said, "Hey, asshole. Tell Arthur this is from Vain." She swung and connected with the side of his head, like hitting a coconut with a bat. A sickening thunk followed.

He dropped like a sack of laundry. Crazy woman wheezed, resting her hands on her knees. Neither of them said anything for several moments.

"I don't know how to drive a car," the woman said.

Despite a lifetime of conversation with other human beings, Emma possessed no experience to draw on that might help her understand how to respond to that statement.

"I enjoy grilled cheese sandwiches," she said. Perhaps they were exchanging random facts. Maybe this was standard kidnapping rescue procedure. Emma felt it best not to disrupt the flow.

"To escape." The woman rolled her eyes. "We can get away in their car, but I don't know how to drive."

"Yes. Right. That makes more sense," Emma said. "The other guy has the keys, and he's inside getting burgers."

"I told you they were coming for you. Why didn't you listen to me? I gave you perfectly clear instructions."

Emma opened her mouth to disagree with the woman's understanding of several words, including 'perfectly', 'clear' and 'instructions', but the woman continued talking.

"There's not much fight left in me." She wiped at the blood pouring from her nose. "Can you throw him away like you did with the other guy?"

Emma's legs wobbled. She was exhausted. Throwing a grown man across half a country with the power of your mind, it turned out, was taxing. "No," she replied. "I don't know how I did that."

They looked at each other for a heartbeat before the crazy woman's eyes snapped to the restaurant. "The last Wyatt is coming back. What are the chances you know karate? Jiu-jitsu?? Even sexy mud wrestling?"

"I don't know any of those things." Emma's stomach knotted. "But he'll have to kill me before I let him drag me back into this car." She surprised herself by saying that; more so because it was true.

Crazy woman smiled, showing blood-stained teeth. "I have a tire iron. We'll be okay."

They stood shoulder to shoulder. By now, Sunglasses had noticed both of them standing by the car.

"Hey!" He jogged towards them, bags flopping at his side. Emma made her hands into fists and held them up. She hoped she'd get at least one decent punch in before he killed her. She hoped her mom would be okay.

Sunglasses picked up speed. With a screech, a cab peeled through the parking lot and crashed into him, sending him flying.

"Pranav!" cheered Crazy woman, punching the air with her fist.

Emma was finding it difficult to keep track of all the people involved in this adventure. On a normal day, she'd be studying, enjoying a glass of wine, some Adele playing in the background. She would not be fighting photocopied kidnappers in a parking lot outside Boston, with a crazy woman as her accomplice. The enormity of the situation came crashing down and panic threatened to overwhelm her again.

Crazy woman ran over to where Sunglasses Wyatt rolled around on the ground. She rummaged through his pockets and pulled out a handful of jingling keys before hurrying to the cab driver's window.

"Pranav, you are the best. This is a great story."

The cab driver shook his head. "I will tell no one. I saw none of this. I am leaving now. Thank you for the generous tip." With that, he rolled up his window and drove off.

"We've gotta move. Here." The woman thrust the keys at Emma and motioned at the SUV. "Let's go."

Emma was exhausted. Her face and chest ached, and she was an emotional wreck. She considered sitting on the curb in the parking lot and waiting for someone to take her somewhere safe. Some of this must have shown on her face and body language because the lunatic woman stopped. For once, her face looked calm.

"I know what you're going through, and I know you're scared, but there are more of them," she said. "They'll never stop."

Three simple words.

Emma got in the car.

Chapter 12

Roman's lack of knowledge about agriculture is a problem.

When Roman opened his eyes, his first thought was of Vain. His second was of how much trouble he was in.

He was lying in a reclining hospital bed, his arms and legs bound to the metal bars that ran along the sides. Aside from a small sink near the door and a single wooden table with a lamp, the pale-yellow room was bare. A camera hung from the ceiling, the red light blinking at him.

He was pantless.

While his memory was iffy after being needled unconscious by the Wyatt, he was positive he'd been wearing pants. Waking up half-naked and restrained could only mean one thing. They had taken him somewhere to do unpleasant things. He wondered how long he'd been out.

"Hello?" He looked at the camera, his voice raspy and dry. "I'm awake. If you're watching, I assume you want to talk." The inside of his mouth was like cotton and he couldn't work any moisture into his lips. He gave the restraints an experimental tug, but they held him tight. There was nothing he could do. Panicking wouldn't help, and he was on his own.

The reality hit him with a thud. Vain was dead. No more Vain. Her expressive, goofy smile, the way she'd talk with her hands, the *hyuk* noise she made when she laughed, all gone. Now she existed only in his memory. What combination of words could he use to describe her absence?

"Vain? Oh, she passed. Quite sad. Quite."

Too British.

"It was an accident. A fluke. No one saw it coming."

The words seemed flat and banal compared to their exceptional subject.

"Vain was my favorite person in the entire universe, my best friend forever, and I am a ruin without her. The world is forever dimmer and I'm fumbling towards an endless night but can't seem to find the light switch."

Passed Away. That's all Vain was, now. She wasn't 'gone to the store' or 'watching a movie' or 'making a joke'. She would never again be any of those things. The singular thing she was, now and for the rest of time, was Passed Away. See that? That was Away; Vain had Passed that. She was waving to Away from far up the road, smiling through the rearview mirror. So long, Away. Time to catch up to Forever.

Christ, that was melancholy. He blinked away tears. Vain would haunt from beyond the grave him if he cried in front of these people.

Why would they even bring him here? He didn't have the Padlock and Vain was dead, so he couldn't imagine what they'd want with him. His energy only worked for Vain, it's not like they could attach him to someone else. Aside from the novelty trick of creating excessive amounts of energy off a single calorie, he was useless to them.

He breathed deeply. He would stay calm and wait and watch and listen, and when the moment was right, he'd get out.

The door clacked as someone unlocked it from the outside. It swung open and a tall figure stepped in, filling the doorway; a shadow blocking the light of the outside hallway. Roman swallowed. If his mouth was dry before, now it was dust.

Trick.

For all their paranoia and speculation about Arthur, neither he nor Vain had ever talked to him. He'd give orders from afar, coming in and out of doors; a person in power they'd whisper secrets and rumors about. Trick was the hands-on guy. If Arthur wanted something done, Trick was the person to do it.

Trick could come and go from the Hotel as he pleased. He wasn't there often, but when he was, it usually meant something bad was about to happen. Roman and Vain had lots of dealings with him, and none were ever pleasant.

He wore a fitted black suit. His simple white dress shirt provided a crisp backdrop to the thin black tie held in place with a diamond-shaped clip. His pocket square was immaculate. He was almost offensively attractive, and he smirked as he approached the bed.

"Hi Roman," he said. "Long time no see."

"Hi Trick. It's been a while. I hoped I'd never see you again."

Trick shrugged and kept up his lopsided grin. "There was never a chance of that. Not after you and your little Utili-bitch stole the Padlock from Arthur. We were never going to stop looking for you." He stepped further into the room. "Do you mind if I sit?" He gestured to the chair beside the bed.

"Yeah, go nuts," said Roman.

"Great. First things first, though." Trick drew back and punched Roman in the face.

Sharp pain exploded through his head and his mouth filled with blood. He tried to open his eyes, but his left one was already swelling shut.

"Sorry about that." Trick shook his hand. "But you're an asshole, and you killed two Wyatts. They wanted me to do worse, but I talked them down to a punch."

Roman tried to answer but choked on the blood trickling down the back of his throat. He coughed and spat bright red splotches onto his shirt. He fixed Trick with an angry glare.

"You know what the best part of killing a Wyatt is?" Roman asked. "No remorse. That's what Vain always said. Killing a Wyatt is like clipping a toenail. They're all clones, anyway. Fuck you, and fuck them too."

Trick rolled his eyes and shook his head. "Technically, they're not clones. A clone would be a duplicate model of an identical Wyatt. It's more accurate to say they're multiple instances of the same Wyatt. They're more like recursions." Trick paused to see if Roman was enjoying the lesson in nuance. Roman was not.

"Honestly, Roman." Trick sighed and leaned forward. "Pairing you up with Vain was a mistake. Normally I'm rather good at picking compatible matches, but you bring out the worst in each other. You were supposed to settle her down, not encourage her to be…" he struggled for the words, "more like Vain. I told Arthur we should eliminate the two of you, but he doesn't like to lose property."

Roman grinned through a mouthful of blood. "He likes me."

Trick grunted. "You led us on a good chase. I didn't expect you to last this long outside the Hotel. You cost me money; we had a pool going. I had you caught in the first month. Do you want to guess how slim the odds were on you lasting over a year?"

"Who won the pool?"

"Wyatt."

"Right."

"That was some move you and Vain pulled in Denver. I told the Wyatts to go in careful. I told them Vain was a tiger. I also told them to ignore you because you're a total weepy, useless puss. I was right about that part."

"What do you want, Trick? Why am I here? Are you taking me back to the Hotel? What's the deal?"

"Yeah, we'll talk about that." Trick adjusted his jacket and leaned back in the chair. "Do you want a drink of water or anything?"

"Yes. That would be nice."

"Sure, no problem." Trick snapped at the camera and leaned back in the chair. Twenty seconds later, a Wyatt entered with a cup of water. He wore glasses, an unusual affectation.

"Are you one of the Wyatts that captured me?" asked Roman

"Yeah. I'm the one that was going to punch you in the face. Remember?"

"I remember." Roman attempted to put menace into his voice. "You'll pay for what you did."

"You're funny."

"Wyatt, be pleasant," said Trick. "At least pretend like you're taking the useless battery's threat seriously."

The Wyatt rolled his eyes. "You want to settle up, you know where to find me."

Roman blushed to the roots of his hair. He'd forgotten how Trick and the Wyatts acted. How had he forgotten? It was horrible. This shrugging indifference was almost worse than the alternative. The Wyatt propped Roman's head up and put the glass to his lips. Roman took a long drink.

Trick said nothing through the entire process. When the Wyatt left the room, he spoke again. "I'm sure you're wondering what's coming next."

"Yes." There wasn't any point in lying.

"Arthur wants you back in the Hotel. He's going to connect you with someone new."

"That's impossible. Once I got connected to Vain, it cut me off from giving energy to anyone else. We can't be re-connected."

"That's what I thought too, but Arthur wants to run some experiments. He has ideas about how he can connect you again. He can't stand waste. His words. He thinks he can give you a purpose again. You're lucky he's as nice a guy as he is. I had other ideas."

"Nice?" Roman barked out a laugh. "Arthur is as far from nice as you can get."

"Oh, I wouldn't say that. Arthur is only doing what he has to. You and Vain and the others don't know ten percent of what goes on in there or why Arthur does what he does. You have it easy. You're fed, you're protected; hell, he keeps you in the life of luxury. And you repay him by running off and stealing his stuff." Trick shook his head in sincere disappointment.

"No matter the accommodations, slavery is slavery."

"How's the view up there on that horse? I know what both you and Vain were before the Hotel. The lives we took you from. Trust me. You're better off now."

Roman's eyes widened in anger. "Fuck you, Trick. I'll die before I go back. You can't understand what it's like."

"A man is not a piece of fruit? Is that where you're going?" Trick stood up, pushing his chair back. He dusted an invisible speck of lint off his immaculate suit. "Here's what's going to happen. Arthur wants you back at the Hotel, so you are going back to the Hotel. That said, we're all a little pissed at Vain killing all those Wyatts, so we planned some light entertainment."

He gestured and the Wyatt from earlier walked back in, shadowed by a second. The first Wyatt carried a small cage, and inside was a creature that looked like a cross between a cat and a giant rodent.

"Do you want to guess what this is?" asked Trick.

"Your last sexual conquest?"

"Seriously? Sex jokes? Do you think Vain would make that stupid a joke? That's barely a step above 'that's what she said'."

Roman could not understand for the life of him how Trick constantly managed to confuse and confound him and make him feel about two inches tall, but here he was.

Trick continued. "Let me give you another run at it. Let's start again. Pretend Wyatt just walked in. Do you want to guess what this is?"

"I'm not playing your stupid games," Roman said.

"It looks like a cat, right? Maybe you could have said, 'you've got to be kitten me'. Huh? Good?"

"That's not bad," the Wyatt said.

"That's without planning either. Boom. Right off the top of my head. The point is, Roman, you're total garbage without Vain. A real bag of crap. Anyway, it's an Australian spotted-tail quoll." Trick took the cage and put it on the bed between Roman's legs.

From inside, the animal blinked at Roman. It was rust-colored, with short fur covered in white spots. It appeared feral and gnawed on the bars with sharp-looking teeth.

"The funny thing about the quoll is their diet," Trick said. "Unlike most mammals in Australia, quolls only eat walnuts. It's the damnedest thing. These little guys are crazy for them. A family of them can tear through an entire walnut patch in minutes. They make a fine mess." Trick tapped the top of the cage. A line of perspiration trickled down Roman's face.

"Now this fella here," Trick continued, "we've been working with him for a while. Want to know what we learned about quolls? We learned they love walnuts so much that they'll go to extreme measures to get them. Heck, they even go for things that *look* like walnuts. Chickpeas, golf balls painted brown, even a baby potato will do the trick. Man, these things will tear into them and rip them apart, looking for the sweet, sweet nutty flesh that lies within."

An icy shiver of fear made its way down Roman's back. Trick was a sadistic bastard, and there was no way this would end well. He had a horrible suspicion about where this was going.

"There's more. You know what else looks like a walnut? Testicles." Trick laughed. "Turns out, if you starve a quoll for a week, and put him in front of a pair of delicious testicles, he won't fuss too much. He'll rip them into pieces."

Trick continued tapping on the cage. "Arthur wants you back, but he said nothing about you having your balls attached. Sadly for you, he was non-specific on that point. 'Bring Vain's Conduit back to the Hotel,' he said, not 'Bring Vain's Conduit back to the Hotel and make sure his balls remain in pristine condition'.

He's usually more precise, but I guess he has a lot on his mind. And I'm almost positive you can still generate energy without testicles."

Behind Trick, the two Wyatts smirked, enjoying the spectacle of an Australian rodent about to savage a man's privates. Roman did not see the humor.

"Tell you what, though, I'll make you a deal." Trick put his foot on the bed, right beside Roman's head. "If you agree to lick my boot, really give it a good tongue-shining, I'll call off the rodent. I'll stop a genuine Australian spotted-tail quoll from eating your dick."

"Fuck you," Roman said through clenched teeth. That horrible scenario explained why they'd removed his pants.

Trick shrugged and stepped away from the bed. "Fine by me. I'm not the one who will be missing his lower parts in two minutes." He pulled back the latch and flipped open the cage. The quoll strolled out, sniffing everywhere. The animal rubbed at Roman's legs.

Roman choked back a scream and concentrated on grinding his teeth together. His hands clenched into tight fists. He wouldn't satisfy Trick by screaming.

The quoll continued its lazy walk up the bed. The animal's nose tickled the inside of his thigh and he moaned in panic. He couldn't help it. He honestly did not want his balls eaten. He strained and struggled against his restraints, which startled the quoll, who stopped his sniffing and looked right at him. It moved up his legs to his exposed groin.

"God, no," moaned Roman, shaking. The quoll brushed against him again, and he flexed with all his strength. The restraints wouldn't give. He closed his eyes and gritted his teeth, waiting for the inevitable hot rush of pain. He wouldn't scream.

Something tapped him in the balls, and he screamed.

He yelled as loud as he had ever yelled and pulled so hard against the restraints he thought his muscles would tear. Through his agony, he heard Trick and the Wyatts laughing.

Roman flopped against the bed, exhausted. He was in… no pain at all. Like, nothing. His balls weren't shredded. He opened one eye. The quoll was still sniffing around his legs. It yawned and made its way back into the cage. Trick laughed so hard that he couldn't breathe.

"Jesus," said Trick. "That was awesome." He slapped Roman on the shoulder. "Oh man, you should have seen your face. That was so worth it."

Roman realized the quoll was paying no attention to him or his testicles, which remained completely un-chewed.

"Do you know how much money it cost me to import an actual, authentic quoll from Australia? A goddamn lot, that's how much." Trick wiped his eyes. "That was worth every penny. Just a tip, Roman, I'm not even sure what quolls eat. Probably insects or something. I'm also positive walnuts are not indigenous to Australia. Wyatt, check where walnuts grow, will you?"

The Wyatt pulled out his phone. "China."

"China. Way to know your agricultural geography there, dummy." He smacked Roman on the side of the head.

Roman's face flushed with rage. Goddamn Trick and his goddamn tricks.

"You miserable piece of shit," said Roman. "One day, I'm going to kill you."

Trick was still chuckling to himself. "Sure you are, buddy. Man. That was fantastic. I'm telling everyone about this. I mean, everyone. Arthur, the Wyatts, everyone at the Hotel, you name it. A quoll eating your nuts. I never thought you would buy it. It's so absurd. You know what, I considered going with a marmoset or ferret, but the authenticity of an actual quoll sold the whole thing. I've had that thing forever, waiting for a moment like this. Seriously, I've been feeding it and everything. Now I'm stuck with a quoll. Worth it."

He turned to leave, gesturing for the Wyatts to follow, but paused when he got to the door. "Listen, man, let this happen. It will take a few days to arrange transportation to the Hotel and I bet you'll come up with a bunch of ideas about escaping. But you have nothing to escape to. Vain's dead. Where would you go?"

Roman opened his mouth to respond and realized he didn't have an answer to that. He gaped like a fish.

"Exactly," said Trick. "Stay here like a good battery. If you screw around with me, I'll do shit so bad that you'll beg me to let an Australian mammal eat your ball sack." He paused. "Huh. I never envisioned a world where I would say that sentence."

Trick slammed the door and left Roman alone with his thoughts.

Chapter 13

Vain does not appreciate the difference between a minor detail and an important detail.

Vain hopped into the passenger side of the SUV. The scared red-headed woman from the hospital got in the driver's seat and attempted to put the keys in the ignition with shaking hands.

"Hey," Vain said. "They're gone for now. We're good." She gave a thumbs-up. Her face ached with bruises, and her hands trembled with exhaustion, but she was alive. Alive, and she saved this woman from the Wyatts, and now she had a vehicle. Aces. This whole thing was turning into a real plus.

The red-headed woman took a few breaths and closed her eyes. She didn't say anything for several moments, and Vain used the time to look around the vehicle's interior. Maybe the Wyatts left a clue behind, something to use against them; but aside from stale food wrappers and crumpled newspaper on the floor, there wasn't much.

When the woman opened her eyes, the shaking had stopped. "Where are we going?"

"West," Vain said without hesitation. That's where Roman was. "Keep going out of Boston and head West."

The car started, and they drove around the back of the parking lot and onto the main road.

"Can you please tell me what's going on? Who were those men? Who are you? Why is this happening? Why were you so crazy at the hospital?" The woman seemed bothered by something, although Vain couldn't fathom what. She was totally, one hundred percent un-kidnapped by Wyatts. She should be grinning from ear to ear.

"Crazy?" replied Vain. "I warned you. I was trying to help."

"For future reference, coming up to someone in an emergency room, grabbing their wrist, and telling them they are about to be kidnapped by duplicate men reads higher on the 'crazy' scale than it does on the 'helpful' scale. Just, you know, an FYI."

Vain chewed on that unhelpful and unwelcome feedback, trying to figure out how to respond. The woman glanced over. "I'm Emma, by the way. Thank you for helping me."

"I'm Vain."

Emma blinked and positioned the rear-view mirror so it showed Vain her reflection. "Is that better?"

Vain shook her head. "My name. My actual name is Vain."

"Are you, like, a street artist?"

Vain sighed. "I'm just me."

"How did you know who those men were? How did you know they were after me?"

"They're not men," replied Vain. "They're things. Their name is Wyatt. Their only job is to find people like you and take them back to a place called the Hotel. It's a place I escaped from."

"How are they all called Wyatt? Why do they look the same?"

"They're from alternate Earths." Vain waved her hand, shooing away the explanation.

"I don't believe you," Emma said. "I'm sorry. I know I'm supposed to humor crazy, but I'm exhausted. Please tell me the truth."

"How about this? You go first. Explain how you threw a person with your mind in a way that doesn't violate a couple dozen natural laws, and once you're done, I'll come up with a better explanation for duplicate psychopaths from various incarnations of Earth."

Vain didn't mean to raise her voice, but she couldn't understand why Emma expected her to have all the answers. Same as everyone else, she was trying her best. Emma, for her part, clutched the steering wheel with her eyes fixed on the road. She opened and closed her mouth a few times. Finally, she took a deep breath.

She started to cry.

It wasn't big, heaving sobs; more like the broken weeping of abject misery. She made gulping noises and squinched her eyes.

Vain was not one to show emotion and was a rock of stability; she couldn't even remember when she'd last cried. Probably never. Watching Emma collapse like that made her insides go twisty, and the air conditioning irritated her tear ducts. Time to give this Emma some tough love and get her out of this unreasonable bout of self-pity. Really yell at her.

"I'm going to help you," she said softly. She wasn't sure how Emma felt about physical contact, so she kept her hands tucked under her legs. "Emma. I promise. They don't get to have you. Not while I'm alive. Not while I have a single drop of blood left in my body. I know you're scared. I know this is all new and overwhelming. I don't know why you're part of my story, but we're in this together. Okay? But for this to work, you have to believe me."

Vain felt a little bad for being so hard on Emma with her brutal, tough-love speech, but Emma took it like a champ. Her tears stopped and after a few final sniffles and nose-wipes, she shook her head and sat up straighter.

"Stop being like Thomas Covenant, is what you're saying," Emma tried to smile at her.

"You mean the Pierce Bronson movie? I thought that was called the Thomas Crown Affair."

"No. The book. The Unbeliever series?"

Vain arched an eyebrow. Apparently, Emma liked to sprinkle obscure references into her everyday conversation. Rude.

"If you're ready to listen, I can tell you what I know."

Emma took a moment to collect herself before nodding. Vain told her, in brief, about The Hotel and about being a Conduit. She left out components that weren't that important, like falling off a building, the Padlock, Trick, or how she was working on a plan to fix everything that also might kill them. Minor details were not important.

The telling only took a couple of minutes, and Emma didn't ask questions. Vain didn't mind the silence and watched the twinkle of cars passing by.

"I killed him," Emma finally said. "I killed another human being."

"Stop," Vain said. "You didn't kill a human, you killed a Wyatt. It's not the same thing. You have nothing to feel guilty about. He would have done worse to you."

Emma glanced at her, apprehension written all over her face. "You're sure these guys aren't the government or something? Is this some secret FBI thing?"

"It's an Arthur thing. He's the guy who runs the place. Now you've shown them you're activated, he'll be more interested than ever in finding you. He doesn't like people running around outside his control."

"I should go to the police."

Vain had expected that, and it was an effort not to roll her eyes. "Emma, I want you to walk me through what would happen if you did that."

"I'd tell them they kidnapped me."

"Okay. Then what?"

"I'd give them descriptions and tell them everything you told me. I'd tell them they will come after me again."

"Great. Let's pretend the police believe your insane story about hotels and duplicate kidnappers and superhuman powers. Then what?"

"Then they'd help me," Emma banged her palm on the steering wheel. "How am I supposed to know? They're the police."

"They're people," replied Vain. "People who have families and normal lives and other cases. They'd take your statement, fill out some paperwork and send you home. The Wyatts will not stop. They'll wait another month and try again. If they didn't succeed that time, they'll wait and try again, and again. Even if the police were around, even if they stopped the Wyatts and sent them to jail, Arthur would send more. There are an infinite number of Wyatts." Vain drilled into Emma, emphasizing each word. "You've killed one of them and somehow you can absorb energy without a connection to a Conduit. Arthur will want to examine you, and Arthur always gets what he wants. If that means throwing an endless stream of Wyatts at you, that's what he'll do."

Emma seemed like she would argue, but instead, she focused on the road and didn't respond. She chewed at her inner lips. They drove in silence, and Vain shut up to give her the time to figure it out.

"Let's say I agree with you," Emma said. "What am I supposed to do? Run? Is my family in danger too? Do you have a plan?"

Vain thought about the fight with the Wyatts; how Emma threw the guy halfway across the planet. Vain could never do that. Shoving people was the extent of her power, and what Emma demonstrated easily surpassed Vain's abilities. Emma was the table spot in her wrestling match, so to speak. But Emma didn't need to know that.

"First, we're going to find my Conduit. He's the guy I pull my power from, his name is Roman. He's great, you'll like him a lot. He's really smart. Like, school smart." Vain chewed her lip. "He doesn't smoke a pipe, but don't let that throw you off. I'm sure he'd be willing to start."

"What?"

"Anyway, we became separated a day or so ago. No biggie. You might say I planned all of this. In fact, you should literally say that. Those exact words. If anyone asks, that is. Not that they will. But if they do, say 'You can't even be mad at Vain for this'. Can you remember that?"

"Seriously, what?"

"Say it wasn't my fault," Vain insisted. She couldn't seem to control her breathing. This conversation was getting away from her.

"Vain, I don't know what you're talking about. But yes, I agree the Wyatts coming after me wasn't your fault."

Not quite what Vain meant, but close enough. Emma was right, though. None of it had been her fault, and was doing the best she could with what she had. She continued.

"I'm not sure where Roman is, but he's somewhere off in that direction." She waved her hand. "We'll find him, and after that, we'll talk about what to do next. While we're on our way, I can teach you about your powers."

Emma shook her head. "None of this makes any sense. I can't go with you, I have a life. Friends, school, my parents."

"What good will it do your friends and family if you forget all about them?"

"What do you mean?" asked Emma.

"As a part of the activation process, Arthur takes your memory. That's why my name is Vain. Well, technically, Vanity, but I don't like that. A guy from the Hotel gave it to me."

"This is unbelievable. It's crazy."

"Yeah, I'm not sure about the process he uses. I think your name would be something like Bookworm, but honestly, I'm guessing. They tend to be slightly more poetic."

"I didn't mean that part."

"Precocity?"

"Stop. Just… stop. I'm so exhausted."

"You're in this now, Emma. I don't know why you can do the things you do. All I know is, you're something Arthur wants, and that's enough for me." She stared straight ahead, into the darkness. It seemed to go on forever, it's presence barely disturbed by the headlights that strained to penetrate through it. That didn't stop the headlights from trying, though. Stupid, stubborn things. Impulsively, Vain made a promise.

"He will not get you."

She left out the part about how they might need to run right at him to stop him.

Minor details.

Chapter 14

Emma does not learn anything important about Sweden.

At dawn, Emma turned off the highway and drove them to a run-down, two-story motel beside a pawn shop with bars on the windows. The counter was sticky with some substance Emma didn't want to think about. A single fluorescent light flickered in the spotty, water-damaged ceiling. Vain paid, pushing cash across the counter with the tip of her finger, trying not to touch anything. Emma had nothing to contribute. She was lucky enough to have her phone. Her wallet hadn't been on her when the Wyatts came.

"Single room, huh?" Behind the checkout counter, the clerk waggled his eyebrows, eying Emma up and down. Of course. Two women checking into a single room. Hilarious.

"You remind me of Andy Griffith," Vain said.

"Why, because of my good looks?" The guy snorted, impressed at his joke.

"No, because you're a fucking asshole."

Both the clerk and Emma glanced at Vain, waiting for further explanation of the punchline. But, no. That was it. Andy Griffith was an asshole, apparently. Vain stared back at the clerk, unblinking, until he stopped smirking and dropped his eyes. He muttered under his breath and handed over the keys. Emma shook her head.

Vain hadn't wanted to stop, but she was fading and struggled to keep her eyes open. They needed a break. Emma also needed time to ingest everything that had happened. This sudden rush of power, the near-kidnapping, the frantic flight with this insane woman— she needed to work through it all.

The room was as miserable as she expected, two single beds separated by a scratched and battered nightstand. More water stains covered the ceiling, and she swore she saw mouse droppings along the edge of the baseboards. The thought of lying down on those beds turned her stomach, but Vain didn't seem to share her disgust.

"I call closest to the window," Vain said. She threw herself onto the nearest bed and burrowed under the covers.

Emma gagged a little.

The moment Vain's head hit the pillow, her breathing slowed, and small snoring sounds followed soon after. Emma huddled up on top of the covers and closed her eyes, but the acrid odor of cleaning supplies and damp mold gave her a headache. Every individual spring in the mattress pushed against her back and she threw her arm over her eyes, hoping to at least settle her nerves. Vain was a distracting hot pulse of power. It was like trying to sleep beside a furnace, albeit one powered by rage and bad hair choices.

Emma tossed and turned, and after about an hour of fidgeting, settled into a light doze. It only lasted a few minutes before she woke up again, restless and brimming with stolen energy.

She got out of bed, being careful not to wake Vain, and went into the bathroom. One look at the tub discouraged her from a bath, but she took a long, hot shower and let herself relax as the water washed over her. The marks from the Wyatts had faded to almost nothing. It was creepy. She had been punched and roughed up. Bruises should cover her face, but nothing showed. Did she heal faster now too? She wished she had some makeup. Such a stupid thing, but a normal thing. She needed normal right now.

She pulled out her phone from the sweatpants that lay crumpled on the floor and sat on the toilet. A harried, fifteen-minute texting binge ensued, first to her mom, followed by her friends, letting them know she would be offline for a while. A 'study bender', she called it. Doreen joked she was the only person who made the word "bender" sound dull. Regardless, it bought Emma some space while she tried to figure out her next steps; and more importantly, investigate these strange new powers she had gained.

She opened the notes app on her phone and got to typing.

One: She could absorb energy from everyone. This gave her limitless stamina, and while getting punched still hurt, she healed faster now.

Two: She could form the energy into something physical, external from her body.

Three: She didn't need to sleep.

Some small amount of tension melted from shoulders. Working the problem like that gave her something tangible to hold on to, a way to break the challenge down into its composite parts. If she'd had access to a notepad? Look out.

When she was little, she had to get her tonsils out, and during the week leading up to the surgery, she learned everything about the procedure. She poured over medical texts, reading about the parts of the throat—epiglottis, pharynx, and palate, what they would remove—tonsils and adenoids, and the type of gas they would use to put her under—desflurane, isoflurane, or sevoflurane. Her doctor joked that she'd be able to perform the operation herself.

Life was mechanics, chemical and electrical reactions. There was no man behind the curtain, no pot of gold at the end of the rainbow, and the only magic in the world was losing yourself in the delightful whimsy of an episode of Parks and Recreation. Everything happening to her had a solution. Every effect had a cause. She'd figured out everything else in her life, and she'd figure this out, too.

Time for some experiments. She got dressed and tiptoed from the bathroom so as not to wake Vain, who still snored on the bed with her head wrapped underneath the blankets.

Emma tried to recall the sensation of throwing the Wyatt. The energy became like a physical extension of her thoughts, like taking a song that only existed in your head and singing it. Turning thought into something. She focused on the small lamp on the nightstand and imagined it smothered in energy. The tips of her fingers tingled with cold as power dripped out of her and flowed outwards. It was alarming, but not uncomfortable. She did the same thing to the small TV and the pillow on the bed. Three objects, all wrapped in her mental energy

She lifted.

The lamp, TV, and pillow rose as if held by an invisible hand. It was effortless, taking only a fraction of her control. Once she had it locked in place, the energy maintained itself. Next, she created a small set of stairs in front of her, like a footstool. She took a cautious step forward, half expecting her foot to meet no resistance. Instead, there was something firm underneath. One step up, and another, and she stood atop a solid platform. The floor remained two feet below her. It looked like she was floating.

"This is crazy," she murmured.

It took about as much mental effort as doing the higher end of the multiplication tables or remembering the words to a song. It required concentration, but it wasn't difficult. As a reaction to the energy leaving her, the amount coming in increased. She focused, and it slowed back down to a trickle. Whatever this thing in her brain was, it tried to replace the energy going out with more coming in. That was its natural reflex, but she could stop it if she wanted to.

"Neat," she said.

The noise woke up Vain, who groaned and rolled onto her back. Her eyes opened. She rubbed at one with her hand and looked around the room.

She yawned. "I can do the thing you're doing, standing in the air, but not the making objects float trick. How does that one work?"

Emma had expected more reaction to a room filled with magical floating hotel items and was slightly disappointed. "I imagine them wrapped in energy and once I get them covered, I can move them around."

"Huh," said Vain, either bored or half asleep. "Well, that's great. I'm not sure I could do this much. It would take everything I have. Can you put all this stuff down?"

Emma hadn't considered how she would stop it. She tried to reduce the energy and put the items back, but it all vanished at once. The TV smashed onto the table, the lamp tumbled to the floor, and the pillow hit the bed with a flop. Emma's stool disappeared, and she lost her footing, landing awkwardly and falling onto her backside with a clumsy thud.

"Tada!" She raised her hands in an exaggerated flourish.

Vain's expression didn't change. Tough crowd. "You can use it as a weapon, too. I can create shields strong enough to stop bullets. I can also fire energy blasts, although not for very long. Either of those will help if the Wyatts come near you again."

"How is it for you?" Emma stood up and dusted herself off. "How do you do it?"

Vain tilted her head. "You know how when everyone tells you what to do, tries to get you to act in a certain way, but when their head is turned, you punch their dick into slush?"

"I do not. Not at all. I'm not even sure you've described a real thing."

"Well, that's what using the power is like to me. I channel that emotion."

"If I ever encountered a culture where the emotion associated with genital-punching as a response to be being told what to do was so commonplace they needed a word for it, I would never, ever visit them."

"Sweden must have a word for that. Aren't they constantly incoherent with rage?"

Emma shook her head. "Without knowing one word of Swedish, I'm positive they do not have a specific word for that."

"Meatball."

"How is this helping me? You said you'd teach me how to use these powers."

"I will," said Vain. "Think of me as your own personal Yoda."

"The tree frog from the Star Wars movies? You're nothing like that. Didn't he have a series of pithy sayings? How about working on draining the energy from me? That would be helpful."

Vain considered for a moment, then grabbed something out of her front pocket. It looked like a broken padlock.

"Do you think you can focus your energy on this?" she asked.

"Why?"

"Can you do it, or not?" Vain gestured to her hand. "Try. Or, if you prefer, do or do not do. There is no try."

Emma wasn't sure what Vain even meant. She noted the dented, chipped locking section on the padlock and the dull, rusty base. A word was scratched into the side. The longer she examined it, the more it drew her in. A small pull emanated from the tiny object and she found she could push energy into it. The padlock seemed alive and hungry. At first, she gave it a trickle, but soon more and more flowed through her. The trickle became a stream, and the stream became a deluge.

Energy ripped through her in a wave, the padlock drinking it all in. She tried to break the connection, to focus her attention elsewhere, but she couldn't. The padlock took everything. She gasped and dropped to her knees, eyes still focused on Vain's hand.

"I can't stop it," she said, struggling for breath. "I can't break the hold. Help."

"What do you mean you can't stop it?" Vain asked. Her eyes widened, and she grabbed Emma by the wrist.

Emma couldn't draw enough air to respond. Her gaze remained fixed on the padlock, her head frozen in place. Every one of her muscles clenched as she struggled against the pull. The light in the room dimmed, fading to a single point: the shining glow of the padlock. Energy coursed through her in hot, painful waves. She wanted to scream, but there was no air in her lungs.

Vain staggered and fell against the bed. "Emma, stop," she said. "You're pulling from me, now."

Emma tried to shut it off, but it was like trying to stop a waterfall with your hand. She resisted with all her will. The padlock had an insatiable hunger and was determined to suck every ounce out of energy from her. She closed her eyes and concentrated, but it was pointless. Whatever this padlock was, it would kill her.

She heard, more than felt, the sharp, meaty thud of a fist hitting her face. Her head snapped back and she fell back to the ground, clutching her cheek. The link to the padlock broke. She gasped, sucking in a monstrous breath.

Vain stood over her, shaking her hand. "Hitting you is like hitting a wall."

Candy was sweet. Night was dark. Vain spoke to Emma in that exact same tone, unconcerned that she'd just punched her in the face.

"What happened?" She couldn't muster the strength to lift her head off the ground. "Why did you make me do that? Did you know that would happen? What is that thing?"

"This is our ticket out of this mess." Vain gave the padlock a quick kiss before slipping it back into her pocket. She looked happy enough to dance a jig.

Emma thought she heard Vain mutter *suplex,* but that couldn't possibly have been right.

"It warmed up when you put your energy into it," Vain continued. "I don't know how much juice this thing needs to reset, but it will take more sessions. We'll try again once we get moving and once you get your strength back up."

"Are you insane? I never want to do that again. I think I almost died."

"You didn't though, and we got rid of your excess energy. Win-win." Vain winked and shot her with a single gun finger.

"What is the second 'win' in that statement? Is the first 'win' me not dying? Because if so, I'd like to make an observation: you have the bar for winning set way too low."

"You've got to learn to trust me, Emma."

Emma's eyes nearly rolled out of her skull. "What is that thing, anyway?"

"It's a Device," said Vain. "Something I stole when I escaped the Hotel."

Emma cracked an enormous yawn. She rubbed at her cheek where Vain slapped her. It had been a hard smack, but it may as well have been a tickle with a feather. "Can I go to bed first?" she asked. "With the energy pulled out of me, I'm sleepy for the first time in days."

"Sure, Emma," said Vain. "I'll watch over you. When you wake up, we'll get going."

"Do you know where we're going next?" Emma crawled into the bed.

"To solve every single problem that has ever bothered anyone, ever, anywhere." Vain held up her fist.

"What?" Emma sighed.

"Or, you know. To find Roman. Either is good."

Chapter 15

Roman tries to escape. Again.

Roman could describe every scratch on the wall of his tiny prison in perfect detail. The baseboards were uneven, and there were four hundred and eighteen dirt-brown floor tiles. Every three minutes and eleven seconds, the overhead lights flickered. Water dripped from the faucet into the stained sink, creating a plinking rhythm that made it impossible to sleep.

Three days. Three solid days since Trick left, taking his stupid rodent with him, leaving Roman alone with only his thoughts for company. Late into the second day, after a restless sleep filled with nightmares and large, accusing eyes, a Wyatt cracked opened the door and tossed in an armful of books. Curious, Roman got out of bed to see what they were.

Jackie Collins romance novels.

He tried to figure out the joke. Did they pick these books to screw with him because they thought Jackie Collins was bad? Or did they think he liked romance novels? Sometimes, Trick's pranks veered so far into the esoteric as to be unfathomable. Joke or not, it gave him something to do and kept his mind off Vain.

By the third day, he had established that while Jackie Collins was a credible writer, he did not care for her specific style of novel. Oddly though, it helped clear his head and focused his thoughts. It was while reading Chances that he decided to escape. He'd be like Dario Santangelo, who had become trapped in his apartment after his male lover took his keys. The parallel between the circumstances wasn't exact, but close enough. Roman would craft his own escape, using Jackie Collins as his inspiration.

He needed a plan. But planning was Vain's thing, and she was gone. That was neither the place nor the time to grieve, so he forced himself to focus. Think. The room was locked tight; there were no windows. The camera on the ceiling with its blinking red light watched his every move. Aside from the sink in the corner and the nightstand beside the bed, the only other item was the box of granola bars they'd left him.

Hmm.

Since they had activated him as a Conduit, he didn't need to eat much. A granola bar had over a hundred calories. For a normal person, that would be half a million joules of energy; or enough to power a single light bulb for an hour. For people like him, the energy output from a calorie was increased. One granola bar for him would be closer to twenty million joules, or forty times the energy of a normal person. He didn't know where his upper limit sat. He only knew that without Vain there to siphon it, it would keep building.

When he'd first woken up in the Hotel, he'd been confused and disoriented with no memory, only knowing he was in a terrible place. The Wyatts ushered both him and Vain into a cavernous round room with high ceilings. A plain white table stood in the middle, a set of high-backed wooden chairs on either side. Vain's long blond hair covered the bruises on her face. She looked as scared as him and he remembered feeling protective towards her even then.

A flexi-hose tap connector rested on the table, the type used underneath sink drains. A Wyatt barked at them to pick it up and focus. Focus on a piece of plumbing equipment? It was disorienting and confusing, but the Wyatts bullied them into it. One punched him in the back of the head. Anxious to avoid any more abuse, he did what they asked.

The moment he picked it up, his head started buzzing. Something was compelling about the connector; the curve of the hose, the way the muted grey plastic seemed to pulse and undulate. He couldn't look away. Everything faded and his vision blurred.

The world crumbled into blackness, an absence of light so profound he thought it had struck him blind. His body shook with tension and he couldn't catch his breath. Thick, wet pressure surrounded him. Across the endless void, he perceived Vain; not seeing her, but experiencing her as a physical presence in his mind, both repellent and intimate. An experimental tug came from her direction, an attempt to harness the pressure that surrounded them, to draw it towards her. Curious, he tugged back.

White-hot rage exploded from Vain, and her gentle pull became a gut-wrenching yank, ripping away his sense of self and causing him to gasp in pain. The entirety of the wet pressure flowed towards her in a tsunami, leaving him shuddering and empty. It was no contest.

In seconds, it established her as the Utility and he as the Conduit. After that, they were bonded, him and her against the world. Much later, Trick laughed that he had never seen a person cave so quickly; normally, the struggle between Utility and Conduit took a couple of hours.

Trick had never been on the other side of Vain.

More than anything, he wished she were there with him. In the Hotel, she'd been the one to figure out how everything worked. Asking the Wyatts had been pointless; it would only earn a cuff to the ear or a harsh curse. Soon enough, they all figured out what their sole purpose was.

Put energy into the Well.

Like every other Device in the Hotel, the Well was literally that. A huge, bottomless chasm that took up an entire room on the ground floor. Every week, the Utility and Conduits shuffled into the room, grabbed onto a pair of handles, and poured in their energy. God help them if it wasn't enough.

Roman let his head fall. Remembering her brought back the sadness and helplessness he had crammed into the back of his brain. Time slipped through his fingers. Every day he stayed here, doing nothing, he got a day closer to the Hotel. He needed a workable solution. He sketched out a plan so bare bones that to call it an idea would be offensive to the word. Basically, he'd punch his way out. Vain would have liked it.

Everyone in the Hotel underestimated Conduits. The Utilities got all the attention; they were the ones with the ability to harness energy and do wonderful, magical things with it. They viewed conduits as passive, plodding dummies, only good for following instructions and fading into the background. Truth be told, they were kind of right. Being a Conduit didn't have many advantages, but there were a few. He'd make use of what he had.

Without Vain to siphon off his energy, it would continue to build within him. Some would dissipate on its own, but not all of it. Without her, the only way to self-regulate would be to stop eating. Instead, he gorged himself on the granola bars.

Shortly, energy infused him, filling up his body. He tasted copper and his hearing became dull and thick, like his head was

swaddled in cotton. Having this much in him made everything…
more. That was the only way to describe it. It didn't make him
invulnerable, but it made him harder to hurt. It didn't make him
superhumanly strong, but it made him slightly stronger. Normally,
he didn't have time to experiment with these side effects, because
Vain would take the power as soon as he generated it. Today, he'd
use what minor advantages he had. They thought he was useless?
He'd show them.

A small table lamp sat on the nightstand by his bed. He
tugged and strained at the electrical cord and ripped it from the base
of the lamp, leaving the wires exposed. When he touched them
together, he got a satisfying pop and smelled burned rubber. The
wires were hot and active.

He grabbed his bedding and sparked the wires above it,
sending fiery sparks cascading down. The blankets smoldered and
smoked, and soon a small flame rewarded his efforts. He blew on it
until it caught and crammed the flaming pile of sheets against the
base of the door. Flames engulfed the plywood, and the room filled
with smoke. He coughed. Maybe not one of his better ideas, but too
late to change course.

"Hey!" he yelled, to make sure he had their attention. "Stupid
Wyatts! My room is on fire, somehow!"

The noxious smoke burned his lungs. He wondered if they'd
watched him set fire to his room through the video camera? It didn't
matter, it's not like they'd let him burn to death.

Would they?

The door was ablaze and the fire spread to the nearby walls.
Moments ticked by. As it turned out, when trapped in a burning
room, every second seemed like an eternity. What the hell was
taking them so long? Why weren't they coming? Jesus, they were
going to let him burn to death.

"Hey!" He pounded on the door and inhaled a lungful of
smoke. Coughing, he fell back against the bed and covered his
mouth with his arm.

Finally, Wyatts yelled at him from the other side of the door.
Roman had never been so relieved to hear their voices. Time to
execute part two of his barely-a-plan-plan.

Roman rushed towards the small sink in the corner and
kicked at the faucet. Once, twice; three times. With a *pop,* it

detached, spraying water everywhere. A pool collected on the floor and hissed where it met fire.

The door crashed open and two Wyatts burst through. Glasses was one of them. Roman owed Glasses some punches. The other had a crew cut, which helped to tell them apart. Both looked angry.

"What the fuck?" said Crew Cut.

Both Wyatts stomped on the bedsheets, creating a smoky, soggy mess. The floor was soaked. It was almost impossible to see anything through all the smoke. Roman jumped onto his bed where he had left the exposed wire, still plugged into the wall. He held it up for dramatic effect.

"Hey guys," he said. "I hope you don't find my exit too... shocking." He threw the wires onto the wet floor and covered his head with his arms.

Nothing happened.

He peeked out from behind his forearms. The Wyatts ignored him and continued stomping out the fire, coughing from the smoke. The last of the flames sputtered and died and, in the background, water gurgled.

"For fuck sakes, dude," said Glasses. "Was this meant to be some kind of escape? I am going to kick the ever-loving shit out of you."

The exposed wire in the puddle of water crackled to life, and blue electricity lanced through the room. The lights flickered. Both Wyatts convulsed as electricity coursed through their bodies, making horrible *nuh-nuh-nuh-nuh* sounds while they twitched.

After ten seconds, a *pop-pop* noise came from the outlet and the room was plunged into darkness. Roman heard the double thump of two thoroughly electrocuted assholes hitting the ground. He crawled off the bed and moved across the dark room, holding his hands out in front of him. His foot hit a Wyatt and he stumbled to the ground, grabbing a meaty thigh. There was something hard and metal attached to it.

Deliriously, he said, "Is that a gun in your pocket, or are you happy to see me?" But no. It was a gun. Roman had no experience with firearms, but one might come in handy if he ran into trouble. He stuffed it into his pocket and made his way to the door.

The frame was still hot. He covered his mouth, trying to avoid breathing the smoke that now filled the hallway. Edging past the smoldering pile of blankets, he stepped outside. At the end of a short hallway, stairs led to the rectangular outline of a door. There was light on the other side. It looked like he was in the basement of a house.

He rushed down the hallway and took the stairs in two giant leaps. The doorknob turned without any resistance, and he experienced a burst of triumph. The door opened into an ordinary kitchen with white counters and a large wooden table in the middle. It was daytime. The kitchen windows looked out onto a quiet suburban road.

It was a safe house. But why were there only two Wyatts guarding him? Where was—

Trick walked into the kitchen. He had a newspaper tucked under one arm and his eyes widened at Roman's presence. He waved his hand against the smoke that drifted upwards from the basement.

"Hey buddy," he said. "Trying to escape?"

"Yep," Roman took cautious steps towards the door that would grant him freedom.

"That's super." Trick smiled. "I didn't think you had it in you. I mean, this is pointless, I will absolutely stop you, but it's nice to know you aren't a total dishrag." He took a menacing step closer.

Roman pulled the gun out of his pocket. It snagged, and he had to yank at it, causing it to clatter to the floor. With a startled curse, he dropped to his knees, retrieved it, and rose again. The entire sequence took eight agonizing seconds and Trick watched with a bemused grin.

"Ha!" Roman, triumphant, pointed the gun right at Trick's face.

"The safety is on."

Unable to stop himself, Roman checked the side of the gun and then Trick was beside him. In seconds, he disarmed Roman, punched him in the ribs, and flipped him to the ground where he landed with a hard thud.

"What's the endgame here, Roman?" Trick stood above him, twirling the gun. "Are you going to run out of the house? Do you think we didn't plan for this possibility?" Trick stepped away from him, gun hanging at his side.

Roman got to his feet, holding his hands up over his head. Trick now stood between him and the door.

"Actually, yes," said Roman. "You always treated us like talking toasters. I wouldn't be surprised if this whole operation was you and those two guys down there."

"Heh. You're right. I was messing with you. We didn't waste people on this. We figured we'd sit on you until we were ready to take you to the Hotel. You're like a garbage bag full of milk."

Roman blinked. "I don't understand. Is that meant to be insulting?"

"I mean, you're soft and squishy and punchable like if you took two hundred liters of milk and poured it into a garbage bag."

As Trick explained his stinging bon mot, Roman lunged at him with a vicious shoulder block. He threw blind haymakers, but few connected. Trick recovered, lashing out with fast punches that got through Roman's defenses. He took a shot to the jaw, the chin, the temple. Roman countered with a punch, but Trick contemptuously swatted it away. Another blow to the head sent Roman reeling, and he fell to the ground. He covered his head while Trick kicked him over and over.

After twenty seconds, the kicking stopped. Trick stood above him, panting. The beating hurt, but he had enough energy stored that it was like getting punched through a blanket. He'd have bruises tomorrow, but nothing was broken. Trick didn't know that, though. Roman groaned and rolled over onto his back, making sure to appear hurt. He squinted at Trick who pulled out his phone.

"Hey, it's Trick. Send more Wyatts. Four, at least. It looks like our battery is a double A." He paused. "He tried to escape, but I stopped him. I'm not sure what he did to the other Wyatts, I haven't checked yet. I didn't think this milk bag had any fight in him." He frowned while he listened. "Because picture a bag of milk. Would you find it threatening?" He shook his head, still frowning. "Well, agree to disagree, then. It's a perfectly good insult." He hung up, complaining under his breath. He reached down to hoist Roman to his feet.

Roman attacked.

He pulled Trick's arm towards him and head-butted him in the face. Through his blanket of energy, Roman barely felt it, but Trick's nose exploded. With a scream, he fell back, dropping the gun and clutching his face. Roman grabbed Trick's hair and slammed his head into the cabinet. *Thud. Thud. Thud.* He brought his knee up into the side of his head, once, twice, a third time for good measure, and stepped back.

Trick slid to the floor, unconscious. Roman stood over him, breathing hard, unable to believe his plan worked. He beat Trick. One on one. Without Vain. A rush of excitement flashed through him and, for good measure, he kicked Trick one last time in the stomach.

"Watch out, Trick. This milk has gone sour."

Trick didn't seem to appreciate the zing, what with being knocked senseless. Oh, well. Roman wished he had sunglasses to put on. On a whim, he rooted through Trick's pockets and took his phone and wallet.

Grinning, he ran out of the kitchen and into freedom.

Chapter 16

Emma references Michelle Obama to get herself out of a jam.

Emma had been driving since the Motel. Releasing pent-up energy into the Padlock let her sleep for a few hours, but eventually, the non-stop trickle flowing into her body woke her up. During the car ride, she'd attempted to draw Vain into a conversation, all without any success. If she asked about the Hotel or the Wyatts, Vain would grunt something unhelpful and retreat into her head. If she asked whether Vain believed the Corey Feldman character from The Goonies was the same character as Corey Feldman from Lost Boys, she was suddenly a Rhodes Scholar on a lecture tour.

Emma had long since tuned out, turning towards increasingly morose thoughts, when she realized Vain had asked her a question.

"I'm hungry."

Okay, so not a question. And kind of insensitive, given Emma was unable to eat now. Was there a term for that? Differently-appetited?

She pulled off the exit ramp and into a gas station beside a fast-food place lit by a gaudy neon-orange sign that read 'Mink Burgers'. Mink. Was that supposed to be someone's name? What in hell was a mink burger? It was a silly thing to call a burger place, and to lighten the mood, she sang, "If you like your burgers mink, get them here, we'll cook them pink."

"That's great Emma, I can't wait to hear your tight five at the Improv." Vain pointed. "There's a spot over there."

Miffed, Emma pulled into the back of the parking lot beside a field full of scraggly brush and half-dead trees. "How are we going to pay for any of this?" She asked. "Do you have any money left?"

"Barely, but I found a few bucks in the glove box. Can you grab the food? We'll eat outside. It's less crowded." She pointed to a patio that had lime-green plastic tables bolted to the ground under limp umbrellas. She crammed a fistful of wrinkled dollars into Emma's hand and hopped out of the car.

Emma headed into the large building to hunt down lunch. Vain had not been specific on what she was looking for, so she got the Mink Combo #1, a cheeseburger and onion rings. Even surrounded by the smell of a fresh meal, Emma had no appetite. This condition was going to help with weight loss, at least.

Families walked by, each one a blinking pulse of energy. They talked to each other, they ordered food, they sat down. They weren't being chased. They were normal. It had only been days since this whole thing started, and already, she missed that. Being normal. The routine of day-to-day life. Not being saddled with a choppy-haired psychopath who struggled to make eye contact.

But Vain had been going through this for much longer, and she'd endured. Sure, she was sharp angles and emotional elbows, but it was understandable, given everything she'd suffered. How much would Emma change if she went through all the same horrors? If Vain could make it, so could she.

Balancing the tray of food, Emma spotted Vain at the furthest table away from the entrance. She sat with her back to the scrub forest, biting her fingernails, her lips moving soundlessly. Her knees were tucked under her chin and her head constantly swiveled, trying to look at everything at once. Twice, she flinched, turning at something behind her, even though there was nothing there. She was the very picture of anxiety, and Emma's heart softened a little. The poor woman. Again, she experienced a tingle of selfish fear for herself. Is this what she'd become? Vain was right about one thing, they needed to stop this. But how?

Emma walked over and plopped the food down, earning a grunted thanks.

"We might have to leave." Vain thrust her chin out at a group of three younger guys a few tables over. "They've been staring at me. I don't know what they want."

"They're guys," said Emma, glancing to where Vain gestured. "They don't want anything. They're looking at us because we're girls."

Vain arched an eyebrow and tore into her burger. "Anytime anyone looks at me, it gives me the creeps. And I'm all out of dick punch."

Emma frowned at the randomness of that last sentence but ignored it. "I'm sure it's nothing, Vain."

"You never know. Arthur is a clever guy."

"I thought Arthur only sent Wyatts after us?"

"You can't be too careful." Vain picked up a fry and waved it to emphasize her point before popping it in her mouth. "There's no reason a guy should look at me."

Emma scratched her head. "Vain, do you know what you look like?"

Vain stopped eating for a moment and squinted at Emma. "What do you mean?"

"You're not ugly. Not at all. You're just unpolished."

Vain arched an eyebrow at her but said nothing.

"That came out wrong," said Emma. "Let me try again. It's not outside the realm of possibility that a guy your age would stare at you because he wants your phone number. If a guy was into the angry goth-slash-emo sort of thing, you might be their type, even if you're not what people would consider traditionally attractive." She made air quotes around the last word and realized she sounded even more horrible.

Vain blinked at her, chewing slowly.

Emma panicked. "But hey, you know who else wasn't considered traditionally attractive? Mona Lisa. And now look at her! She's the hottest painting in the world. Ok, so she's no Comtesse d'Haussonville, but then, not everyone can be Jean-Auguste-Dominique Ingres, am I right?"

She got no reaction from Vain. Not a fan of classical French painters, apparently.

"You know who else doesn't follow traditional standards of beauty? Michelle Obama. And, she was the president's wife. The first black president, I might add, which, while not making her more attractive, per se, certainly adds to her mystique. So, what I'm saying is, you need to be yourself, like Mona Lisa and Michelle Obama taught us. Maybe get a normal haircut and boom. We'll have guys hitting on you in no time. Or, I mean, people. Whatever your thing is. You need to be yourself, and yes, I recognize the inherent contradiction in telling you to both be yourself and get a new haircut, but also consider this. Equality." Yikes. That one was uneven. That said, she was confident she'd recovered near the end. Was there any speech a Michelle Obama reference couldn't improve? Probably not.

Vain snorted, shook her head, and continued eating.

Emma realized that a Vain-snort was equal to a laugh for a normal person and was relieved the moment passed. She played with her hair as Vain continued to inhale French fries.

"I want to try something," Vain said around a mouthful of food. "Do you think you could hold energy outside yourself? Not do anything with it, but just hold it?"

"I think so." She sort of understood what Vain wanted. "Once I imagine the energy outside my body, I shape it and keep it in place."

"Try this," said Vain. "I want you to form an energy ball the size of a marble. Can you do that?"

"Sure." Emma focused and did what Vain asked. She created a small dot of energy, hovering between the two of them.

"Okay, now send it to those trees over there." Vain gestured behind them. "Once it's there, tell me."

"It's there," said Emma. One moment, it was between Vain and Emma, and the next, it was in the clearing behind them, one hundred feet away. "It's a little harder to control from this distance," she said. "It's like it's slippery."

"Don't worry about that," said Vain. "I want you to release all the energy in the ball at once. Try detonating it."

Emma did what Vain asked. The energy ball burst with a loud pop. It sounded like a firecracker going off. "Neat," she said. "That took hardly any energy, if that's what you were trying to figure out."

Vain tapped her fingers on the table. "Hmm. Roman was right. Maybe we would have blown up the money."

"Come again?"

"Nothing. I'm done here, let's get gas."

"Do we have any money left?"

"Don't worry about it. I have an idea."

Emma rolled her eyes. There was no getting through Vain's explanation aversion. It was frustrating, but she was getting used to it. They got back into the car and drove around to the gas station. Vain got out, put the hose into the car, and poked her head in the window.

"I need you to make a bigger energy ball. The biggest you can do."

"Why?"

"Because. Put it in that meadow behind us, away from everybody."

Emma wasn't sure what Vain was up to, but she was curious, and she enjoyed doing these experiments. With every step, she inched closer to understanding, with understanding came control. Maybe if she did a bigger one it would suck out some of the excess power, too.

She focused on the meadow behind the gas station and created a shape about the size of a yoga ball. She anchored it as far away as she could, well into the growth of trees.

"As big as you can make it," said Vain.

"I'm at my limit. It's about the size of a yoga ball, but it's getting slippery. Any bigger and I won't be able to control it."

"Okay, now detonate it."

"Are you crazy?"

A man at the pump beside them glanced over, arching his eyebrow. Emma realized she was almost shouting.

She forced her voice to a harsh whisper. "It's two hundred times the size of the one I did before."

"It will be fine," said Vain. "If this works, it gives you a reliable way to siphon off energy. Make sure you shut your eyes."

"It will blow everything up, though."

"I don't think size affects the explosion. I'm sure it will be a small puff. The detonation is inversely proportional to the amount of energy you put in."

"Why would it be inversely proportional? That makes no sense. That's not how energy works. In fact, that's the exact opposite." It was getting harder to hold the energy ball, and sweat dotted Emma's forehead.

Vain was now staring at her with her giant eyes, not blinking. "The law of thermodynamics says the further energy is from a Conduit, the smaller the release of that energy. It's x over y. That's the math."

"That's not even close to what the law of thermodynamics says. You know I go to actual school, right? I pay people to make me smart."

"Entropy," replied Vain. "It's a closed entropic system, so you're golden."

Emma gritted her teeth and groaned. The strain was becoming untenable. "You're just throwing out random science terms. Nothing you're saying has anything to do with explosions. You can't say a bunch of gibberish and expect it to make sense."

"It's quantum physics. Reverse the polarity. Quarks and vectors such. All Hotel things." Vain hadn't blinked once during this entire exchange. "Trust me, I know way more about this stuff than you do, Emma. It will be safe."

Emma didn't think it would be safe at all, but it was becoming difficult to hold on to the ball and she didn't know how to pull the energy back. She had no choice.

"Okay," she said. "Here goes."

She held her breath and released the energy all at once.

The resulting explosion was the furthest thing from a puff Emma had ever seen. A massive detonation rumbled through the ground, loud enough to be heard miles away. Trees burst into the air and bits of destroyed timber rained down on the gas station. The car trembled beneath her, and her ears rang. Vain took a step back.

"Holy shit," Vain said.

Holy shit was right. People screamed and ducked and howled, yelling about terrorists and being under attack. Families poured out of the restaurant, parents clutching children to their chests. One woman tripped, and another walked right over her, stepping on her back. In the meadow, a giant crater smoldered where her energy ball exploded. The remaining trees were ablaze, and smoke filled the air. Absolute chaos surrounded them.

Vain ran into the gas station, knocking two teenagers aside. What was she doing? Around Emma, cars were pulling out, some still attached to the gas pumps. Two of them crashed, adding to the confusion. People crept towards the meadow, hunched over with their phones out, trying to record whatever was happening.

This was madness. She did this. Her. The same Emma who wouldn't even cross the street without making sure the walk signal was on. Part of her recoiled, but another part clapped in exhilaration. This was power.

"Let's go." Vain climbed into the passenger seat. "With all this noise, they won't notice we didn't pay for the gas. I also grabbed sandwiches, beef jerky, cash from the register, and these super sweet sunglasses." She held up her prizes.

"Jesus Christ, did you have me do that to create a distraction?"

"Sort of. I didn't know the bang would be that large. You're really powerful." She gave Emma an encouraging thumbs up and put on the sunglasses. They were not 'super sweet', they were five dollars of cheap, pink plastic that made Vain look ten years younger. Emma wanted to bang her head against the steering wheel.

"Next time, at least warn me."

"I did warn you," replied Vain. "Remember? I was totally transparent. I said you should shut your eyes. Did you need a four-hour lecture with visuals? I thought you said you were smart."

Emma goggled at Vain, unable to formulate a response. Transparent, she said. With a frustrated head shake, she pulled the SUV away from the noise and chaos of the parking lot, weaving around traffic and following the line of cars racing back onto the highway.

"How is that a warning?"

"It's the same as saying brace yourself."

Emma sighed and rubbed the bridge of her nose. Arguing with Vain was pointless. "Where am I going now?"

"Keep driving in the same direction. We're not stopping again until we find Roman."

Chapter 17

Roman takes a nap.

The bus rumbled and bounced across the weather-stripped highway. Roman rested with his head against the window, not paying attention to the landscape as it sped by. Every time he blinked, it took a little longer to open his eyes again.

After the fight with Trick, his escape from the safe house had been refreshingly anti-climactic. He sprinted through white-picket suburban streets until he hopped on a local bus that took him to a central terminal. From there, he used the money in Trick's stolen wallet to buy himself a ticket to the only place available to him, now that Vain was dead.

Minnesota.

His jaw cracked with a huge yawn and he nestled in closer to the side of the bus, trying to find a comfortable spot. The next blink pulled him under for seconds. It had been so long since he'd seen them, the others he and Vain escaped with. How would they react when he walked through the door? The flight from the Hotel had been horrible and he tried not to dwell on it, but it was hard to stop. Each blink dropped him further into the memory of that horrible experience.

Blink.

Blink.

Bl-

*

"-ink we should wait."

"What?" Roman kept his voice below a whisper.

"I said, I think we should wait," Hush repeated.

They hid behind a clump of bushes within the garden at the front of the Hotel. It was night, or at least what passed for night. The lightning-striated skies never darkened. More accurately, it was when most of the Conduits and Utilities slept. There were always a few up and about, roaming the hallways, but this was as quiet as it got.

"No chance," Vain said. "Now or never, Hush."

"There is neither a 'now' or a 'never' in this place, Vain," he snapped back. Still, he nodded, his mouth forming a tight line.

Roman rubbed at his wrist, hardly able to believe Vain figured out how to remove the handcuff Device the Hotel required them to wear. Without it, they could use their powers and stood a chance.

The vibrant green of the bushes and lawn stuck out in vivid contrast to the faded red of the sky and exhausted grey of the barren landscape surrounding the Hotel. The garden acted as a lush paradise, a place for pairs to sit and relax and pass endless minutes in quiet contemplation, reading books or magazines.

The Hotel grounds were immense, easily three miles around. Right up front, near the garden's edge, stood the Portal. Unlike the Elevator at the back of the Hotel, the Portal only went to one place; the version of earth they'd all come from. Home.

"Come on," Vain said.

Six of them were in on that insane scheme together: him and Vain; Hush and Blunt; and, bringing up the rear, Patience and Charm. Hush and Blunt were fraternal twins, although you'd have a hard time guessing it from their appearance. Both were dark-skinned, but where Blunt was a large, athletic guy with an easy way about him and an open, honest face, Hush was much smaller and wore a permanent scowl. Charm and Patience were older women, although grey hadn't yet started to appear in their brown hair. They held hands and exchanged worried glances.

Keeping close, the group crept across the deserted path towards the Portal and freedom. He believed in Vain, but this part of the plan was the hardest to swallow. Literally walk into the Portal. About eighty percent of her idea consisted of that one step. She reasoned they'd never expect it, and, to be fair, she wasn't wrong. It wasn't like they guarded the Portal; the mere fact that Wyatts flowed in and out of it was enough to keep everyone at bay.

As they descended the sloping path that led to the periphery of the garden, their destination came into view. A grass-covered clearing surrounded a single, massive door in the center. The Portal. Roman tried to remember the first time he'd woken up, but it was

99 | Michael James

hard to think straight. Had he been here before? It was only yesterday he'd arrived. Yesterday, or one hundred years ago.

A group of Wyatts stood around the Portal, laughing and smoking cigarettes. Charm gasped, but Vain shushed her with a sharp motion.

"We knew this would happen," she whispered. "Hush will get us past."

"Hush will get us past," Hush mimicked. Vain shot him a glare that could draw blood, but he ignored her. Hush was the Utility and Blunt was the Conduit. Their powers worked a little differently. Where Vain's ability let her make shields, Hush used his energy to manipulate people for short periods. If he focused on you and told you to eat an apple, or jump up and down, you'd do that as nice as you please and wouldn't think anything of it. Pretty handy, considering they needed to walk past a group of Wyatts.

"Can you do that many?" Vain chewed at her bottom lip.

Hush snorted. "It's a little late to worry about that. Someone needs to help Blunt. I'm going to pull."

Blunt's lips were fixed in a firm line. "I can do this. Take as much as you need."

Roman and Charm slipped on either side of Blunt and supported him. When the Utility pulled, it was exhausting. They sucked life's energy from the Conduit's body. Even a little was too much. Blunt wilted and Roman figured Hush was working.

"You're taking too long," Vain snapped.

"Christ Vain, it's been four seconds." Hush scowled at her. "Give me a break."

"Stop!" Someone yelled from behind them.

Roman flinched. Even though they were almost a full football field away, the voice cut across the distance. A group of Wyatts. They'd been discovered, somehow.

"They have the Padlock!"

"What?" Charm's face drained of all its color. "You took the Padlock?" She hugged herself and groaned. "You've killed us all."

Patience looked like she was going to be sick. Even Roman couldn't believe what he heard. Vain took Arthur's Padlock? How? How had she even gotten it?

Everything happened all at once. The Wyatts by the Hotel ran at them. At the same time, the ones by the Portal spotted them. They were caught in the middle and exposed, with nowhere to hide.

"We have to go," Vain said. "It's our only chance. The worst they can do is take us back. It's now or never."

Without looking to see if anyone followed, she ran down the sloping dirt path towards the Portal and the Wyatts. Roman trailed behind. Surely, Hush could handle a few Wyatts.

A noise like an explosion broke the stillness; a sharp crack that echoed through the air. Something hot whizzed past Roman's cheek.

"They're shooting at us," Blunt said, mouth agape. "Vain, they're shooting at us. You said they wouldn't."

"It's because of the Padlock," Hush yelled. "If you don't drop that thing, I'm holding you responsible for murdering every single one of us."

Vain didn't respond. She charged right at the Wyatts. One of them pulled a gun from under his jacket and pointed it at her. Roman yelled, only knowing he needed to do something, but his muscles turned to syrup and he stumbled. Vain was pulling from him.

The Wyatt fired and Patience screamed, followed by another whizz as a second bullet ricocheted off Vain's energy shield.

"Drop your guns!" Hush yelled.

Blunt became a sack of flour in Roman's arms, and he and Charm were unable to support the bigger man's weight. All three tumbled to the ground. As he struggled to his feet, the Wyatts threw their guns to the ground.

For a second.

The Wyatts looked at each other, shrugged, and picked their guns back up. Hush's instructions had been a little too vague. He had said drop your guns, not drop your guns and leave them on the ground.

"It's over," Hush said. "I surrender! Don't shoot!" He put his arms over his head and approached the Wyatts.

"The hell it's over," Vain ripped more energy from Roman's body.

A Wyatt's head exploded with a sound like the breaking of a water balloon. The other Wyatt yelled and fired. Something splattered against the side of Roman's cheek. Charm screamed, a sound of incomprehensible agony.

Roman tried to turn his head, but he couldn't make his muscles respond. He knew why. He knew what he was going to see and the moment he did, his life would be sharply divided into before and after.

Patience was dead, her face ripped up by the bullet, leaving only chunks of debris and brain. Charm cradled her lifeless body to her chest, wailing. For once, Vain was speechless. Her mouth hung agape and her hand reached towards Patience. Small moans escaped her throat.

Another bullet seared through the air jolting him back to awareness.

"Fucking die!" Hush yelled.

The Wyatt blinked once in surprise and dropped to the ground like a puppet with its strings cut.

"We have to go." Roman grabbed Charm under the arms and hoisted her up.

She kicked at him and tried to wrestle free. "Leave me alone," she sobbed.

Roman dragged her to her feet, but she resisted.

"We can't leave her!" she screamed.

"We have to go," he repeated, and pulled her towards the Portal.

She fought like an angry house cat. He was exhausted. So, so exhausted. Even simple tasks were overwhelming after feeding Vain most of his energy.

The Wyatts behind them yelled and fired again. A puff of dirt exploded beside Roman's feet. The Portal loomed above them. It was enormous, fifteen feet high, at least; a midnight-black frame with a purple, gurgling glow where a door should be. Hush and Blunt went first. Charm was now limp, sobbing in his arms. Vain reached out to touch Charm's shoulder as they stumbled past.

"You." Charm's red-rimmed eyes burned holes into Vain. "You did this. This blood is on your hands." She spat at Vain, a thick glob hitting her right in the face.

Vain flinched but didn't move; didn't blink. Her left eye twitched.

"I hope you die." Charm said and dove through the Portal.

And that was their escape from the Hotel.

The Portal led to a weird, circular room with a door on the other side. It acted as a waypoint. That door took them to Earth. When they burst through, there were more startled Wyatts, some further yelling from Hush and more of Charm screaming at Vain. They ran and escaped and had been running ever since.

Months later, Vain made them go back. To see, she said. To make sure. But it was gone. They'd moved the Portal to a new location. Vain nearly pulled her hair out in frustration. Roman had no idea why. Who cared where it was?

Roman stirred in his sleep, jolted awake by the combination of horrid memories coupled with the bus squealing to a halt. He covered a yawn with his fist and looked through the window. A sign hanging over the entrance to the terminal read 'Welcome to Minneapolis'. End of the line.

After the Hotel, they split up. Hush, Blunt, and Charm were furious at Vain for taking the Padlock. They parted on bad terms, but still gave vague indications of where they'd settle. For whatever reason, Hush picked Minneapolis. Roman kept tabs on them using library computers and burner phones.

They'd opened a restaurant, and he was sure they lived in the building above it. Hush had always talked about his plan after the Hotel. It was pretty straightforward: make people tell him their secrets and use those secrets to get rich. What chance did anyone stand against twins with mind control?

Roman came back to himself and sighed heavily. The Hotel, and everything after, had been terrible, but it had given him purpose. Meaning. Protect Vain, make peace, try not to get killed. All good goals. What would he become without her?

With the last of Trick's cash, he paid for a cab. After a half-hour ride, it stopped in front of a multi-story brownstone building. A generous awning spanned across a picture window with the words 'HBC Bar and Grill' stenciled on the front. It was before noon and the bar was opening. He patted down his hair and rubbed his face. The events of the past week had left him disheveled and unshaven, and he was sure he looked terrible.

He stood in front of the restaurant for several minutes, unable to make himself go inside. Were these people even his friends anymore? After everything? He didn't know them, not really. They might take one look at him and tell him to beat it. Well, if that happened, he'd deal with it. As Vain would say, get through the scene, not the entire movie.

With a butterfly-filled stomach, he swung the door open and entered the cheerful pub. A large amount of natural light came in through the picture window, shining on the wood-trimmed booths. A large man puttered behind the bar, wiping the gleaming countertop while a busboy set up tables. Roman couldn't stop wiping his hands on his jeans. The bartender noticed him.

"Sit anywhere you'd like," he said. "We're just opening, but we can be ready in about ten minutes."

Roman smiled weakly and slid onto a stool. The large man flicked him a glance, taking in his disheveled clothes.

"Coffee?"

"Water, please." Roman looked around the restaurant. "Nice place. Homey."

"Yeah, it's got a good atmosphere."

"Are the owners around? I'm an old friend. I'd like to say hi."

The bartender raised an eyebrow and stopped mid-polish. "You know the owners?" He said it as a flat statement with the emphasis on 'you'.

Roman shrugged and dragged his fingers through his tousled hair. "I know what it looks like, but we're old friends. I'm good to talk to any of them. Either twin is great."

From behind, soft hands wrapped themselves around his eyes and a female voice said, "What about me, handsome?"

He spun around on the bar stool. Charm. She wore a huge smile and some of that exhausted look from the Hotel had left her eyes. Her brown, straight hair was longer than he remembered. He stepped off the stool, unsure of what to do next.

"Charm," he said, "I-"

Charm gathered him in a hug. He stiffened for a moment, then leaned into it, the tension draining from his body.

"Oh," he said, and found his voice breaking. "I missed you."

"We missed you too, Roman." She pulled away and dabbed at her eyes. "It's been so long. Why didn't you ever call?" She looked around the empty bar. "Where's Vain?"

"Gone." He tried to smile but his voice broke. "I lost her." The floodgates opened and he started to babble. "I tried, Charm. I promise. I tried so hard. But she's impossible to manage, and she wanted to keep moving. The Wyatts found us. They never stopped looking."

She wrapped him in a tight hug, cutting off any further explanation. "It's okay. You're here now," she murmured into his ear while he buried his head in her shoulder.

The stress and tension of the past week poured out of him. "I tried, Charm," he said again. He needed her to understand. "I tried. I wasn't good enough."

He repeated it while she hugged him and told him it was okay. Even though he didn't believe her, it was wonderful to be in a place where he had someone to hug; someone to whisper lies to him.

Despite his agony over losing Vain, for the first time in ages, Roman felt safe.

Chapter 18

Vain does not understand how phobias work.

Vain exhaled a breath she hadn't realized she'd been holding. Roman was close; close enough to point at, even without being able to see him. Only a few miles away, and again like a stable rock in her head. She sagged with relief.

She and Emma had followed the slow, steady pull from Roman for about a half a day. Vain had expected to find him with the Wyatts. Instead, the highway signs pointed them towards Minneapolis. He'd run to the twins. If he was there, it meant he had escaped.

How, though? She ran through scenarios in her mind. After she fell, everyone probably stopped for a moment to admire how awesome she was. The Wyatts must have talked about how she beat them and how they were dumb, stupid losers. Roman used that time to ninja-roll away. Maybe he shimmied down a rain gutter, or something.

It made sense. The Wyatts would have been like, "even though Vain kicked our asses and we're total morons, she's also the best." Roman, agile gymnast that he was, would have scaled down the side of a five-story building. Once he realized she wasn't a squishy corpse on the sidewalk, he'd understand what the Padlock did. Roman was so smart. Knowing she was safe, he came to Minneapolis to wait for her and maybe say hi to the twins and Charm. It was literally the only scenario that made sense.

"Is this it?"

Vain blinked. Beside her, Emma was a pale, exhausted mess, her skin the color of expired yogurt. The past few days had been difficult for her. She fell into that world without asking for it; but then again, none of them had asked for it. As far as Vain figured, life represented a non-stop series of problems that needed solving. Some required a subtle approach, but for most, punching did the trick. Either way, when the problems stopped, it meant you were dead.

"This is it." Vain motioned towards the restaurant. The name on the front read 'HBC Bar and Grill'. Cute. Emma parked a couple of spots down and they hopped out of the car. She'd have to figure out what to do with it later; they couldn't keep driving around in a stolen Wyatt vehicle.

"We'll find help here?" Emma asked. "Your friends?"

"Yep." Vain ignored the nervous flutter in her stomach. "Great friends. Chums. Real buddies. Certainly not a shred of unresolved animosity, if that's what you think, Emma. That's quite forward of you, why would you say that?"

"I didn't say anything."

"Don't worry about a thing." Vain couldn't take her eyes from the restaurant. Roman was in there. She felt him. Charm would be in there, too. "I like Charm," she said, in case Emma had doubts.

"Like, the cereal? Lucky Charms? What?"

"Okay." Vain clapped her hands. Her voice was too loud. "Let's go visit my good friends who will be happy to see me."

Emma sighed at her, but Vain was getting used to that. She suspected Emma had undiagnosed asthma and made a mental note to talk to her about it.

They shuffled through the front door into the din of the crowded restaurant. Cheery faces filled the tables; families with kids who drew on placemats with worn-down crayons. These were people who seemed happy and relaxed, as if they were not being chased by psychopathic rejects from an alternate earth. She couldn't relate.

"Table for two?" An aggressively cheerful young girl with a brown ponytail approached them, holding out two menus.

Vain flinched. "Charm, Blunt or Hush. Get one of them. Now."

The young frowned. "Is that a reservation? Under Charm Bluntenhush? Am I spelling that with a 'C' or a 'K'?" She looked at her reservation sheet. "Is that, um… Orthodox?" She smiled helpfully at them.

"Get the owners of the bar," Vain enunciated. "And tell them Vain is here."

"Are you with the health inspector? Should I get the chef?" A look of concern crossed her face.

Vain's head pulsed with an oncoming headache. Roman was only fifty feet away; she sensed him in the building. He was so close, and this dumb idiot stood in her way. She should knock her silly. Vain's nerves were all over the place, which was odd. She had nothing to be nervous about.

"We're meeting friends." Emma pushed in front of Vain wearing a big friendly smile. "We're the first ones here, we'll wait."

"No problem," said the hostess, visibly more comfortable dealing with Emma. "We have a bar around the corner. You can grab a table there and order appetizers while you're waiting."

The hostess gestured, and Emma plucked at Vain's shoulder, pulling her along. The noise of the restaurant surrounded Vain, smothering her. Trapping her. Everywhere she looked, people. The constant rumble from conversation made it difficult to hear anything, and as they got further in, she lost sight of the exit. Although not that warm, her clothes stuck to her body and she couldn't work saliva into her mouth.

Emma and the stupid hostess led her through the crowd, and Vain concentrated on putting one foot in front of the other. They slid into a booth and, as soon as she sat down, Vain's shoulders climbed up into her ears.

Emma tilted her head. "Are you okay? Your face is flushed."

Vain tried to say, "I'm fine" but no words came out. Her mouth flopped open and her breath exhaled in a puff. She felt like she was choking.

"Vain?"

"Perfect." The word out dribbled out. A heaving gasp followed, her heart beating a mile a minute. It was nothing unusual though, she was only eager to reunite with Roman. That's all. Perfectly normal. No need to worry that her heart was being crushed in an invisible vice.

"I need…" she said, but couldn't get any further. The booth was shrinking, pressing in around her shoulders. Why did stupid Emma pick a stupid booth? Her breathing increased to a pant.

"Vain, you don't look good. Should we find a place to lie down?"

Vain gaped at her.

"Wait," said Emma. "Are you… you're not enochlophobic, are you?"

"No, I like Mexican food," Vain gasped. She had picked up a paper napkin and ripped it into tiny pieces. She didn't remember picking it up.

"It appears you're having a panic attack," Emma said.

"I'm super-duper." She took deep breaths. It helped a little. "I don't like crowds, and I'm excited to see Roman."

"Yes, that's what enochlophobia is."

"There's a word for being excited to see Roman?"

Emma shook her head. "It means 'fear of crowds'."

"Why wouldn't you say it that way, then? Do you use big words to make people confused with your secret, multi-syllable language?" Vain talked faster, the anxiety escaping out. Breathing exercises weren't working. She wanted to punch Emma in her smug, non-terrified, pretty face. It probably wouldn't alleviate her panic, but then again, punching never made anything worse.

Emma flagged down a passing server. "Can we get a glass of water?" She tapped her chin, thinking. "You know what else? Two shots of whiskey, and a paper bag."

"Panic attack?" he asked. On Emma's nod, he continued, "My boyfriend gets them all the time. The paper bag might help, but if it doesn't, I can round up a sedative, if you think she needs it."

"We should be alright," replied Emma.

"I'll be quick." The server skipped off without missing a beat. Apparently, he was no stranger to dehydrated, alcoholic, bag-needing women.

The fist clutching Vain's heart gave a quick squeeze, and she gasped.

Emma put her hands on the table and leaned forward. "Vain, I need you to listen. You'll get through this, but you need to do what I say. Can you take some deep breaths for me?"

Vain nodded, but the rumbling noise overwhelmed her. There were people everywhere, all laughing; and the jarring and broken sound came from every direction. It pierced her skull like a cold headache. Somewhere behind her a child wailed, and she jumped. Was there a Wyatt hiding in the crowd? From the table next to them, a man looked at her strangely. He wasn't a Wyatt, but he had a mustache, which was almost as bad. Never trust men with mustaches: that was practically rule number one.

"I have to get out of here," she whispered. She wanted to move but couldn't. If she ran, she'd be further away from Roman, but if she stayed, they'd get her.

"Vain, look at me," Emma spoke in a slow, measured cadence, and Vain tried to pay attention. "Take one deep breath. Stop thinking. Breathe."

Vain didn't love the condescending way Emma was talking to her and she didn't like being told what to do, but the hand clutching her heart had a tight grip and oxygen sounded like a good idea. She took a giant breath and her panic diminished from a frantic yell to a persistent lecture. It wasn't exactly peaceful, but it was progress. She took another, and another. The room swam back into focus.

At some point, Emma had taken hold of her hands to stop her from tearing at the napkin. Touching. Yuck. She tried to pull away, but Emma had a firm grip. "That's good, Vain. Keep breathing. You're doing awesome. Is your friend close? Roman?"

Vain hated the way Emma looked at her—like she needed help—and for a moment, anger bubbled up and took over from the panic. Where was Roman? She concentrated. There.

"Above us," she said. "Above the restaurant" She pointed toward the kitchen, not looking up from the table.

The waiter returned with their drinks along with the paper bag.

"Thanks," Emma said. "We'll be okay. Can you do us a favor? We're here to meet old friends, and I believe one of them is with the owners. I think they're upstairs, there's a separate space up there?" The waiter nodded. "His name is Roman. If you get a moment, can you run up and let him know that Vain is here?" She gave that big, winning smile again, and the waiter smiled back.

"Yeah, you got it. Can you say that name again?"

"Vain," replied Vain through clenched teeth. "Vee ay eye enn. Vain."

"Neat. Are you, like, a magician?"

"Thanks very much," said Emma, smiling again. "Can you let him know we're here?"

The waiter walked off and Emma turned back to Vain. "Drink your water and whiskey. Once that's done, breathe into the bag. If Roman isn't here in five minutes, I'll go upstairs myself."

Roman. He would come down and see her like this, a flustered mess. That terrified her more than the crowd. She clutched the water with a trembling hand and drank half of it in a gulp. The whiskey came next, burning an angry path down her throat and settling like fire in her stomach. She took deep breaths into the paper bag.

"You don't do anything halfway, do you?" Emma gave a rueful chuckle. She sipped her water and made a face. "Nothing goes down right anymore. Not since I've gotten this thing."

Vain took the bag away. "Roman said eating and drinking were the two of the things he missed the most. Well, that, and having a memory and a life, but a close second was eating and drinking. You don't need to do it anymore."

Emma pushed the glass away. "I hope your friends can help me get rid of it so I can get back to my life."

Vain wasn't sure they could turn the power off, but she said nothing. Numbness spread through her nose and cheeks. The whiskey was getting to work. The hand clutching her heart relaxed its grip a little. The chatter faded, and, after a few seconds, became background noise.

The sensation of Roman grew in her mind. His presence came closer and her nerves spiked for different reasons. The doors to the kitchen swung open and there he was, looking around the restaurant.

His eyes were red and tired, and he had a little stubble on his chin, but he looked like he had recently cleaned up. His brown hair was combed and washed, and someone had gotten him a beige wool knit sweater that made him appear quite responsible. She approved and decided Roman should only wear wool knit sweaters from now on.

A faded red welt also marked his face. Someone had hit him. Motherfucker. Someone had hit her Roman. She clenched her teeth and made a mental note. 'Someone' needed to be punched in the face with a tire iron.

He frantically scanned the restaurant before settling on her. His mouth dropped and his eyes tried to erupt from his head. Why was he surprised? He broke into a huge smile and the grip released her heart. She sagged with relief. He pushed his way through the crowd towards her and she stood up from the booth. She needed to do something with everything inside her, so she wrapped her arms around her body. He stopped in front of her.

"Vain." Was he crying? "How are you alive?"

"I'm aces." She smiled. He *was* crying. "Why are you sad? Are you watching Field of Dreams?" That movie always made him cry at the end.

"I thought you were dead."

"Why would I be dead?"

"You fell off a five-story building."

"Oh, that. The Padlock doesn't keep a *thing* safe, it keeps a *person* safe. You figured that out, good for you."

"Wait, you fell off a building?" Emma interrupted. "You never told me that."

"How would I have figured that out?" replied Roman. "The Padlock saved you? I don't know what you're talking about."

"Right. When I pulled the Wyatt off the building, the Padlock opened and exploded me to Boston. Then you shimmied down the side of the building."

"Shimmy? What? You exploded?" Roman appeared to be getting frustrated, which was weird because he knew all of this already.

"How else would you have gotten away from the Wyatts?"

"I didn't get away. They took me to a house and Trick was there."

"Trick?" Her chest constricted with fear. "When did you see that piece of garbage?"

"It's a long story." He considered it for a moment. "Actually, it's incredibly short. Trick captured me, but I escaped and took a bus here. The bus had inadequate foot space and smelled like ham. The end."

"You saw him?"

He nodded. "Yeah, the Wyatts took me to a safe house. I head-butted him and broke his nose."

"Good," said Vain, trying to process this information. "I told you to stay close, why didn't you?"

"You fell off the top of a building."

"Did the Wyatts at least mention how cool it was?"

"No," Roman replied, now obviously irritated. "No one thought it was *cool* when we all thought you were dead. I've been in misery for the past week. I thought I had lost you forever."

"Well, I'm not dead, I'm alive and I have the Padlock and I brought along this Emma."

He looked over at 'this Emma', who rang her finger around the lip of her water glass. "And she is?"

"She's like us, but everyone is her Conduit. She let the stupid Wyatts kidnap her, even though I warned her about it." Emma objected, but Vain knew she'd mess up the story, so she kept going. "I saved her by hitting them with a tire iron, like, a bunch of times. It was great. A cab driver ran over one and she energy-shot another into space. Then we blew up a gas station, but that's not related to the main story, I just thought it was cool. I'm sure Arthur will keep coming after her, so we have to help." Now that she was in front of Roman and talking, her panic disappeared. She waved her hands around her head while she talked, increasingly excited. It was so great to be with him again.

Roman shook his head and looked back and forth between Emma and Vain. He opened his mouth a few times, but nothing came out. Vain fidgeted. Was she in trouble? Was he mad at her? That worried her more than the Wyatts. Eventually, he took a deep breath.

"Vain," he said. "I'm glad you're okay. I missed you. A lot."

"I'm sorry the Wyatts captured you," she said, happy he wasn't angry. "I'm glad you're okay, too. But honestly, Roman, you should have escaped when they talked about my awesome disappearance and how kick-ass I am. You could have ninja-rolled."

"They didn't…" he started to say, but then shook his head. "Emma, it's wonderful to meet you. I'm sorry you've been dragged into this." He held out his hand and Emma took it and smiled sweetly.

"I've heard a lot about you, Roman," Emma said. "Vain didn't tell me the full story, but she spoke highly of you. It's nice to meet you. I'm sorry I've been dragged into this too, I only want my life to go back to normal so I can go home. Vain said you'd be able to help me."

Roman gave her a sideways glance Vain recognized as his 'oh-god-what-did-you-say-now?' look. "We'll figure this all out together. Why don't we head upstairs and meet the rest of the group?"

Vain's stomach flipped over, once, for good measure. Yes. Good. Nothing stressful about that at all.

Time to say hello to the group.

Chapter 19

Emma meets new people under totally normal circumstances.

Emma followed behind Roman as he led them through the noisy kitchen to a small set of stairs at the back. He was much younger than she'd imagined. From the way Vain described him, she expected someone more mature, but he looked the same age as her. He had a mild presence about him, with his tousled brown hair and quiet, expressive eyes. His concern for Vain was obvious, and she concentrated on him with laser-focus. Every time she said something, she'd glance over to gauge his reaction, of which he had very few. He was clearly recovering from the shock of seeing Vain alive, something he obviously hadn't expected.

Vain hadn't mentioned to Emma that she fell off a roof. Apparently, that little tidbit didn't rank highly enough to bother with, even though she had spent three solid hours in the car talking about the movie Labyrinth. Vain believed the size of David Bowie's codpiece held deeper meaning, and the song "Magic Dance" directly referenced global warming.

Roman stood to the side of the stairs, gesturing for them to go up first. As Emma passed, he chuckled, asking whether she needed any sedatives after spending time in a car with Vain. Vain retaliated with a glare that held no real heat and Emma smiled and said it was okay.

The stairs opened into a hallway with rooms on either side and wide French doors at the end. In front of the French doors stood a shaved gorilla that had been stuffed into a suit. Or, so it appeared. In truth, it was the largest man Emma had ever seen. He towered over her with muscles that had muscles that said hello to other muscles. The goatee and shaggy dark hair that hung past his ears gave him an air of menace. As they walked through the doors, he grunted a greeting and followed them in. With the way his suit creased, there might have been a gun under his jacket. More likely, it was a monstrous rib muscle she'd never heard of.

They entered a large recreation room complete with a mahogany bar, a pool table, and several leather couches arranged around a low glass table. A circular, open staircase led to the next level. The exterior walls had floor-to-ceiling windows and the whole room screamed wealth and opulence. It would have cost more than Emma's annual tuition.

By the pool table, a dark-skinned man with a pinched expression lined up a shot. He wore a gray suit and was playing with an older white woman with long brown hair. Her eyes were kind and soft and she was in the middle of ribbing him. Another dark-skinned man sat at the bar, hunched over a crossword. He was bigger than Roman and his head was closely shaved. All three sets of eyes locked on them as they walked into the room. No one said anything for several moments. Several incredibly uncomfortable moments.

"Roman told us you were dead," said the one with the angry expression.

"Okay," said Vain.

Both men glanced over at the woman playing pool, who stared daggers through Vain. For her part, Vain tried to appear relaxed, but it was obvious she was uneasy. This was her idea of friends? The tension had physical weight.

"What a large pool table," Vain's words fell over each other. "I bet you go swimming in it, ha-ha. Are those windows made of glass? How neat. I like your couches. Is that a real ceiling or one of those fake ones? Hi, Blunt." She waved to the man at the bar.

"Hi, Vain. I like your hair. Black suits you."

"This?" Vain patted her head. "Yeah, I thought the Wyatts had our descriptions."

"Smart," Blunt responded. "You always had good ideas."

"I don't know about that." The woman by the pool table rested her cue on the green surface and approached Vain.

The room took a collective breath, and Emma realized she'd walked into the third act of a drama those five had been living for quite some time. Vain regarded the woman warily.

"Charm. Don't," said Roman.

"It's alright, Roman. Hello, Vain."

"Hello, Charm." Vain kept her head down, fixated on the floor. Emma had never seen her so out of sorts.

"When Roman told us you were dead, I was surprised to find myself genuinely sad. Perhaps not as sad as I would be had it been someone else, but certainly unhappy. There aren't enough of us on the outside."

Vain mumbled something about James Gardner, a reference whose relevance Emma couldn't even begin to imagine. Roman hung on their every word.

"I forgive you for Patience, Vain."

Whatever that sentence meant, it got Vain's attention. She looked at Charm with anger written all over her face.

"Me? Why would you forgive me? I didn't kill her."

"You didn't pull the trigger, but you loaded the gun. It's okay. I forgive you."

"I don't accept you forgiving me because there's nothing to forgive. I didn't do anything wrong." Vain folded her arms over her chest and jutted her chin out.

Charm hands clenched into fists at her sides. Her nostrils flared and she took several deep breaths to calm herself.

"Jesus Christ, Vain," said the man by the pool table. "Can't you say thank you like a normal person? You haven't changed a bit."

"That's not true. I like red licorice now." She looked at Roman. "Why didn't you tell them about that?"

Roman gaped at her and shook his head. He made a settling motion and addressed the group.

"Okay everyone, let's all take a deep breath. Plenty of time to work through this. Let's get a drink and relax. No need to fight. We're together now, and that's what matters. We're all safe. Right?"

Charm didn't look any less angry, but she nodded once. A small fraction of the pressure drained from the room. Whatever was going on, it centered on Vain and this woman. And who was Patience? How many corpses lay in Vain's wake?

Taking a last breath, Charm turned to Emma. She put a megawatt smile on her face, and Emma had no choice but to return it. "My name is Charm. I'm so sorry we haven't introduced ourselves yet. Are you a friend of Vain and Roman? The angry-looking fellow at the pool table is Hush. His brother, Blunt, is the one at the bar."

Emma waved, self-conscious now that all eyes were on her. "Hi. I'm Emma. Nice to meet you all. I'm, um, with Vain, I guess."

"Emma is activated." Vain gave a staggeringly inaccurate recap of how they met. In Vain's version, she planned the meeting with Emma as a willing participant. No mention at all of the Wyatts or the attempted kidnapping.

She wanted to interrupt, but Vain steamrolled through.

"Emma is a Utility and can pull from everyone. She can wield more power than all five of us combined. I said we'd help her." Vain looked at the huge man behind them. "Who is this, by the way?"

"That's Tank," replied Blunt. "He's ex-military, knows five types of judo, and can kill you by looking at you. He keeps us all safe." Blunt mimed a karate chop to emphasize his point.

"My name's Mark." The giant man stepped forward, shaking his head at Blunt's exaggerations. "I own a company that provides protection services. I make sure no one gets near the twins and Charm."

"You should call yourself Tank," said Blunt. "It's way more badass."

"Sure."

"Does he know about us?" asked Vain

"He knows enough," said Hush. "Although, I don't know how much of it he believes."

Mark shrugged. "It doesn't matter. I've seen weird stuff around you guys. I get paid either way."

"Why do you need him? Have you seen anyone? Wyatts, or anyone else from the Hotel?"

"No one," Hush said. "We haven't been bothered at all."

"They bothered us plenty," said Vain. "They've been at us since we left."

"You had the Padlock." Vain opened her mouth to retort, but Hush begged her off by raising his hand. "It's not a criticism. I'm stating a fact. They never wanted us, they wanted that stupid thing you stole. We'd all be better off without it and we should give it back to them."

"No," said Vain. "I took it, and it's mine. Don't even think about it. If that's what you want, we'll leave right now."

"All right, take five, everyone," said Roman. "No one is going anywhere. We don't need to decide right now. We can take our time figuring out what to do next." Roman, Emma was learning, was the peacemaker of the group. She wondered how exhausting it must have been for him, always putting out Vain's fires.

"I agree with Roman," said Charm. "Vain, Emma, come sit and tell us what happened to you. We've heard Roman's story, but nothing about what you've been through. You look a fright, poor thing."

Emma let the older woman guide her to a seat. She wrapped her in a throw and somehow made a cup of tea materialize from nowhere. In moments, she had Emma bundled up and was remarking on how pretty her sweater was. Bemused, Emma sipped at her tea, enjoying the reassuring sensation of being mothered.

They all sat on the plush, luxurious couches in the middle of the room. Now that the immediate tension had passed somewhat, the mood softened. Vain gave them a thorough retelling of events, one that stuck more closely to reality. She told them about waking up in Boston, finding Emma, fighting with the Wyatts, and the explosion at the gas station. Their expressions alternated between surprised, concerned, and suspicious. Blunt was the only one who seemed happy, and he whooped with joy when Vain told them about hitting the Wyatts with a tire iron.

"You showed them good, Vain. That's great." He reached out for a high five. A hint of a smile crept onto Vain's lips and she air high-fived him back. By the end of the story, Hush had stood up and was pacing.

"Give me the Padlock," he said, snapping his fingers.

Vain didn't move at first, but Roman gave her a nearly imperceptible nod, and she pulled it out of her jacket and handed it over. Hush turned it over, fiddling with the clasp.

"You broke it," he said.

"Maybe." She shrugged. "I think I can fix it, though."

"It's cold," he said. "Ordinary metal. After it teleported you, it opened, right?"

"When I woke up, it was the next day and I was in Boston. And the Padlock was like that."

"Did you know that would happen?"

"No. But it would explain why Arthur wants it back. With this, he'd not only be powerful, but also unstoppable. Immortal." She nodded to herself. "He'd do anything to get this back."

"And that's why we need to return it. So he'll leave us alone," Hush said.

"We're not giving it back to him."

"We are giving it back to him." There was heat in his voice. "If you want to stay here, you need to get rid of this thing."

"Like I said before, if that's your price, I'll leave." Vain stood up and Roman pulled her back down.

"No one is going anywhere," Charm said. "Hush, watch your tone. We didn't all come together to send her back out into the world again. We'll figure this out as a group, and we'll decide what to do next. Together. We should never have split up in the first place. All we have is each other."

"None of this explains Vain's latest catastrophe." Hush pointed at Emma.

Emma's shoulders tensed and she looked to Vain for help.

"She was just there," Vain said. "Nothing but random coincidence. She was getting kidnapped when I teleported to Boston."

"What time was it when you fell?" Charm asked.

"I wasn't timing it. I was busy fighting Wyatts and kicking ass." Vain's voice raised in pitch. It was clear she wasn't used to being questioned like this. "Dusk, maybe. Eight or eight-thirty."

"I had my seizure at about a quarter to nine." Emma got where Charm was going.

"So?"

"So, the two are related," said Charm. "Assuming you're right, and the Padlock protects the person holding it from mortal harm, the energy would get released when the Padlock opened. Any excess energy would have to go somewhere, so what if it looked for the next closest repository?"

"Almost like a battery deposit," Roman rubbed his chin. "The Padlock releases all the energy in one burst to protect Vain, but needs somewhere to put the leftovers, so it bounces around until it finds the next closest person who can take it."

"That's why I'm like this?" said Emma. "Vain fell and now I'm a freak?"

"Welcome to our world, kid," said Hush. "That's what Vain does. She hurricanes through life and leaves garbage behind her." He pointed at Vain. "That's why you two need to clean up and get gone. We don't need your trouble here."

"You better be real careful with where you point that finger, Hush." Roman took a step toward him. Vain hadn't reacted to the accusation at all. "None of this is her fault."

"Stop protecting her." Hush stood and pushed himself into Roman's space. "Everything she touches turns to trash."

"You wouldn't be here without her. She got us out of the Hotel."

"Settle down," said Charm, also standing. "Roman is our friend. Of course, we're going to help him."

Emma noticed she didn't say 'they'. Roman is their friend. Not Vain.

Now, everyone was standing. Roman and Hush squared off, Charm was trying to pull them apart, and Mark jumped in to help. Blunt stood separate from the group, watching them with confused eyes.

Emma buried her head in her hands. These were the people who would help her? They could barely keep themselves together. To call this hopeless would insult the meaning of the word.

"Everyone, shut up," said Vain, holding up a finger. Remarkably, everyone did. "Do you hear that? What's that noise?" She looked around the room.

Emma heard it, too. It was the distinctive chiming of a phone ringing.

"It's Trick's phone," Roman said. He pulled it from his pocket and waggled it.

"What do you mean, Trick's phone?" said Hush.

"When I escaped, I stole his phone."

"Yeah, you did," said Vain with a half-smile.

Emma was beginning to think that Vain might be a kleptomaniac. She certainly seemed to love stealing.

"That is Trick's phone," said Hush. "In your hand. You are holding Trick's phone."

"Yeah. So?"

"It will have GPS in it. GPS which is probably enabled and will lead Trick right goddamn to us. "

Roman stuttered a protest but stopped and regarded the buzzing phone in his hand with horror. "Phones do that, now?"

"We should answer that." Vain lunged and grabbed it before anyone could stop her. She clicked the speaker button. "Hello?"

Chapter 20

Vain hates Trick, like, so much.

"Is this Vanity? Wonderful. How are you? You found Roman. That's super." Vain put the phone on speaker and Trick's voice came out. Her blood turned to ice. She thudded on to the couch.

"Trick." She tried to work moisture into her mouth.

"You sound congested," said Roman. "How's your nose?"

"Don't worry about my nose, Roman. You got lucky. Although I have to give you credit for that escape. I won't make the mistake of underestimating you again."

"You will, Trick, because you're an idiot," Vain said.

"Oh, stop. We're all friends here, having a casual chat. There's nothing to get angry over."

She was flustered. Trick had been the source of so many horrible memories from the Hotel; always smirking at a private joke, always playing pranks on people. Horrible, awful pranks. One of his hands would distract you while the other pulled the quarter from your ear; except, it wasn't a quarter, it was a knife. And he didn't pull it from your ear, he stabbed it in your back. You never saw it coming and it always hurt.

"Is she with you? The redhead who killed the Wyatt by throwing him halfway to the Atlantic Ocean? We'd like to have a word with her."

Before Emma could do something stupid like speak, Vain piped up. "I left her behind after I took care of your idiot Wyatts outside of Boston. It's only Roman and me."

"Well," said Trick. "I somehow doubt that, given we've been following you at a distance for quite some time. The Wyatts watched you get in the SUV with her, and every compass in North America is pointing right at you. That girl gives off more power than a nuclear reactor. I assume you're with the others? The twins and the Conduit? I'm sorry, I don't remember their names."

Vain wasn't sure what to say. Hush and Charm glared at her. Blunt looked confused, which wasn't unusual for Blunt.

"I'm going to guess from the pregnant silence that you're not sure how to answer," Trick said. "That's okay. Let me catch you up. Number one, thanks for getting everyone in one place. It's remarkably convenient and makes this so much easier. Number two, I want the Padlock back. That's all I've ever wanted."

"Bullshit," Vain said.

"Vain, let me give you a brief lesson. Do you know what a provision for a loan loss is?"

"I do." Roman blinked in surprise.

"Oh right," said Trick. "That makes sense. Roman, why don't you tell us?"

Roman looked around the room. "It's an accounting term. A loan loss provision is an income statement expense set aside as an allowance for uncollected loans and loan payments. It covers bankruptcy and stuff." Roman seemed confused. "Did I used to be an accountant?"

Trick ignored him. "Thanks, Roman. You got it. Here's my follow-up: why do companies use this? Why do they accept the loss instead of going after the delinquent loan?"

"Because it's cheaper to write the loan off," Roman said. "It costs more money to recover the funds than it does to drop it."

"Exactly," Trick said. "You, my stupid, frustrating friends, are the loan. It is easier and cheaper to write you off. There are hundreds of you in the Hotel. Do you think Arthur cares he lost a couple? We only want the Padlock back."

"If we give you the Padlock, you'll leave us alone?" Hush said.

"Is that one of the twins? Yes, I'll leave you alone. In fact, I'll do one better. You give me the Padlock, and I'll reverse the activation. No more Utility and Conduit active connection thing. You'll all be normal, ordinary people, free to live your lives. It's good for both of us. I don't love the thought of literal superheroes walking around and you get left alone. What could be fairer than that?"

"What about Emma?" Vain asked.

"Her too." A noise, like the crunching of an apple, came through the phone. "Here's the deal, gang. In the book of your lives, you're all the main characters. Everything revolves around you. I'm in a different book. Arthur's book. And in that novel, you barely register. You're like the guy who walks into the bar on page two hundred and eighty for a single scene. Why do you think anyone cares about you? Arthur only wants his property back. I think my offer is fair. I'm going to give you a half-hour to talk it over. Ta."

Trick hung up and the pregnant pause lasted only a moment before the group exploded into yelling and arguments, each person providing their own stupid idea. Vain tuned them out.

Trick lied. No matter what he said, it was a lie and a trick. She already knew how this would go. Hush would settle down the room with his smarmy logic. Charm would hand out smiles like ice cream, and sturdy, dependable Roman, the born peacemaker, would lead them to the path of least resistance. They'd already decided. The next half hour would be window dressing so they could pretend like they debated it.

"I'm going for a walk." She stood and the room quieted. "I need to clear my head."

"You can't go anywhere, Vain," said Roman. "We need to talk this through and figure it out."

"You figure it out for both of us. I'll go with whatever the group decides."

Roman gave her a frown and she realized she'd screwed up. Going with the group wasn't her thing, and he was suspicious.

"What are you planning, Vain?"

She held up her hands in a show of surrender. "I'm not planning anything. I don't want to fight about this, I'm too wrung out. You guys hash it out. None of you like my plans anyway, so I'll stay out of it." Vain walked to the door. "I'll be back before he calls. I'm going to circle the block. Hey, is there a hardware store nearby?" Again, she got a suspicious look from Roman. He knew her too well and she was getting clumsy. She wasn't used to having other people around.

"Vain?" Roman raised his eyebrows.

She scrambled to cover her tracks. "Also, is there a convenience store? I want to buy some licorice, a bottle of whiskey and some pizza. I'm going to party. It's been a tough week."

Hush stuttered out a response and tried to explain that they were over a bar and had liquor and pizza on-premises. Vain provided assurances that the walk would give her time to resign herself to their choices. She slipped out the door, followed by Roman's considering glare.

Mark followed her and stopped her with a hand on her shoulder, "Do you need any help with whatever it is you're doing?"

"I'm getting food and going for a walk." Vain shrugged away his hand. "You heard me. I'm stressed, and the combination of candy, booze, and pizza helps me relax."

"You're lying." Mark folded his arms and leaned against the wall. "I was watching you during that call. I don't know you, but I know that look. You're planning something. You had your mind made up about five seconds in."

"I thought you were security. Is getting up in my business part of your job description?" She had to crane her neck back to look him in the eye.

"I can do two things," Mark rolled his enormous shoulders in what Vain assumed was supposed to be a shrug. "I like to be useful. Why don't you tell me what's going through your head?"

Vain considered it. There might be a brain behind those layers of muscle. She made a snap decision to test him a little. "I know how this ends. Those idiots in there will agree to meet with Trick. They think he'll stop once he has the Padlock, but they're wrong. They've let themselves forget what he's like. What he did to us in the Hotel."

"Okay. So, what are you doing?"

"I'm going to go for a walk and maybe eat candy, then figure how to keep us all safe when shit goes sideways. Because shit will absolutely, one hundred percent, go sideways."

"Keeping the twins and Charm safe is my thing."

"Yeah, well, you've been demoted to second in command. I've been watching over them since long before you, and I'm not stopping because they found a trained dinosaur made of pectoral muscles."

"You lost me on that last part."

"Listen," she said. "Are you saying I can count on you? If things take a turn, you're with me?"

"I don't want anything to happen to them either, but you need to let me in on what you're thinking."

"I will," she replied, not sure if she was telling the truth. "But we'll talk more when I get back."

She tried to pat him on the arm, but he was so tall she ended up patting his hip. Awkward. She turned and walked down the hallway.

*

When she returned, the room was quiet. Emma sat in the corner with Roman. Was she leaning against his shoulder? The twins were at the bar with Charm, and Mark stood watch as usual. Trick's phone perched in the center of the room on the table, a talisman that the group was studiously and obviously ignoring.

"Did you find food?" Roman got off the couch and Emma tipped over.

She *had been* leaning on his shoulder. Vain filed that away as a problem to deal with later. "No, but I had a nice walk." She gave him a tiny grin. "What did you decide?"

"To hear Trick out." He held his hands up as if expecting a fight. "We'll listen. That's all we agreed to. If he can give us some assurance that he'll leave us alone, we can talk about giving up the Padlock."

"Whatever you want. I thought about it. It's useless now, anyway. We used it once and we don't know how to recharge it. If giving it back secures our safety, I'm game."

Roman frowned. His head turned sideways as if trying to find the problem with that statement.

"I trust you, Roman. You watch my back and I'll watch yours." She hoped that would be enough to get him to stop sniffing around.

He seemed satisfied and walked over to the table with the phone. "Trick should call back any second. Are we in agreement? If the deal seems good, we'll take it and hand over the Padlock. If any of us don't like it, we'll back out." He looked around the room and got nods from everyone. On cue, the phone rang and Roman answered.

"Hi again, everyone." Trick's voice projected through the speakers. "I hope you've thought things through. What's it going to be? Are you ready to work together?"

"What assurances can you give us that nothing bad will happen?" asked Roman.

"The best assurance of all," replied Trick. "Apathy. I do not give one hot shit about any of you. We haven't even tried to find the twins and the woman. Only you. This might hurt your feelings, but we have bigger things to deal with. You give us the Padlock, I un-activate you and we never talk to each other again. Deal?"

"What about Emma?" Roman asked. "You tried to take her to the Hotel."

"Who is Emma?"

"The woman you tried to kidnap."

"Oh, is that her name? Well, that was unfortunate," said Trick. "The Hotel needs energy and a constant supply of people is the only way to get it. But yeah, she's part of the deal too. I'll turn her off and she can go back to studying."

Vain's head jerked at that. He knew she was a student. God, they were being played. But if she said anything, she'd be devoured by their blind hope that this could be over soon.

"Why would I trust you?" Emma leaned towards the phone, her voice getting louder. "Those men kidnapped me. *Kidnapped.* They put their hands on me. They hit me."

"As I said, the circumstances behind that incident were unfortunate. You have my apologies."

"You're a lying piece of shit!" Vain yelled. So much for control. She tried so hard, but he was selling poisonous lies as nectar, and they were all drinking it. "Emma, Trick won't help you. Trick only helps himself. This is all bullshit."

"Let me ask you something, Emma," said Trick. "Since you've been with Vain, has she helped you? Has she explained anything to you? Has she given you a single indication that she has any idea what she's doing?"

Emma opened her mouth a few times, but didn't say anything.

The group stared at Vain. She had lost before the battle even started. She wrung her hands together. "This is garbage. I know you're all scared and looking for a way out. I get it, I honestly do. I'm scared too. But the devil you know *isn't* better than the devil you don't. They're both devils, and this will end badly. Please. Give me time to think of a way out of this."

"You're out of time and options," said Trick. "We'll never stop as long as you have the Padlock. Arthur has work to do, and he can't do it without that Device. I don't know what else I can say. I don't care about any of you."

Vain glanced over at Roman to see how he was taking this. He was nodding, along with everyone else. Their eyes met, but she dropped them before her anger gushed out. They all wanted it to be over as quickly as possible and weren't listening.

"Okay," said Roman. "You have a deal."

"Super," said Trick. "I knew you'd make the right call. I'm going to text an address. Meet me and my guys there tomorrow at two p.m. You give us the Padlock, we turn you off, everyone goes their separate ways. No funny stuff."

"No one will do anything funny," replied Roman. "We'll be there."

"This is great, team. I feel really good about this. We made spectacular progress today. This will all be over soon, I promise."

The phone clicked off, cutting the connection. No one said anything. Vain stood up.

"You're all making a terrible mistake. I want this on the record."

"It's over, Vain," Hush said. "Enough. There's nothing more you can do or say."

"Not true. I can think of several insults to use when we see him. I'm probably going to throw an egg at him, at the very least."

Roman coughed out a chuckle and covered his mouth. "You can throw an egg at him, Vain. That's fine."

Vain took a last look around the room, daring anyone to challenge her. No one did.

She walked out.

Chapter 21

Roman visits Vain who, in turn, lies to him.

Roman woke with a jolt.

He'd been having a nightmare, but the details were foggy. A vague sense of being chased lingered. He wiped his hands on the bedsheets. When, in the past year, had someone not been chasing him? He'd been on the run for so long now that staying in one place seemed stranger than moving. Always hiding. So many close calls. So many times when Vain had nearly died.

He smoothed down his hair with a weary hand and crawled out of the massive queen-sized bed the twins put him in. They had made a life for themselves here. They built the two floors above the restaurant like a fortress. Hush said the construction cost over a million dollars and included top of the line security, cameras everywhere, and Mark's hired guards watching them around the clock. Arthur and Trick couldn't get within ten miles of this place without him knowing.

When they'd first escaped the Hotel, he agreed with Vain's decision to leave. Staying in one place seemed dangerous and the animosity towards Vain was causing constant friction. But looking back on the past year, had it been the right decision? The twins built something, constructed a life. Charm was in a book club, for God's sake. If Roman had stayed, he could have helped. Instead, he'd run with Vain; and what did he have to show for it? Bruises, a weary soul, a broken Padlock, and not a single step closer to safety. He couldn't even collect air miles because he didn't have a frigging identity.

He showered and put on the new clothes Hush had secured. For whatever reason, a couple dozen wool knit sweaters filled the drawers. Hush was eager to prove that money wasn't an issue and sent one of his 'people' out for supplies. Charm filled him in on the details of their wealth before bed. Hush was unstoppable in his quest to get money and build power. He owned land, buildings, stocks, the works. He even started a holding company to manage their various investments. It had been effortless. Hush started by approach bankers in the downtown district and telling them to give him insider stock tips. Then he bought the stock. Every single one made money. In months, he was a millionaire. Once you hit a certain level of wealth, it became self-sustaining. It was impossible not to earn more. Charm wasn't sure how much Hush was worth, but estimated it to be millions.

Charm spent her time walking the streets of Minneapolis, going for jogs around the lakes, reading books, and watching movies; always followed by Mark or one of his team. She seemed quieter than he remembered. Some of her confidence and lighthearted way with people had returned, but she was still dealing with the death of Patience.

And now Vain had introduced a new person into the mix. He wasn't sure how Emma fit into all of this. She was quiet, probably intimidated by the family drama. She had strength, though; a quiet core of determination. An intelligence worked behind those eyes that studied everything. If trading a broken Padlock saved her and gave him and Vain their freedom, he'd take that deal.

Given that Vain agreed to the plan without complaint, it meant she had something brewing in her head. He needed to find out what that something was; preferably before they met Trick. He was relieved she'd survived, but that little scare hadn't taken any of the fight out of her. She'd plan something. Something she believed would be best for everyone, even if it meant a path they didn't want to take.

He wandered into the hallway, trying to remember which bedroom Vain and Emma were sleeping in. This place was enormous. A door that he thought led to their room was ajar, and he knocked before poking his head through.

"Hello? Anyone in here? Vain?"

Vain sat cross-legged on the bed with a laptop on her knees, wearing giant headphones that dwarfed her face. She wore the polka-dot pajamas the twins had given her, and her big eyes were wide, staring at the screen. Her lips twitched while she watched.

"Hello," he said again to get her attention, waving his arms above his head.

Looking up, she paused the video and gave him a tight grin. For Vain, that was the same as a hug and a laugh.

"Hi Roman," she said. "What's up?"

"Hi." He sat on the bed beside her. "Where's Emma?"

Her brow furrowed. "I bet you'd like to know where Emma is."

"Yes. I wanted to talk to you alone," he said, ignoring her weird reaction.

"Oh. She got up early. I don't know where she went."

"Have you been awake long?"

"Yeah, I didn't sleep that well. Too keyed up, I guess. Hush let me use this laptop. I'm watching the Back to the Future trilogy."

"We never saw that one, did we?"

"I have," said Vain. "I didn't realize until I watched it, but I've seen this before. I don't remember, but…" she finished with a shrug.

Roman understood. Neither of them had memories before the Hotel, but parts of their old life lingered. They would hear a song for the first time and know all the words. They would read a book and know the ending. He remembered how to drive. There was so much left in his head, like a jigsaw puzzle with no box illustration to help them put the pieces back together. They had lost so much of themselves.

"I'll finish regardless, it's a good movie." She shut the laptop. "What's on your mind?"

"Nothing. Can't I come in to say hello? We've barely talked since Denver."

"Sure, but you're not wearing a just-came-to-say-hello face, you're wearing an I-need-to-have-a-talk-with-Vain face. You only have about four faces, Roman. It's not rocket science to figure them out."

"Oh, really? Since you're such an expert on my face, what do I want to talk about?"

"You're worried that I'm planning something because I agreed to this stupid idea without arguing. Also, you're fretting that we should never have left the twins, and you're going to argue that the Padlock is worthless so there's no harm in giving it up. Did I miss anything?" She thrust her chin forward and batted her eyelashes at him; a picture of insincerity.

He couldn't help but smile. Behind the dumb jokes and the unblinking stares, Vain had a brain that never stopped moving. "Yeah, that's about all of it. So?"

"Of course I'm planning something, Roman. It's what I do. I'll go along with this, even though it's a dumb, dangerous plan, but I'll also keep us safe. We'll try your way first, and if that doesn't work, I'll make sure there's a way out."

"You think Trick will come after us?"

"I know he will. Arthur needs his property back."

"They can't need all of us." Roman sat on the bed and Vain scooted over to make room.

"For Arthur, it's about the principle of it. He needs to bring us back to show the others what happens if you run." She wore determination on her face like a shield. To call Vain a pessimist wasn't even close. She wouldn't say the glass was half empty, she'd say the glass was filled with a sentient alien that only looked like water and was trying to kill her while she slept. She never stopped.

Roman snorted. "A full three-quarters of the people in the Hotel wouldn't leave if the doors were wide open, leading to paradise. They have it too good there."

"But some would," she replied. "It's not good for business."

"He left the twins and Charm alone. You heard it, too. They haven't even sniffed a Wyatt since we left."

"Yeah, because he focused on us. We're giving him the store, tied up in a neat little bow."

"But you're willing to give up the Padlock? Even though you think it's a mistake?"

She fiddled with her fingers. Roman knew that body language well. Vain wasn't the only one who could read people. The answer was no, but she wouldn't lie to him, not directly, and was trying to come up with a different answer.

"I've been thinking about that day in Denver. They knew we had the Padlock when they came after us. It wasn't supposed to go down that way, they made a mistake."

"It must have been horrible, thinking you were going to die. I'm sorry."

She shook her head. "No, you're missing the point. They never shot at us. I'd be willing to bet they had orders to take us, not kill us."

"Okay," he said. "I'm not sure why it matters though?"

"Don't you get it? The Wyatts screwed up. They caused the Padlock to activate." She became more agitated, but he wasn't following her line of thinking.

She hopped off the bed and grabbed something from beneath it. Facing him, she held out both hands, palms flat. In each hand, she held an identical padlock. Both had the small word 'safe' scratched into the corner. He couldn't tell the difference between them.

"Which is the real one?" She dumped them into his hands. "You don't know, do you?"

Both were cold and lifeless. He turned them over.

"Vain," he said. "We can't give them a fake. They'll know. Just because I don't know the difference doesn't mean they won't recognize a decoy. They'll kill us." He squinted at one of them. "How the hell did you scratch the word 'safe' into the side? Did you use a knife?"

"We can try." Vain ignored his question and leaned forward, her eyes intent on his face. "We give them the fake one and if they take it, great. Everyone walks away. And, more importantly, we keep what's ours."

"They'll figure it out, Vain. Even if they fall for it tomorrow, they'll go back to the Hotel and they'll try to recharge it. It won't work, and they'll know."

Vain crossed her arms and jutted her chin. "By then I'll have figured out how to fix it."

"We can't do this. We have to give them the real one. I can't run anymore. This is our chance to stop and build a life."

"What life can we make, Roman?" she said. "We don't remember anything. Are you going to walk into an office and say, 'Hello, my name is Roman. That's not my real name, I'm not sure what it is. Work experience? I probably have some, but I've been spending my time in an interdimensional Hotel at the nexus of time and space and my memory is spotty. I can do simple math and I know how to eat with chopsticks. May I have a job?'"

"Hush has contacts, he has a business. He has money. We can find lives for ourselves, lives that don't include running from goddamn mercenaries for the rest of our days. I can't carry on like this, Vain. Something's got to give." Frustration crept into his voice. He had to make her understand.

She frowned. "I'll stop when you're safe. When we're safe. If they can get to us, if the connection between this world and the Hotel stays open, we'll always be on the run."

"You want to close the Portal?" He shook his head. "There's no way. I want to support you, but I need you to give a little, too, and support me."

Vain looked like she was going to argue, but instead, she took a deep breath and dropped her arms to her sides. "Fine." She frowned. "We'll try it your way." She opened the nightstand drawer and pulled out a third Padlock.

Roman tugged his hair in frustration. "How many of these did you buy? Did you find an all-night padlock store? How is that even a viable business model?"

"Here." She thrust the Padlock from the drawer at him. "This is the real one."

It looked identical to the other two. Did it hold a slight warmth that wasn't present in the others? Tough to say.

"You give it to Trick," she said. "I won't be able to do it."

He studied her, trying to pick up on any signs of subterfuge, but she fiddled with hair and chewed her lip, all candy-sweet innocence.

"Thank you, Vain. This will work out. I promise."

He gave her a big smile that she returned with something that was not exactly a smile, but not a frown either.

"Can I pull from you today?" Vain bit her lip and picked at the bed cover. "Can you start storing? To be safe?"

"That's a good idea. I'll start right now with a big breakfast." He stood up to leave, but she looked like she still wanted to say something. "Vain? Was there something else?"

"Can I throw an egg at him? At least?" she asked. She fake-batted her eyelashes at him.

"It would be weird if you didn't," he laughed. "Want to pause your movie and see what the others are doing? Trick should call in a few hours."

"You go ahead. I'm at the part where Michael J. Fox is about to make out with his mother, and I want to see how he handles it in case it ever comes up in my own life."

He shook his head. No matter how much time he spent with Vain, he'd never understand that twisted brain of hers. There were entire sections of her thought process he couldn't even begin to unravel.

He got up and headed downstairs. With the sounds of activity all around him, he could almost pretend the day was an ordinary day; and his life was a normal life. A guy waking up in the morning, on vacation with friends. A pipe dream, but maybe one that would be closer to reality after they got rid of the Padlock. He'd give anything for that.

Chapter 22

Emma learns about coffee makers.

Vain wasn't pleasant to sleep beside. She tossed and turned all night, murmuring and calling out, and besides that, she snored. Emma barely needed to sleep anymore, so she'd spent most of the night reliving the events of the past few days.

Was she safe now? Is that what safety meant? Forced together with that strange group? Hush made her uncomfortable, with his deep, piercing stare that regarded you like an unsolved puzzle. Roman seemed nice enough. More than nice, if she was being honest with herself, but they had just met. Vain was not a friendly woman. Last night, with the two of them in the room, she'd tried to get Vain to talk, but all she would say was that they had to see it through.

Emma crawled out of bed before the sun rose and found her way into the massive, marble-slathered kitchen. Something resembling a coffee maker sat on the counter, except it had more controls than a jet engine and an incomprehensible set of instructions. The interface had a digital screen, with a button that read 'push here'. She did, and the display changed to two icons, both of which were coffee mugs. One had steam coming out of it and one did not.

She pushed the button with steam on it and the display switched to 'cleaning mode engaged'. The machine whirred. The readout blinked. 'Please wait 15 minutes for cleaning to complete'.

She sighed and settled for a glass of warm tap water.

The noises from the restaurant below reminded her she hadn't eaten in days, which further reminded her she never needed to eat ever again, which then sent her into a mild-to-severe panic at that thought of trying to fend off her mother at Christmas. God, she'd need to invent an entire fake system that mimicked actual eating. Maybe a flesh-colored tube strapped to the back of her neck that connected to a pouch beneath a turtleneck? She'd need to sign up for an engineering course and a knitting elective. Ugh. How would she handle soup? It was too much for her to deal with and threatened the fingernail grip she had on her emotions. She needed to think about something else.

The power, for instance. She couldn't deny that it held an undercurrent of desire. The way it felt to stop that Wyatt. One moment, she'd been helpless. The next, in control. What would that even be like, to have that sort of power all the time, that knowledge that she could out-muscle her way through any situation?

Emma recalled an incident a few months ago. She'd stayed late at the library and when she left it was approaching midnight. But the library was only a mile from her house, and in a safe neighborhood. No reason not to walk. So, with her books pressed to her chest, she headed for home. Was she walking faster than normal? Maybe she was, but she only wanted to get to bed. That's what she told herself.

She turned a corner, and at the end of the block, a group of guys stumbled towards her. Drunk and loud and laughing, they were obviously on their way home from the bar. A small knot of fear formed in her stomach and she ignored it because it was twenty God damned twenty and a strong woman didn't need to cross the road, not at all.

One guy laughed, a braying sound that pierced the silence of the night. Even as her conscious mind said no, her feet had other ideas and she scurried across the road, feeling small and worthless. Even the way she walked, she shrunk into herself and whispered, "don't notice me don't notice me don't notice me."

The guys passed, barely paying attention to her, and she hated the wave of relief that came over her. Because three guys in the middle of the night were scary, full stop. And they were scary because if they decided to do something, there wouldn't be a single thing Emma could do to stop them.

Until now.

Now, with this power, she'd never be scared again.

She shook her head to clear it. Such dark thoughts. Where were these even coming from? In a couple hours, she'd be normal again, and that would be that. Good. She was glad. She was.

"Good morning," said a voice from behind her.

Startled, she whirled around. Charm stood in the doorway, wrapped in a thick bathrobe and wearing giant fuzzy ladybug slippers. She had a newspaper tucked under her arm.

"Did I wake you? I'm sorry," Emma gestured at the machine. "I was trying to make coffee."

"With that thing? Good luck. We normally have the restaurant whip us something up. You want me to call them?"

"No, I don't want to be a bother."

"Don't be silly. Did you sleep well?"

"Not really," Emma said. "This thing makes it hard to sleep."

"Tell me about that." Charm took a seat at the kitchen table. She pushed out another chair for Emma. "You can pull energy from anyone? Arthur's the only other person I knew who could do that. Did Vain tell you anything about him?"

"Not much. She talked a little about you guys, though. She said Hush can make people think or behave however he wants?"

"Yes. It's been helpful in setting us up here."

"What else can people like us do?" Emma leaned forward on the table, resting her chin in her hands. Unlike Vain, Charm seemed to be willing to explain things. Emma was desperate for someone to talk to.

"I've only seen a handful of manifestations." Charm had an easygoing way about her, smiling as she talked. It put Emma at immediate ease, like she could trust the woman with anything. "Energy manipulation is, by far, the most common one. Some people can turn the energy inward and gain physical augmentation, like increased strength, speed, whatever, but that's not as helpful as you'd think."

"Really?" said Emma. "Super strength would be handy to have."

"Sure, with super bone density. One guy used it to jack himself up to be as strong as a gorilla. He tried to lift a giant tree trunk and snapped his forearms in half. Muscle is only half the equation. Let's see, what else?" Charm tapped her chin. "What the twins can do is rare, only a handful can do that. Healing is another. That's rare too. Some people can warm things up, make them super-hot. Can't freeze things though, they'd kill themselves trying."

"It's because of the energy displacement, isn't it? You'd be taking energy out of something to cool it, not adding it. We can only add energy to things."

"You got it, sugar," said Charm. "There are practical limitations, like the amount of energy available in our sources. Unless they've been storing, there's only so much you can pull before they run out and get hurt, or worse."

"Every time Vain uses her power, it might hurt Roman?" Emma recoiled. Another piece of information Vain neglected to give her.

"Well, she's pretty cautious when it comes to him. But yes, it's a theoretical possibility. Some of the other people weren't as considerate."

"You're like Roman, right? A Conduit? Vain told me a little about your partner, Patience?"

The easy smile faded from Charm's face, but she nodded.

"What was her power?" From Charm's expression alone, she knew she'd messed up. "I'm sorry, I shouldn't have asked."

"It's okay." Charm gave a sad shrug. "It's getting to the point where it doesn't hurt the way it used to, and it's nice to remember her. She'd want to be remembered by someone who loved her. Patience could turn her powers inward and enhance her senses. Mostly, her eyesight. She detected reflections of energy, or physical injuries, which was helpful if anyone in the Hotel was hurt."

"How did people get hurt?" The words were uncomfortable in Emma's mouth. She didn't quite believe some of the stories Vain had told her about it, but these people acted as if it were all true.

"The reason Arthur collects people like us is to pour energy into his Well. It's a giant physical hole that sits in the center of the Hotel. Every few days, after the sources had had enough time to build up energy, we'd march in pairs and grab these handles." Charm closed her eyes, lost in the painful memory. When she opened them, she had a faraway look. "For Conduits, people like Roman and I, it wasn't that big a deal because they created us to output energy. Not the Utilities. Patience compared it to having your veins flossed with electricity that had been set on fire. She'd scream every time, and it would last for a full thirty seconds while the energy poured into that damn thing."

Emma didn't know what to say. Was that the life she'd be facing if she let the Wyatts take her? She'd die first. "That's how people were hurt?"

"One of the ways. It was temporary though, and some of the people in the Hotel convinced themselves it was no different than getting a flu shot or going to the dentist." This time, Charm's smile didn't reach her eyes. "Not everyone, though. Some people, the ones who were stubborn enough, or maybe crazy enough, would fight back against the pull. If you wanted it bad enough, you could stop the flow and only deposit a little."

"Vain," said Emma.

"Vain." Charm nodded. "Stubborn, angry Vain. She'd resist every time. Oh, she'd put on an act like it was killing her, but she'd leave with most of her energy intact. Trick didn't reach the point where he had free run of the Hotel by being stupid. He knew when a Utility was holding back. And, every so often, he'd catch Vain not pulling her weight. I never knew how much of what happened was Arthur and how much was Trick. Arthur was a hands-off guy. Regardless, Trick would signal to the Wyatts and they'd pull Vain into a back room and work her over a little. Break her fingers, snap a couple of ribs, maybe cut on her a bit. Sometimes they'd just beat the holy hell out of her. The worst part was how functional they were about it. The Wyatts didn't even seem to like it. It was a job."

Emma swayed in her chair, dizzy. She took a sip of her water and Charm continued.

"There were some healers, but Trick wouldn't let them get to her right away. He'd leave her overnight with whatever injuries the Wyatts inflicted. He let Roman in, though. Roman would sit with her and try to settle her until they'd let one of the healers do their thing. Vain would come out, good as new, with only the memories. And she'd behave, for a while. But, sure as the sun rises, she'd get antsy, and she'd get up to her old games. From there, it was the same dance all over again. I swear that girl is the toughest, most stubborn thing I've ever crossed paths with. Roman would beg her to give Arthur what he wanted, but that girl doesn't know how to quit. If Trick threatened her with a twig, she'd spit and tell him to get a branch."

"Is that what pushed you all to escape?"

"No. If Trick is nothing else, he's practical. He'd find the most efficient way to make you cooperate. For Vain, that was the stick. For others? It was the carrot. They had the Hotel set up almost like an all-inclusive resort, if you can believe it. There was a spa, a library, a games parlor; all the books you could ever want to read. Some people liked it there. We had our own rooms, which were quite lavish; we were well fed; and some of the pairs never tasted the lash. Quite a few became institutionalized. Arthur found one doorway that led to an unpopulated version of Earth. Every few months, he'd let us go to that world and have a day on the beach; the most beautiful water you've ever seen." Charm smiled. "That was nice."

Emma's head spun. It seemed so unreal. Energy wells? Alternate Earths? She leaned forward, eager to hear more.

Charm's eyes still had that faraway look, like she wasn't even seeing Emma. She was fully back in the Hotel. "None of it worked on Vain though. No matter what he offered, she'd spit it back in his face. Eventually, Trick tried something else. One day, when it was her turn to give power, she held back. Trick noticed and, as usual, she geared up for what came next. This time though, they didn't take Vain. They took Roman." Charm hugged herself and the blood drained from Emma's face.

Even though she'd only known Roman for a day, she couldn't imagine hurting him. He was such a kind and gentle soul.

"They strapped her to a chair and gave her a front row seat. They took their time. Vain screamed so much through the whole thing that she ripped her vocal cords. When it was over, there was no fight left in her." A single tear rolled down Charm's cheek, and she sniffled and wiped it away. "It wasn't right, what they did."

"But she didn't stop," said Emma.

"No, she redirected. She'll never stop, not if she's doing what she thinks is right. And Vain always, always, thinks she's right. That's why she's Vain."

"Ah." Emma smiled sadly, getting the joke.

"But, Trick made a mistake. He went after the one person Vain cares about more than anyone in the world. If he'd stuck with hurting her, she would have continued screwing around with mini acts of defiance, but now that Roman was involved? Now, the entire Hotel needed to crumble. That's when she came up with the plan to escape."

Emma tried to wrap her head around all these new concepts. "What kind of person could be that driven?"

Charm tapped her chin. "I don't know what Vain was like before the Hotel. None of us know anything about ourselves. But I have a theory that life lingers."

"Lingers?"

"Take you, for example. You're a strong, intelligent, self-possessed woman." Emma blushed and waved a hand, but Charm continued. "If they ever took you, you'd still be those things. The Hotel can only strip your memories, but they can't strip you of being you. Vain came into the Hotel angry and latched on to Roman like a life preserver. Trick didn't make her like that."

"She was always herself." The pieces clicked together in Emma's head.

"You got it. What makes a person like Vain, become Vain? Closed off, angry, distrustful, and ruthlessly, psychotically loyal to the one person who has ever shown her any kindness or protection? There's no way to know, but I have my suspicions about the person she was before the Hotel."

"A mime?"

Charm laughed and rubbed Emma's hand "Cute. You remind me of Vain, sort of. A little less rough around the edges, but that same core of determination."

Emma rubbed her finger around the edge of her glass. "Are you scared about today?"

"A little." Charm said, slowly. "But I think we have to get rid of that Padlock. It's the only way we'll find peace."

"What if Vain is right and they try to take us?"

Charm bared her teeth. "Then God help the poor person who tries to take Vain back to the Hotel. Because I honestly think she'll kill anyone who gets in her way."

Chapter 23

Vain carries an egg in her pocket for some reason.

Mark drove them down an ill-used side road surrounded by a thick forest. Even though the sun was high in the sky, the densely packed trees only let a little of the light through. He had to slow the van down to drive through the twisting roads. Vain felt like the forest was smothering her. This area was isolated and had so many places to hide. Through the open window, the sounds of birds happily chirping set her teeth on edge.

"This was the only thing available?" Vain gestured at the minivan Mark had secured. It was a newer model and included every accessory possible, which somehow made it even worse, like they tried to make it cool and failed.

"There's a bunch of us, we wouldn't fit in anything else," replied Mark.

"Two cars weren't an option? We look like assholes."

"Who cares?" said Mark.

"Trick will bust our balls for this. You think it's fine now, but just wait."

To keep her mind off the upcoming disaster, Vain assaulted Mark with a steady patter of inanities, which he handled with Roman-like aplomb. A definite plus in his favor. She wasn't nervous though. Not at all. Life-threatening standoffs with Trick were her bread and butter. Were the trees getting closer? She rolled up the window. Stupid birds.

"We're almost there," Mark checked his phone one final time. "About two minutes. Everyone, get ready."

"There are a lot of Wyatts," Emma said. "I can feel them."

"Probably a precaution," Hush said. He didn't sound convinced.

Rocks crunched underneath the van's tires as paved road gave way to crumbly gravel. The address Trick provided led to an old state park, albeit one that had apparently been shut down for years. They were so far off the main road, and there had been so many twists and turns that Vain became disoriented. Whatever Trick had in mind, he'd picked a spot with privacy. Even if they screamed for hours, no one would hear them. That, more than anything, made a bubble of fear work its way into her stomach.

The road opened into a large, circular parking area surrounded by ancient, towering pine trees. Above them, the sun burned brightly, casting deep shadows that covered the open space. Near the back, two Red SUVs were parked in front of two white ticket booths. Behind them, gates opened onto a winding path that went deep into the forest. Vain's stomach had a dead weight to it, a cold knot of tension. She took deep breaths.

In front of the ticket booths, four Wyatts stood at attention, armed with assault rifles. They wore mean-looking body armor and had mean expressions to match. Two open umbrellas sat on the ground in front of them, the tops pointing toward the minivan. Two TVs perched on giant stands with wires running to a portable generator.

Umbrellas and TVs. What new trick was that?

Mark pulled the van to a stop, perpendicular to the Wyatts, twenty-five feet away. He turned the key, killing the engine. No one said anything or moved or made any motion to get out. They sat there in hushed silence, soaking in thoughts of what would come next.

Vain leaned back towards Roman and whispered, "I'm pulling now, okay? Just in case."

Roman's lips pressed together in a straight line and he nodded.

She opened herself up and let power drip in, only a trickle. The sense of Roman in her head intensified, and some tension and fear made its way through the link. "I'll protect you." She wanted to pat him on the knee, or his shoulder, but she didn't. Instead, she crossed her arms. "Roman, trust me."

With that, some of the tension left his body. He lightly smiled at her. "I do, Vain. I really do."

To the group, she said, "Let's get this over with. Open the doors. Chop, chop."

"Something's wrong," Emma said. "There are only four of them, but there's more energy around. It's fuzzy. I can't get a read on where it's coming from."

"Okay." Vain wasn't surprised. "Stay focused. Remember what we talked about, what I need you to do if this goes badly."

Emma chewed her lips and nodded. Roman raised his eyebrow at her, but she ignored it. It would be up to Emma to get them out if it turned into a trap.

They crept out, keeping one eye on each other and one on the Wyatts. Before they left, they had agreed that Hush would do most of the talking, since Vain was likely to let her diplomacy devolve into a series of insults.

They kept their backs to the minivan and stopped within fifteen feet of the Wyatts. The profoundly uncool vehicle blocked off Vain's view of the entrance, so she attempted to position herself where she'd be able to see everything. The Wyatts wore sunglasses and earpieces. Couple that with the riot gear and they looked ready to airdrop into some war-torn third world country.

"Why don't any of your gloves have fingers?" Vain called out. "Is that like a fashion thing? Do you all shop at the same store? Is there some website that tells you what to wear?" She put on an affected voice, climbing to a falsetto that she sprinkled with a British accent. "Today's fashionable thug will want to tell the world they mean business with our selection of black, tactical hunting boots. Your guns aren't the only thing that can bring suppression. Surprise them all with your military green flak jacket, in a soft hypoallergenic cotton blend. Now only forty-nine ninety-nine."

"Vain. Shut up," Hush said without turning his head.

The Wyatts didn't respond or even acknowledge her. They stood there with their angry faces and military-grade combat gear, looking both bored and terrifying. There was something unsettling about all those duplicate faces staring at her, each one capable of acts of horrific violence. She knew first-hand what those things could do if given free rein. That they never seemed to take any pleasure from it somehow made it worse.

The door from one of the ticket booths opened and Trick walked out. As usual, he was dressed immaculately, wearing dark jeans and a long-sleeve, green shirt buttoned halfway up. Not even the bandages covering his nose and the dark circles surrounding his eyes ruined the look. With his irritatingly attractive face, he looked like a magazine cut-out, albeit one with less depth.

"Hi gang," said Trick, eying their vehicle. "A minivan, huh? There weren't any PT Cruisers?"

Roman nodded. "It's economical and spacious."

"It makes you look like assholes."

"Shit," said Vain. "I told you."

"I like your hair, Vanity." Trick waved. "Black suits you."

"Don't call me that."

He grinned. "Sure. I'm glad you all made it. It's been a while since I've seen most of you." He looked at Emma. "We haven't met, so I'm assuming that makes you Emma. My name's Trick."

Emma shook her head. "Why do you all have such weird names?"

Trick shrugged. "It's a Hotel thing, part of the check-in procedure. Roman, I want you to know that there are no hard feelings about this." He pointed at his nose. "It was a well-executed escape and I'm a little proud of you."

"Can we get this over with?" said Roman.

"Sure. Before we get down to business, I want to explain a few things. You might wonder why we have umbrellas scattered around without the slightest trace of rain. Well, they're—"

"They're Devices." Vain had figured it out. "Dampeners that block energy. Our powers won't work past the umbrellas. Got it."

Trick appeared miffed and fiddled with his shirt sleeves. "Yes, that's exactly it. I know all of you well enough—especially Vain—to know that trusting you is a lousy idea. You have something planned, don't you?" He looked right at Vain.

She nodded and reached into her jacket pocket.

The Wyatts stiffened and raised their guns, but Trick made settling motions, and they lowered them.

"Easy," he said. "Everyone take it easy."

Vain pulled an egg out of her jacket and held it between her thumb and index finger. She showed it to Trick and the Wyatts, who appeared confused. "Yaaa!" she yelled and threw it at Trick. "This is for Roman!" It missed by several feet and it sailed past his head, hitting the ticket booth with a splat.

"Did you throw an egg at me?" asked Trick.

She nodded. "It's the form my protest is taking."

Trick chuckled. "I've missed you, Vanity. I know it never seemed like it, but you were always my favorite. It's great to see you again." His eyes grew soft, with a whisper of sympathy behind them. "Listen. I'm sorry about how the attack played out in Denver. For the record, those Wyatts had instructions to subdue you, not throw you off a building."

Emma interrupted their back and forth. "After this, you'll leave me alone, right?"

Trick nodded. "Emma, I also want to apologize for your treatment. The Wyatts broke standard protocol when they took you, and I understand it was jarring. In fairness to them, had Vain not interrupted, you wouldn't have remembered any of it anyway."

"Is that supposed to be reassuring?"

Trick shrugged. "It's whatever you want it to be. Either way, I'll honor my part of the bargain. Once I get the Padlock, I promise you that the Wyatts won't hurt you. Tell them, Wyatts."

"I don't even like violence. I like women's studies." A Wyatt said. He received withering looks from his colleagues and Trick sighed.

"Settle down, Alan Alda. Now, to make it extra certain that you'll hold up your end of the bargain, I've prepared a little surprise for you. A movie, if you will." Trick giggled; a high-pitched noise that echoed off the trees.

Vain licked her lips. It was starting. Whatever he was planning, it was starting.

The screen flickered to life and projected images of a dimly lit room. A person was tied to a chair with their back to the camera. With the bag over their head, Vain couldn't tell if they were male or female. A single Wyatt stood beside the chair, looking menacing. He held up a knife.

Trick looked at the group expectantly. "I'm sure you're wondering what this is about." He pulled a walkie-talkie from behind his back and turned it on. "I wanted to make sure there was no chance you'd back out of your end of the agreement. So, we found someone that one of you cares about very deeply. You could say we hit the... *Mother*-load." He smiled. "Now."

The standing Wyatt pulled the bag off the other person's head. A shock of long red hair tumbled out and flowed down the back of the chair. Whoever she was, she gave a frightened and gravelly scream.

Trick threw back his head and laughed. "We have your mother, Emma. That's right. We tracked her down. Ha!"

Vain gasped. Of all the things she expected from Trick, that wasn't one of them. She had no contingency plan for this. How would Trick have found Emma's mother? It changed everything, and there wasn't time to figure it out. She looked over to gauge Emma's emotions. How would she react?

Emma blinked. Vain was impressed by how calmly she was taking it. From her behavior, you'd think none of this bothered her, but Vain knew better. Several moments passed, with no outward reaction. Emma cleared her throat and looked around at the group.

"That woman has long, red hair," she said.

"That's right, Emma." Trick laughed again.

"My mom is a brunette with short hair. I don't think that's my mom."

The two groups considered each other. Trick licked his lips. On the monitor, the Wyatt facing the camera did some neat knife maneuvers. Vain squinted at the screen, taking a closer look at the woman tied to the chair. Hmm. Awfully broad shoulders for a woman.

"But you're a redhead. " A note of worry entered Trick's voice. "So, your Mom should also be—"

"It skips a generation sometimes. My grandma was a redhead."

Trick whispered something to the Wyatt beside him.

The Wyatt shook his head. "I'm positive it doesn't skip."

Emma looked at the group and shrugged. "I don't know what to tell you. That's not my mom. I mean, I don't want anyone to get hurt, but I don't know who that person is."

"God damn it." Trick barked into the walkie talkie. "Call it off."

On screen, the person slipped out of the ropes. A Wyatt wearing a red wig and a woman's blouse turned to face the camera.

"I told you this wouldn't work, Trick," the Wyatt said. "No one was going to buy me as a woman. This was a dumb idea. You don't pay me enough for this." He threw the wig to the ground and walked off camera.

The remaining Wyatt did a few more awesome moves with the knife.

Trick made a slashing motion across his neck and the Wyatt beside him turned the TV off.

"Well," said Trick. "This is awkward. I guess they can't all be winners," he giggled into his sleeve. "Still, I think I get credit for trying. I thought it would be a funny gag. I should get some points for convincing a Wyatt to wear a wig. Right? Sorry, Emma. I don't know who your Mom is. I don't even know your last name."

Oh, right. Trick was also helplessly, deliriously, insane. How had Vain ever forgotten? How had any of them forgotten?

"Jesus Christ, Trick," said Hush. "We brought the Padlock. You didn't need to do whatever the hell that was. We've held up our end of the deal, and we're all here. Take away our powers like you said, and we'll hand it over."

"You know it, buddy." Trick winked and gave him a single gun finger. "Padlock first, then powers. Not the other way around. Hand it over."

Roman reached inside his pocket and pulled out the padlock she had given him. The real one hung on a chain around her neck, hidden under her shirt. There was no way she'd hand over the real thing; she just hoped Trick wouldn't be able to sniff out a phony.

Roman bent over and put the padlock on the ground. He pushed it toward Trick with his foot, but the ground was rocky, and it wouldn't roll like a soccer ball. It moved an inch. An awkward silence followed.

Trick sighed. "Roman. Come on, man. Get your shit together. You're embarrassing yourself. Everyone's watching."

Roman flushed and picked it up. He tossed it at Trick. "Here you go."

Trick snatched it from the air and inspected it. "How do I know this is the real thing?"

Vain said, "Give me a gun and I'll shoot you. If it's real, you'll be safe."

Trick glared at her, but she didn't drop her gaze, and she kept her eyes wide and innocent.

"You may have broken it," he said, twirling the lock. "Arthur will be very unhappy if that's the case."

"Your Wyatt broke it when he pulled me off the roof."

Trick rubbed his earlobe with his right hand, looking around. No one else caught the gesture, but Vain did. She squinted into the thick forest surrounding them and made out shapes moving through the tangle of brush and undergrowth.

That was it. She pulled energy from Roman, preparing to create a shield. He noticed, and they made eye contact. After a moment, he nodded. He took a few steps back and leaned against the side of the van, bracing himself in case she pulled so much he fell unconscious.

"I'll assume this is the real thing." Trick's voice sounded suspicious. "We'll know in a couple of days, anyway. For your safety, and ours, we're going to ask you to come with us for a bit. Just until we figure things out."

"You didn't say anything about that." Hush pointed an accusing finger. "You get the Padlock and de-power us. That was the deal."

"Oh, that. Listen, man, I don't even know if it's possible to de-power you. I made that up. I guess I could ask Arthur to make a Device, but what would he even use?"

"Vacuum cleaner?" said one of the Wyatts.

"Breast pump?"

"Toilet plunger?"

"These are all great ideas, guys," said Trick. "I love the enthusiasm. But no. Now that we have the Padlock, you're coming with us." Trick made a spinning gesture with his free hand, and more Wyatts appeared; over a dozen at least, stepping out of the forest from all sides. Some carried guns and some umbrellas. Vain threw up a shield between them and the group and Roman sagged against the van.

"You're betraying us?" Hush sounded shocked. Vain rolled her eyes.

"Ha. Yeah. Here's the plan, everyone," Trick said. "If you look around, you'll notice you're surrounded. You walked right into the center of this. You can save us all time and surrender now. Vain, I assume you've thrown up a shield." He put his hands out and walked forward until his fingers touched something. A small crackle sparked his hand, and he pulled back. "I thought so. Save your friends the trouble, Vain. Drop the shield and come nicely. These guns are loaded with rubber bullets, but they'll still hurt and break bones. You can't keep this up forever. Look, Roman's already exhausted."

Hush spat on the ground. "I don't think so, Trick. We're leaving. Everyone, into the van."

Trick seemed disappointed. "Have it your way." He gestured to the men surrounding them. "Light them up."

Vain braced as the guns screamed to life. Time slowed to a crawl. The rubber bullets thudded against her shield. The Wyatts circled on all sides, taking positions and firing into it. The bullets drained her energy faster than she could pull it from Roman. The noise was deafening, the sound of the rifles firing echoing off the surrounding forest. Blunt cried and dropped to his knees, screaming. Hush stepped in front of him.

Vain cupped her hands around her mouth and yelled at Emma. "Now, Emma, now! Do it now!"

Emma only chewed at her bottom lip, pale and wide-eyed. She looked much younger than her years, and Vain felt a small twinge of guilt for what she was about to make her do. Very small. Vain would pay the price later.

Emma dropped to her knees with tears streaming down her cheeks. "I don't know how," she yelled.

Beside her, Mark pulled a gun and shot at the Wyatts, weakening Vain's shield even further. She heard the whine as his bullets bounced off the inside and whizzed past her head.

"Stop it, you idiot dinosaur, you're making it worse!"

Outside the shield, the Wyatts advanced, still firing. Vain crouched beside Emma and took her by the shoulders. "We don't have time. I can't hold my shield up much longer." She looked at Roman, who rested with his head folded in his arms. "You have to do this." Vain tried to make her voice calm over the din. "It's the only way."

"Give it up, Vain," yelled Trick. "We're going to get through."

The Wyatts stopped shooting and held their distance. One of the braver ones approached the edge of the shield, stepping in front of the energy-dampening umbrellas. Vain struck. Faster than thought, she dropped him with a blast to the head and he fell with a thud. A puddle of red expanded beneath him, soaking into the gravel.

Trick yelled, "Stay behind the umbrellas, you idiot photocopies!"

"Jesus Christ." Vain turned back to Emma. "Emma, please. They'll kill us."

Tears ran down Emma's face and she wiped them away. "I'm so scared. What if I can't control it?"

"Then say goodbye to your memory, because we're checking into the Hotel."

That seemed to get through. A smolder of fire burned in her eyes and she clenched her jaw.

"Get as close to Emma as you can," Vain yelled. "She's pulling everyone's energy."

This was Vain's Hail Mary plan, the one that had scared Emma so badly. Vain suspected Trick would figure out a way to nullify her powers, but Emma could pull from anyone. His umbrellas stopped energy from getting to him, but it didn't do anything about the energy leaving. She glanced back at Roman, who was crumpled on the ground in a heap. That was an affirmation. It was going to work. Because what happened to a person when you pulled too much energy from them?

They dropped unconscious.

Emma gathered herself and pulled. Vain felt it almost immediately. Everyone else crowded around her. Even on a regular day, standing beside Emma was a little exhausting; she always drew a small amount of energy from everybody. She couldn't help that. But, now that it was unleashed, thick waves of it passed over her, around her, and through her. It was staggering.

Emma stiffened, her arms at her sides, palms upwards, pulling. Trick realized something was going wrong. A Wyatt dropped to one knee, his gun falling to the ground. That was all the confirmation he needed.

"They're doing something." Trick backed up and looked around frantically. "Stand back."

"Emma, it's working," said Vain. "Pull harder, you have to pull harder. Take it from all of them."

Emma raised both her hands to the sky and yelled. The waves of energy became a waterfall, then a tsunami. Christ almighty, she was pulling fifty times the amount of energy Vain had ever gotten from Roman. How was she keeping it all? How powerful was she?

Around them, the Wyatts dropped one at a time. They staggered and resisted, but they all fell. Trick also dropped and fell silent.

Vain sagged in relief. It worked. She looked at Emma and a shiver of raw, unconstrained fear ran up her spine.

Emma floated four inches above the ground. Her hair stuck out as if she had rubbed a balloon against her head. Her arms were outstretched and blood dripped from her fingertips. Two fingernails dropped to the rocky earth with a horrible plink. She was screaming, her voice a raw tear of agony that cut right through Vain.

Across the clearing, a tree fell over with an enormous crack. Three birds fell from the sky, dead or unconscious, and the power kept coming, more every second. It was growing and growing. From where Vain was standing, it looked like it would never stop.

"Vain!" Emma's voice sounded amplified and electric. Blood from her bleeding gums ran down her chin. "I can't stop it! I can't turn it off! I'm going to explode!"

Vain ripped the Padlock from around her neck and pressed it into Emma's hand, cupping it together with her own. "Pour it all into the padlock! Like we did at the motel. Put it all in there!"

Emma turned her attention towards the Padlock, but nothing happened. The energy continued to batter Vain, flowing ceaselessly into Emma. As Vain considered a punch-based solution, the sickening, overwhelming waves of energy slowed, then stopped. For a pregnant second, there was complete silence.

Then, Emma screamed again, and power erupted into the padlock.

Vain felt all of it. So much energy. Such a fucking terrifying amount of energy that, for a moment, Vain worried it was *too* much. No one should have that much power. Emma could wipe entire cities off the map with the amount she was handling. What if she ever used it on something other than a Wyatt?

Emma grabbed the Padlock like a talisman and sank to her knees. The sensation of being smothered by energy faded, but Vain shuddered at the ungodly amount of power that flowed into Device. It had physical gravity, and Vain struggled not to lean into it.

"Everyone, get in the car." Vain's voice was thick and syrupy.

The group crouched by Emma's feet, huddling like terrified sheep. No one moved.

"Now!" She clapped her hands to bring them to attention. "Charm, help Roman into the van. He's done. Mark, grab one of the Wyatts. It doesn't matter which one. Let's go, everyone. Time to jet."

"Mark should do what to a Wyatt?" Mark asked. She held up a single finger, challenging him to say another word. He frowned, but moved to follow her orders.

Vain crouched beside Emma, who lay curled up in a ball on the ground, still clutching the Padlock to her chest. The waves of power had dropped to a trickle. She was crying a little. Emma's bloodshot eyes flicked back and forth. Her hands were a bloody mess from her missing fingernails, and a thick rope of blood poured from her mouth.

"I stopped it myself this time," she said to Vain. "You didn't need to hit me. Progress." She gave a tiny smile.

With shaking hands, Vain reached out and smoothed down Emma's hair and made soft, comforting noises. She wasn't sure how to do this part. "You did great, Emma. You saved us all. Let's get you in the car and we'll get back to the restaurant and figure this out. You need to give me the Padlock now." She looked over to Blunt, who was getting the van. "Blunt, help Emma."

Blunt looked like he would rather do anything else. He approached her warily, like you would approach a tiger that someone claimed was domesticated. He tried to appear unfazed. Vain unclasped Emma's hands and pried the Padlock out. It was back to its original, pristine condition, like it had looked when she stole it from Arthur. The lock was shut, and the gold base once again held a polished glow and was warm to the touch. As Vain suspected, all the padlock needed to function again was staggering amounts of energy.

God damn it, the whole plan worked. She couldn't believe it. The bad guys were out cold, her friends were uncaptured, the Padlock wasn't broken, and—most importantly—that proved that Vain's scheme to free them from the shadow of the Hotel would work.

It had been a tough fight and in stark contrast to the group that had exited the van; they were a ragged, shell-shocked bunch.

And now, they carried one extra passenger in the form of an unconscious Wyatt. But still, Vain couldn't contain her elation.
This time, not even Arthur would stop her.

Chapter 24

Emma and Roman have a moment.

Emma sat on a cushioned, cube-shaped footstool at the edge of the bathtub. Like everything else in the apartment, the bathroom dripped with over-the-top wealth, filled with objects that were either perfectly square or imperfectly square. Apparently, spheres were for poor people? The bathroom was the size of her kitchen. A shelf ran around the circumference of the room and held a confusing collection of knick-knacks, like random bottles of shampoo and soap in black unlabeled containers, a bust of a head, candles, and the occasional container of potpourri. The whole thing indicated two rich bachelors who had never once set foot into that room.

Emma struggled to keep her eyes open as dizziness assaulted her in waves, the result of channeling that much power. The ride back to the restaurant had been awful. Hush lost any semblance of control and wouldn't shut up about what he would do to Trick. He had contacts all over the world and he would call all of them. To do what, exactly, he wasn't clear on. But, by Christ, phone calls would solve everything.

Barely anyone else talked. Mark and Vain exchanged quiet words, but Emma couldn't hear what they said. No doubt it had something to do with the unconscious henchman they kidnapped, and any number of other crazy schemes Vain had cooking. Was it still kidnapping if you stole the person who tried to kill you? Did one negate the other?

Charm and Roman sat with her in the back seat while she wept, overcome by fatigue and fear. During those horrible moments when she became a whirlpool of energy, her bones swelled and expanded, leaving her sore. Her skin stretched, like she had swallowed lightning. The whole of her insides became too big for her outside. No wonder her fingernails popped off.

The more energy that had come into her, the less of herself remained. Her core sense of self, the center that made her Emma, rubbed down to nothing, leaving only hollow anger. There was a

157 | Michael James

moment where she thought she might kill them all.

Even now, safe in the bathroom back at the restaurant, the scab in her mind remained, and she kept picking at it.

Everyone had been ants scrambling around her. One stomp from her boot and she would have ended them all. The Wyatts, that baffling Trick person, even her new friends. God help her, she had wanted to do that. At that moment, she felt compelled to. She shuddered at the memory and her eyes welled up. Was that life, now?

Roman sat next to her, searching through the medicine cabinet for Band-Aids. Her hands flared with bursts of searing pain. There had only been time for a hasty field dressing in the van using paper towels they found in the glove box. Every part of her hurt, but her nails were the worst.

"Okay, found them." He produced a small box of bandages and crouched down to her level and noticed her tears. Gently taking her hands, he started removing the towels. She flinched in anticipation.

"The bonus of having your fingernails fall out, I think, is the money you'll save on nail polish." He smiled at her while he worked, and the soft kindness in his eyes made some of the pain go away.

"That's the stupidest thing I've ever heard." She sniffled. She kept her voice easy, so he'd know there was no anger in her words.

He concentrated, making sure he was removing the makeshift bandages with speed, but in a way that caused her no further discomfort.

"I mean, I don't know what you ladies spend on nail polish in the first place, but I'd bet it's in the high thousands. So, that's a plus. A feather in your cap."

She snorted. "Step three on any good financial plan will include removing your pesky and expensive extremities."

"Right," he agreed. "You know who the real idiots are? Suckers with functioning fingernails. Poor bastards don't understand the maintenance associated with them. Don't get me started on cuticles."

Her hands were now exposed. He reached over to the sink for a wet towel and dripped water onto her nails to clean them. They still wept bright red blood, and each drop of water sent paroxysms of pain through her entire limb. She inhaled and held her breath for a moment.

"What about the bleeding gums?" She turned her head to face the bathroom wall so she didn't have to watch him repair her tattered fingers. "What're the advantages there?"

"Lipstick. Your lips will always have a healthy red color to them and coupled with your naturally fingernail-less hands, you'll never have to worry about makeup again."

"So, after this is over, I should become a supermodel? Hit the runways?"

His eyes darted to her face. "You could." Starting with her left hand, he wrapped a bandage around her raw nailbed. His fingertips danced in a light tickle across her palm.

"Has anything like this ever happened to you or Vain before? Where your skin erupts?"

"No," he replied. "But I can't pull a fraction of what you do. Not even close. When Vain and I were in the Hotel was as much as I've ever done, but comparing you and I is like comparing a candle to the sun. I've never seen anything like what you did today." He finished up her left hand and placed it on her leg. "There, that's one finished. Not too bad, right?"

"Not too bad," she agreed. Getting fresh gauze wrapped around her fingers soothed her through to her core, and some of the tension melted from her shoulders. Only gauze, but it was enough. "Have you done this before?"

"Vain's gotten her share of bruises. I've never done fingernails before, but I can throw a Band-Aid on with the best of them. Call me Nurse Roman from now on."

"I'm probably not going to do that."

"How did Vain convince you to do that, anyway? It was insane," Roman asked.

"You've met Vain, right? There's not a lot of compromise there. She told me what she needed me to do. In fact, when she first talked about this, her exact words were: 'if things don't work out, I need you to suck everyone.' I told her she might have misunderstood my experience in that regard and asked if she planned on helping. She didn't get the joke."

Roman laughed, a warm and genuine sound. "Yeah, Vain is pretty to the point. Did she do that thing where she stares at you for thirty solid seconds without blinking?"

"Yes." Emma laughed. "Oh my God, what is that?"

"She calls it her Jedi mind trick. In actuality, it's Vain not caring about the norms of standard human interaction."

"Norms of standard human interaction?" Emma teased. "Were you a psychologist, or something?"

"I don't know." He shrugged and went back to work on her right hand. The light mood vanished, leaving behind a heavy silence.

"Not that you need to know what you did before. Memory is overrated." She scrambled to recover. She wanted that easy mood back, the one where they were two people making stupid jokes. "Take milk, for example. I don't remember what I was like as a baby, but I drank milk, so who cares when I first learned to like it? The important thing is that you're you. That is, if you enjoy milk. I don't, it makes me sick, but I hate telling people I'm lactose intolerant. People don't say they're gasoline intolerant, do they? They simply don't drink gasoline. Not that milk would cause your insides to explode like gasoline, but it sure comes close for me." She forced her Judas mouth shut by clamping her teeth together. God, was she babbling about milk?

"Sure, milk is horrible," he said. "I would love to meet the person who saw that dripping out of a cow and thought, 'I bet that's delicious. My kids need to drink that'."

She barked out a relieved laugh, some of the heavy tension evaporating, and said, "Here's a good one. Do you know what type of coffee cows drink after they give birth?"

He frowned in confusion. "What?"

"Decaffeinated."

"Nice," he laughed.

Continuing to move with delicate caution, he finished with her right hand. He stood up and rooted through the medicine cabinet once more. "I think there's some aspirin in here, you should take a couple."

"That would be good. Or wait. I don't eat anymore. Does aspirin even still work?"

"Great question. One way to find out." He turned around with a bottle of pills and shook a few into her palm. "Emma, you were very brave."

"Oh. I didn't have much choice, what with the guns and

shooting and so on."

"Still," he said. "You saved all of us. Thank you." He gazed into her eyes until heat rushed to her face. It was nice to be looked at like that by someone she realized she wanted very badly to look at her like that. It had been a long time, and he really was quite pleasant to look at.

"You don't by chance like rap music, do you?" she asked.

"What?"

"Never mind." The moment was becoming fraught again, but for different reasons. She didn't have anywhere to put her eyes, so she popped the pills into her mouth. Dry. Of course, they didn't go down, and she choked and coughed.

"Careful," he said. "I'll get you some water."

She waved him off and tried to get some words out, but they stuck in her throat. Roman searched around the sink for a glass, but only found a container with cufflinks in it. He dumped the cufflinks on the floor and filled it under the tap.

She drank some water. Seconds later, she coughed it back up, spitting it all over him. He rubbed and patted her back and she leaned over until the coughing stopped, then took another drink of cufflink-flavored water.

"Yes." *Cough.* "I'm a real hero." *Cough. Cough.*

He laughed again and helped her to her feet, taking care not to grip her hands. "Let's get back to the group."

"Roman." She stopped him by resting a hand on his shoulder. "What happens now?"

"We'll go talk to Vain and the others and come up with a plan."

"No." She shook her head. "I mean, what is life now? How does this ever stop?"

Fatigue leaked onto his features. "I don't know how to answer that. We've always kept moving. We try to stay one step ahead of Trick and the Wyatts. Sometimes we get pizza."

He was trying to bring the easy mood back, but she wouldn't let him. Instead, she stepped closer to him and looked up into his weary brown eyes.

"I can't run forever," she said. "I have a life to get back to. I need a goal to all this; something concrete to work toward." She put urgency into her voice. "I need this to end."

"Let's talk to the others. I'm sure Vain will have some ideas."

"No, not Vain," she said. "Us. Plural. If Vain has a plan, she needs to tell us. She can't keep us in the dark like she did this last time."

He thought about it for a moment. "Her plan got us out of a tight spot."

"Yes, but none of us knew about it. She gave you a fake Padlock without telling you. She pulled me aside in confidence and didn't even let me know why. Did she know she was going to get Mark to kidnap a Wyatt? I wouldn't put it past her. None of us got to hear the full idea. We headed into that situation blind."

"But it worked," Roman said, as if confirming it to himself. "Vain came up with something when no one else did, like she always does. Maybe she doesn't always tell us everything, but she's doing it for us. You weren't there in the Hotel, Emma. She was the only one who took steps to get us out. I trust her."

"It isn't about us trusting Vain, it's about Vain trusting us." She crossed her arms under her chest. "Don't you see? That could have gone so badly in the forest. What if she had been wrong? What if I wasn't able to knock everyone out? Vain's plans are a crazy combination of confidence and dumb luck. I can't do that again. We have to come up with something else. Together."

"What do you want, Emma?" He took a step away from her. "Let's play your version out, one where Vain doesn't come up with a plan. In that version, Trick double-crosses us and then what?"

"In that version, we discuss what to do together, beforehand. Vain sets people on edge, Roman. You saw Hush. He was barely thinking straight, he was so angry at her. Charm, too. Without that, maybe we make better decisions. Maybe we don't just drive straight into an ambush."

"Oh, so it's Vain's fault?"

"No, Roman. God. I'm not saying that."

Roman frowned and his nostrils flared. She was pushing too hard. He was blind when it came to Vain. He opened his mouth to protest again, but she stopped him with a wave of her hand.

"What happened to Patience?"

"What?"

"Why does Charm blame Vain for Patience's death? I know

she does, but I don't know why."

"It's kind of complicated," he said. "Does it matter?"

"I need to know."

Roman looked exhausted and her heart melted for him. He was such a wonderful and gentle man. But she couldn't stop. He needed to hear this. He needed to see Vain for what she was.

"A Wyatt shot her," he waved his hand. "Charm thinks the only reason he did was because we had the Padlock. That wasn't part of the plan, Vain didn't tell us she was taking it."

"You don't say."

Roman frowned. "It's not like that. She did the right thing."

"How was stealing the magic immortality Padlock on your way out of a prison the right thing? How has that helped at all?"

"It saved her from dying when the Wyatts pushed her off the roof."

"The roof they pushed her off because she had the Padlock."

"Jesus Christ. Stop. You don't know what would have happened if she didn't take it. You honestly don't. For all we know, if she didn't take it they would have come at us harder, with everything they had. Maybe we wouldn't have lasted a year. Maybe we would have only lasted a day." He pointed at her. "You don't know. And neither do they."

She needed to back off. Roman was becoming too agitated, and she needed to get him back on her side.

"Look," she said. "I agree that Vain's idea saved us. I never would have thought about sucking the energy out of everyone. I didn't even realize it could be used offensively. It's not that Vain has bad ideas. She has great ideas, but I want her to include all of us. I don't want anyone else to be hurt." She allowed the despair that lingered on the periphery of her emotions into her voice. "Do you think that's unreasonable?"

"No," Roman said. He sounded suspicious; as if he were waiting for the other shoe to drop. "That doesn't sound unreasonable."

"All I'm asking is that when we go downstairs, we work this through with everyone as a group. Try to convince Vain to be more forthcoming, all right? You never know." She smiled at him. "Maybe we'll have ideas too."

He didn't smile back, but he nodded. "Yeah, fine. Whatever.

I'll talk to her."

"Great."

The bathroom door slammed open with a bang and Vain stood in its place. "What's taking you so long?" she said. "What are you doing?" She looked at Roman when she said it, but her eyes flicked to Emma.

"Patching Emma up." Roman gestured to her. "Her hands were a mess."

Some of the suspicion melted from Vain's face and she flicked her eyes to Emma again. "Are you okay?"

"I'm good, Vain, thank you." On an impulse, she placed a hand on Roman's shoulder and gave a big, lazy smile. "Roman is a wonderful nurse." She leaned in against him.

Vain's eyes widened and her nostrils flared. Oh, yes. Vain did not like anyone playing with her things. Emma would have to tread lightly.

"I'm glad you're better." Vain's voice was cool. Ice. "Roman, can we go? We have to interrogate the Wyatt we captured."

"What?" Roman's eyes grew wide. "Why did you even make Mark take him?"

"Answers. Come on." Vain didn't wait for a response; she turned and left.

Emma pointedly glanced to where Vain had been standing as if to say, *"you see?"* Roman shrugged and followed.

Plans within plans within plans. She followed Roman out the door.

Emma was done being Vain's pawn.

Chapter 25

Vain hates Wyatt, like, so much.

Vain stomped down the stairs to the main floor. Emma had certainly been quite cozy with Roman. Quite cozy. Quite, quite cozy. Cozy McDozy, that's what she should call Emma from now on. Queen of Cozytown, lording over her subjects with her cozy, Roman-stealing ways.

She tried to put the image of Emma leaning on Roman's shoulder out of her head. Roman's shoulder could be touched by anyone, at any time. She did not own his shoulder. It was a serviceable shoulder, she supposed, and although she didn't really consider his shoulders in *that way*, she understood why other women viewed them as touchable and lean-on-able. Was lean-on-able a word? It was now. The point was, Roman was free to have his shoulders leaned on by whoever he wanted, and it was great and cozy and she was for sure not bothered in the slightest. But he was her Roman, damn it, and she wasn't going to lose his attention to some waif-eyed, pale-faced, redheaded bookworm.

She made a mental note to remind Hush to turn down the fucking heat. Her face was on fire. It didn't even make sense to keep it that hot in there. Weird that she hadn't noticed before.

A few deep breaths through her nose helped her settle. Focus. Plenty of time to worry about all of that later. Right now, she had to talk to the Wyatt they kidnapped before Hush messed it up.

The doors leading into the den were open, robbing Vain of the opportunity to kick them, doing nothing for her mood. They had the unconscious Wyatt slumped into one of the thick leather chairs by the pool table. Mark leaned against a wall with one leg up and his arms crossed. Hush's tight control had snapped, and he wailed into his phone, putting on a show for everyone.

"You get me at least twenty men." He paced back and forth.

Vain was distracted by only getting one end of the conversation. He'd bark out sentences and pause to listen before barking out another.

"I don't care about money. They need to be armed and they need to take care of business. Don't you worry about what kind of business. No, not construction and not light housework." He made his voice ominous and deep. "Business. Capital-B business. I can't give you details. You send men and I'll take care of the heavy lifting." He nodded. "Exactly. A shitload of guys with guns. The more the better." His head tilted. "Why not? It's a legitimate offer. Oh, I'm the crazy one? The only crazy thing here is you and your stupid business."

Vain shook her head and let him continue to rant at the other end of the room. Roman and Emma walked in behind her. Blunt and Charm sat together on the couch, working on another crossword puzzle. Blunt's mouth was twisted in to deep, sad frown, and Charm rubbed his arm. Vain felt a moment of sympathy for him. Next to Roman, he was her favorite.

She walked over to the Wyatt. They'd stripped off his bulletproof vest, leaving him in his green and brown military attire.

"Mark, is this guy secure? Should we tie him up?"

Mark shrugged. "He's not going anywhere. If he tries, I'll stop him."

"Good. Blunt, get your idiot brother off the phone. I need both of you for the next part."

"Do you want to tell us what the next part is?" he asked, getting up from the sofa.

He sounded irritated. That stung a little. Soft, gentle Blunt; why would he be irritated? She was doing all of it for them. "I need you two to work your magic on this guy so we can get some answers. Let's move."

Blunt scowled—he was definitely irritated about something—and crossed the room to get Hush.

Emma sat beside Charm, and Roman sat across from them. Everyone studiously avoided looking at the Wyatt.

"How are you, sweetie?" Charm asked Emma.

Emma held up her bandaged hands. "Never better."

"Oh, your fingers. You poor thing." She gave Vain a withering glare. "Why didn't you tell anyone about this?"

Vain raised her eyebrows. Why the hell was everyone so mad at her all of a sudden? "I told you all that Trick was going to double-cross us. I made sure we had an out."

"But look what it did." Charm pointed to Emma's hands.

"How is that my fault? Since when did pulling energy pop someone's hands off? Maybe little Miss Cozy McDozy should have stronger fingernails, you ever think about that?"

"Cozy what?" said Emma.

"I would have told you," said Charm, "if you talked to me about what you were planning. I'd have been able to tell you the risks. I know more about this than anyone."

Vain chewed her lip. Charm had a point. "I didn't want you to panic and call everything off."

"Like when you stole the Padlock in the first place?"

Not that again. Vain pointed at Charm, fixing to lay into her, when Roman interjected.

"Can it, guys. It's over."

"Stop protecting her." Hush had finished his phone call and walked over to the group. "First Emma's hands, now a fake Padlock? You put us all at risk."

"Give me a break," Vain replied. "We were finished from the moment you idiots trusted Trick. *Trick,* for God sakes. What he's going to do is right in the name. Were you also surprised by the amount of punching in Fight Club? Or when Luke showed up in Return of the Jedi? It's not like Good Will Hunting, where there's no hunting at all."

Hush ignored her. "Did you know about this, Roman? Did she tell you she was giving them a fake?"

Roman glanced over in her direction and stuttered a response. "I knew some things. I knew there was more than one padlock."

"He didn't know anything, Hush. Leave him alone," Vain said. "Blame me if you're pissed off at someone."

"Yes. I am doing exactly that. I am blaming you completely." His face flushed with anger. "Are you unclear on what's happening?"

"Maybe if you weren't such a fantastic idiot, I wouldn't have to come up with plans all the time. Do you think I like this?"

"Yes," Charm said.

"We've been doing great since you left," Hush said. "Number of murderous attacks without Vain: zero. Number in the twenty-four hours since Vain's return: one. The math is on my side."

Vain drew a breath and rubbed her face. Herding those idiots was like trying to get a group of cats to dance the salsa. Even when she was successful, the result was only a group of stupid, dancing cats.

Emma broke the temporary silence. "Are we planning on leaving the unconscious kidnapper in that chair for long?"

Hush opened his mouth to continue arguing, but paused. His shoulders sagged, and he slumped in the chair beside Roman. "All right. What now, Vain? Since you have all the ideas. Why the hell did we kidnap a Wyatt?"

"You'll see," she replied. "First, Mark is going to wake this guy up."

"How am I going to do that?" Mark asked.

"First, Mark is not going to bug me with his problems, and *then* Mark is going to wake this guy up."

Mark grumbled under his breath and walked over to the bar.

Vain looked over at Hush. "When he's up, you and Blunt do your thing with his head so we can ask him some questions. Are you guys in decent enough shape to do that?"

"We should be okay. One guy doesn't take much effort."

"Good. Once you're in his head, we'll find out what to do next."

"You mean you don't know?" asked Charm. She was syrup-sweet, but was she being sarcastic? As it happened, Vain knew exactly what came next; only she didn't want to be the one to tell them. They needed to hear it from the Wyatt.

"I have some ideas." Vain tapped her temple. Did Emma roll her eyes? "Let's listen to him, first."

Mark returned from the bar with a bottle of vodka. Vain didn't recall asking for a drink. He screwed off the cap and poured the contents out on the Wyatt's head.

"What on earth are you doing?" Hush grabbed Mark by the arm and took the bottle away from him.

"I have no idea," said Mark. "My job is getting people to be more unconscious, not less. I figured most people don't like having gasoline-grade liquor poured on their heads."

"This is Stoli Elit Vodka, part of the Himalayan Edition. This is three thousand dollars a bottle." Hush shook his head in genuine bewilderment and cradled the vodka to his chest.

Mark leaned over and gave the Wyatt a couple of light slaps. The Wyatt groaned and rolled his head from side to side. He coughed and wiped the vodka from his face, confused. Vain imagined what was going through his head. His last memory would be of the clearing, shooting at an invisible force field, hiding behind umbrellas. Now, he was waking up surrounded by enemies. Vain couldn't guess what his reaction would be. Violence? Struggling?

He blinked once. "Ah, nuts."

"Ah, nuts, is right." She smiled without any warmth. "Blunt, Hush, now."

Hush focused on the Wyatt with the same intensity Marty showed when resisting his own mother's sexual advances. In retrospect, Back to the Future was a pretty messed up movie. In the seat beside him, Blunt slumped over as his brother pulled energy.

"You're completely relaxed," Hush said. "You really like us. You're enjoying yourself. You're going to do whatever we say. You will answer all of our questions honestly. Do you understand?"

The Wyatt's demeanor completely changed. His posture relaxed, and he leaned back in the chair. He smiled and nodded, but the smile was a droopy, lopsided thing that didn't reach his eyes. His eyes remained hot and angry, but the rest of his face put on the caricature of a happy grin. It was perhaps the single most unsettling thing Vain had ever seen.

"I understand. Why am I wet?"

"I poured vodka all over you to wake you up," said Mark.

The Wyatt laughed. "Ha! You guys. Can I get a towel or something?"

"Soon," Hush said. "First, we want to ask you some questions, okay?"

"You got it. Are you Blunt or Hush?"

"I'm Hush. He's Blunt." He hooked a thumb at his brother.

"Are you doing that thing to me where you're putting the part of my brain to sleep that would be resisting this right now?"

"Yes."

"Yeah, Trick told us about this. Man, does it work well. I mean, I know intellectually what you're doing, but holy smokes, do I like you guys. You're all great. It's crazy." He shook his head and ground his teeth together. Why would he grind his teeth? Was a subconscious part of him resisting?

This whole thing grossed Vain out. To have your thoughts, your agency taken from you. It was wicked. Even though they needed to do that, part of her recoiled. She'd never seen anyone acknowledge what Hush did. "He's aware of what you're doing," she said to Hush. "Is this normal?"

"Not really. Usually, people haven't been briefed by Trick ahead of time, so we're on new ground here."

"Hey gang, just so you know," the Wyatt said. "I bit into a cyanide pill. I've got maybe five minutes before I die. That's a heads up if you want to speed things along, but whatever. Totally your call." He winked.

"Jesus fucking Christ," said Hush, which Vain felt was completely appropriate. "Why did you do that?"

"I'm not going to let myself get captured by the enemy. And you didn't tell me not to, and even though I really like you, I still have some small amount of personal control left. This is so trippy. You guys are the best though, sorry if my killing myself leaves you in a pickle." He seemed unhappy at that thought, and his smile faded. "But if we go quickly, we should be able to get through your questions."

"Throw up," said Vain. "Right now."

"Hmm." The Wyatt considered it. "Weird. I feel sick, but not enough to vomit. Maybe Hush has to say it? But honestly, it doesn't matter. Trick said these things work in seconds."

"Wait," Vain said. "Trick gave it to you?"

"He did."

She waved her hand. "We're cool, then."

"I don't have the resources to dispose of a Wyatt corpse." Hush rubbed his cheeks. "I mean, I own a restaurant, but—"

"Hush, gross." Charm recoiled in horror.

"Oh, stop it, everyone," Vain said. "He won't die. It wasn't a cyanide pill."

"How can you know that?" Charm asked.

It took a real force of will to keep herself from yelling at them. "His name is fucking Trick," Vain said through clenched teeth. "I cannot think of any single way to make this clearer to you. How many times do I have to explain this? Emma, does your fancy school teach de-dumbing?"

"But his own people?" Charm put her hand on her chest. Christ, did she need a fainting couch?

"Okay. Tell you what. Let's wait. Blunt, google how long it takes for a cyanide pill to work." She snapped.

Blunt looked at his phone. "Says he should be unconscious in thirty seconds and dead in another five."

"Super. Time it."

She eyed each of them as the Wyatt sat in the chair, clearly not dying. He watched their exchange with a bemused smile. "I think she's on to something gang. I don't feel anything at all."

"He's not going to die?" Blunt asked.

"No," Vain said.

"Hm. Trick sure is an asshole," Wyatt said. "That's frustrating. I wonder what he made me eat?"

"You can ask him later. Let's get down to business. What were you going to do to us if we surrendered?"

"You're Vain." He started pointing around the room. "And you're Roman, you're Charm, and you're the x-factor that Trick is terrified of."

Confusion and fear in equal parts flashed across Emma's face.

The Wyatt continued. "First, we were going to kill Charm. She's useless without a Utility."

"What?" Charm's face paled, and she covered her mouth.

The Wyatt nodded as if talking about the weather. "Yep, you were done for. The twins we'd haul back to the Hotel. We planned to take Vain and Roman back to a warehouse we rented until Vain told us where the Padlock was. Trick had already figured there was no chance you'd give up the real one."

"I never would have told you," said Vain. "No matter what you did to me."

"Sure you would. We weren't going to do anything to you, we were going to do it all to him." He pointed to Roman. "The plan was to throw him off the top of a boxcar. It's about a twelve-foot drop."

Roman eyed the Wyatt and shrugged. "I'm pretty sure I could handle that."

"Sure. The first time. Even the hundredth time. But eventually, after hours and hours? You'd land funny. You'd go over on an ankle or something. Each landing would get harder. You'd have to favor a good leg. But, again—time's a bitch—you'd land wrong on the other one, too. You'd have to take the fall on your side, or your back, or your arms. They'd all go, too."

Vain's blood froze as if she'd swallowed ice cubes. Roman's mouth hung open in surprise. Emma rubbed his knee. Of all the courses she'd plotted, she never thought they'd use Roman to get to her—again. Shock and horror projected from the faces of everyone in the room. No one made a sound as the Wyatt continued speaking in that awful, just-good-buddies monotone.

"We've done this before. By the end, it's awful. After about fifteen hours, we're throwing you off a twelve-foot drop onto broken limbs until you're nothing but a wet, bloody sack of snapped bones and liquid organs. You'd be begging us to kill you. And you," he looked at Vain, "would absolutely tell us where the Padlock is."

Vain couldn't help herself. She lunged forward and punched him in the face as hard as she could. The Wyatt's head snapped back, and he rubbed his jaw. The dull, droopy smile never left his lips, but his eyes glinted with the promise of murder.

"I need to teach you how to throw a punch," said Mark. "That was horrible."

"Oh, it was complete trash." The Wyatt leaned over and spat blood onto the carpet. "She didn't put her hips into it, it was all upper arm."

"Right? She didn't set a great pivot point either, just flailed from the shoulders." Mark shook his head.

"Don't even get me started on the follow-through."

"Oh my God, can you two shut up?" Hush slapped his palm against his thigh and the Wyatt's teeth clamped together with an audible click. "Let's stay on track. What else were you planning?"

"Sorry. Once we got the Padlock, we were going to kill Vain and Roman. Trick talked about bringing them back in, but after the last week, he's decided neither of them are worth it. Too much trouble, even though Arthur hates to lose property. Hey, you know what's weird? Even though I know you're walking time bombs, I still like you a lot. Wild."

Emma said, "What was Trick going to do to me?"

"He's terrified of you," replied Wyatt. "Normally, he's a relaxed guy, but he wants you under supervision as fast as possible. The plan was to bring you back to Nevada."

"Why Nevada?" Vain didn't take her eyes off him.

"That's where we moved the Portal to after you guys left."

Vain's heart raced, and she wiped her hands on her jeans. Nevada. He'd given the location of the Hotel. She'd fought and scrambled and struggled in the year since leaving, always trying to figure out what she could do to stop them, but the sticking point had always been the Portal. The main conduit from this Earth to the Hotel. The place where all the Wyatts came through. Now that she had the location, the second part of her plan seemed in reaching distance.

Emma recoiled and clutched her chest. "Were you going to erase my mind?"

"Technically, erasing your mind takes everything away. It turns you into a moron. It was going to be more of a memory-wipe, if that helps."

"It doesn't help," replied Emma.

"I don't mean moron pejoratively. Erasing your mind drops your IQ to below sixty-five."

"Understood, Wyatt. I would be an idiot if you erased my mind. Thank you for the clarification."

"Again, technically you'd be a moron. Anyway, back to the Hotel, they bought the land around the Portal for miles and put up a bunch of fences and guard posts. From the outside, it looks like abandoned farm property, but once you get close, there's a whole way station there."

"Where in Nevada?" Vain got right up in his face.

"If you give me a pen, I can write the address."

Vain snatched one off the bar and pressed it into his hand with a notepad. "Here."

He took them both and scribbled an address on the page. Vain wanted to grab it but stopped herself.

"Does anyone have anything else for him?" she asked.

Everyone shook their heads. Emma had fallen back onto the couch with her head between her hands. Charm rubbed her back.

"How about you, Wyatt? Is there anything else you think we should know?"

"Only that Trick has people around the building. We've been watching you for about a day. The plan was simple. If we didn't take you in the forest, we'd take you tonight. We were going to kill you in your sleep and dispose of the bodies." He said it like she might say, "I was going to hit the gym and have a shower."

"There's no way out, either," he continued. "We have guys planted in the restaurant. Obviously, we're not using me for this, you'd recognize us. If you try to leave, we'll follow you and grab you. We have every inch staked out; every exit under surveillance." He gave gun fingers to the group. A buddy helping some friends.

"This never stops," said Emma. "They never quit."

"We were doing great before you showed up. We had a good thing here," said Hush.

"Oh, that," Wyatt said. "We've known where you were since the day you left. The only reason we haven't come after you is we thought she might come back with the Padlock."

"Wyatt," Charm licked her lips, strangely formal. The room quieted. "Would you have left us alone if Vain never took the Padlock?"

"No," The Wyatt said. "You belong to us. You're property."

Charm paled and kept her eyes from Vain. It was all Vain could do not to tell them all to get fucked. She'd been right the whole time. Instead, she said, "None of that is important. We have to figure out how to get out of here. Hush, can you make him forget about this?"

"Yeah," he replied. "Wyatt, I want you to get up, leave the room, and walk out of the restaurant. When you get outside, you'll forget everything we talked about here. Got that?"

"Got it." Wyatt stood. He gave them a big smile and a thumbs up. "Good luck, everyone. I hope you make it out of here alive, even though you almost certainly won't."

The Wyatt walked to the door, showing as much emotion as a mailman dropping off a parcel. As he passed the group, they flinched away like he carried an infectious disease. Vain didn't care if the Wyatt lived or died. She had what she wanted. Her mind flipped through scenarios, picking up some and discarding others. Once the Wyatt got outside, Trick would know he was compromised. They didn't have much time.

Mark paced the perimeter of the room, looking out each of the windows. He closed the blinds.

"They're going to attack us?" said Blunt with a small groan. "Hush, you said we were safe here."

"It's okay," said Hush. "There's a way out of this. We need to work the problem, see if we can find some give. Maybe if we call Trick, try to negotiate again."

"You absolute moron," said Vain. "Did you hear the same thing I did? Trick is going to kill us."

"Not if we have something to bargain with," said Hush.

A thick silence settled over the group, the weight of his threat stopping all conversation. Hush looked down his nose at her, his jaw set in determination. A heaviness settled on her head like the air had calcified.

"Vain," Hush emphasized her name, and a weight pushed against her mind. Syrup wasn't in it. It was like trying to swim through a swimming pool full of gelatin. The room faded into the background and there was only Hush.

"You really like us."

Roman lunged across the room and threw a sloppy haymaker that connected in the middle of Hush's face, followed by a sharp crack, like a whip striking skin. Hush stumbled back into his chair. Vain shook her head as the room came back into focus.

"You miserable piece of shit." Roman jumped on top of him and threw clumsy, awkward punches at his head. Mark ran over and grabbed Roman by the arms and hauled him off. Roman struggled against his grip, but the bigger man held him with ease.

"Settle down, Rocky," Mark said. "Those punches are almost as bad as Vain's."

"Everyone needs to relax." Charm stood, shaking her finger at the room. "Hush, you deserved that. Shame on you for doing that. We're not going to betray our friends. How dare you?"

"We need to think this through, Charm." Hush rubbed his cheek. "Blunt and I didn't create all this to have it taken away. Especially not by *her*." He pointed at Vain.

Rage hit her, and Vain exploded. "By me? *By me?* You wouldn't even have any of this if it wasn't for me!" She screamed. She shouldn't scream. She couldn't stop. "Who came up with the plan to get us out of the Hotel? Me. Who kept us together when we pulled it off? Me. Who, only literal hours ago, saved your ass from Trick? Again! Me. Me. Me, me fucking me." Her voice was a high-pitched screech, and heat covered her face like sunburn. Her hands were shaking. Everything she did, she did for these people, and to have it thrown back at her so carelessly; screaming for days wouldn't be enough.

"Spare me the pity act, Vain," Hush said. "I won't let you kill my brother like you killed Patience."

Vain recoiled as if slapped, and the strength left her legs. She fell back on to the chair with a heavy thud. With a shaking hand, she brushed her hair back.

"I didn't kill Patience," she whispered. "Stop saying that. I only wanted the Padlock."

"You ungrateful piece of shit." Roman lunged at Hush again, but Mark held him back in an iron grip. Roman wrenched himself free and came to stand beside Vain. "We're through. We're leaving right now."

"How are you going to do that, Einstein?" Hush said. "Did you forget that Trick has the place surrounded?"

Vain let their argument wash over her. Charm gaped at her with sad eyes, and Vain waited for her to say something. If Charm defended her, it would be okay. But she didn't say anything. She only wiped a few errant tears off her cheek. Eventually, she shook her head and looked at the ground. Nothing. Vain's heart snapped and she wondered why no one heard it. Did everyone believe that of her? Did they all think that?

It always ended the same way. She and Roman versus everyone. Every single time. Why did she even bother? She set her jaw and let anger replace unhappiness.

"Screw all of you," she said. As she opened her mouth to expand on that central theme, really explore the thesis statement, a wave of lethargy washed over her and she was abruptly exhausted. Roman seemed similarly affected and dropped to the couch. The twins looked around, confusion on their faces. Blunt yawned.

"What's happening?" Vain said.

"I'm getting better at pulling from targeted people," Emma said from the corner of the room. "Everyone seemed like they needed a timeout. Hopefully, it settles you all down. I don't care about any of your history or who did what to who. You're wasting time. We have to get out of here. Somehow."

Charm frowned. "Where would we go? They'll never stop coming after us. You heard the Wyatt. They view us as property. Do we run until we die?"

They all started talking at once, throwing out dumb ideas. They would start over, go to Canada. Mexico had long coastlines where they'd never be found. The Eiffel Tower would make for a great backdrop when eating breakfast. Blah, blah, blah. It was difficult to make herself care. She only needed Emma for her plan. The rest of them could hang.

"Vain." Roman's voice cut through the argument. "Tell us what you're thinking."

Vain folded her arms. "No. What's the point? You all seem to have all the answers. Vain is the worst. Everything Vain does is terrible. Vain killed P...people. I'm through with all of you. Since Hush seems to have all the answers, let's let him tell us what to do next. Over to you, Hush. Tell us what you have planned."

Hush opened and closed his mouth a few times as the weight of the room settled on him. Several moments passed. He seemed to count numbers on his fingers.

"First," he said. "We need a leaf blower."

"Stop it," Emma interrupted. "This is all theatre. None of us are going to follow Hush. No offense."

"Well, what then?"

"We need to apologize to Vain," Charm said. "All of us."

The room quieted and Vain's heart became wedged firmly in her throat. Charm stood up and knelt in front of the chair, her lips set in firm determination. Vain's tried to swallow past the lump, but couldn't work moisture into her mouth. Charm took her hand. Vain tried to pull away, but the older woman squeezed tighter.

"Thank you for getting us out of the Hotel," Charm said softly, "and thank you for saving us from Trick. I heard the Wyatt, they would have killed us no matter what. We've treated you poorly. I've treated you poorly. I was wrong and I understand why you're angry with us. But we're stuck and we need your help."

Vain didn't say anything. She couldn't. She had no defense against this attack. Charm rubbed her hand. The silence stretched.

"Thanks for helping me with my crossword." Blunt gave her a thumbs up.

From her spot in the corner, Emma said, "Thank you for saving me from the Wyatts."

"Thanks for lending me your copy of Back to the Future," Mark said.

Everyone turned to look at Hush, who grimaced. The moments stretched. Finally, he mumbled something that sounded like "Thanksforwhatever."

Vain swallowed several times and blinked rapidly. She pulled her hand away from Charm and wiped it on her jeans. Roman was smiling at her.

"Oh, that. It's nothing," she said. Her voice sounded weird and emotional. "I don't get why you all make such a big deal about everything."

"We won't do that anymore, will we?" Roman said to the room. He received nods in return. "You have something planned, Vain. Tell us what it is. Please."

"All of it," Emma said with particular emphasis.

"Okay. As it happens, I do have an idea." Vain took care with her words. She didn't want to choose the wrong ones. Now was not a good time to complicate matters. "We need to go to Nevada. Once we're closer, I'll tell you more about what I have in mind."

"No." Roman crossed his arms. "Tell us everything. Now."

What did that mean? When did she ever *not* tell them everything? She'd always been completely transparent and forthcoming with her plans. The stuff with the Padlock and Trick didn't count. That stuff was minor. She told them everything important, so what was the issue? Roman had a very Roman look on his face, that stubborn look that said he wasn't backing down.

"Why would we go to Nevada?" asked Hush. "That's the last place we want to go."

"Vain knows how to stop this," Emma said from across the room. "And Nevada is at the center."

"What, are we going to storm their base or something?" Blunt asked.

If Vain told them everything she planned, they'd never do it. That was the problem with telling people great ideas, they always wanted to criticize. Her plan would work. She was eighty percent positive it was doable. Well, more like sixty percent. Okay, if she was honest with herself, it had a one in five chance of working. And that was assuming everything went perfectly. But the way she figured it, they didn't have much to lose.

Roman positioned himself right in front of her. "Vain, we can't do this on faith. You have to tell us what's in your head, or we can't help you."

He was looking at her with his stupid, trusting Roman face. It was hard to say no. She loved him so much. "Can't you trust me? One last time?" Her voice was small.

He glanced at Emma and sighed. "Not on this one, Vain."

She bit at her lower lip. They wanted details of the plan? They wanted to know how to finish this once and for all? Fine. She'd give them just that. She unclenched her teeth to release her lower lip, then did something she thought she'd never, ever do.

She told them everything.

The plan had been building ever since she figured out what the Padlock did, and came together when she realized how much power Emma had. Nevada had been the last piece of the puzzle. She told them how everything fit together and didn't hold anything back. Every card she was holding was face-up on the table for all of them to see.

Emma, always pale, went practically translucent. The twins both looked at her, mouths agape. Charm sat back down on the couch and buried her face in her hands.

"You are the craziest person I've ever met." Mark was the first to break the silence. "You're a hurricane."

"Yeah, she is," Roman said. He smiled at her and everything was okay. "She's our hurricane."

"There are so many ifs in that plan," Charm said. "So many maybes."

Vain thought about it for a moment. Lying about it was pointless, so she stuck to the truth instead. "We don't. We have to hope that it plays out the way I think it will. We need to go all in."

"I'm in." Heads turned to look at Emma. She crossed her arms and jutted out her chin. "I'm not running anymore. I want this to be over with." The look she gave Vain was all eager confidence. "I'm with you, Vain."

"Charm, is this workable?" asked Roman.

"Maybe. I'll have to ponder this a little. Vain and Emma and I will have to pour over the details. It's theoretically doable."

"We can help you get into the complex," said Hush. "It's our escape from the Hotel, but in reverse."

"I can work through that plan with you and cover how we can get close to the building," said Mark. "I've got some experience with that."

Hush walked over to the big man and regarded him seriously. "This isn't your fight, Mark. You can walk away."

Mark shrugged. "I don't think I can. Besides, I owe one to Trick for that business in the forest. I can't believe I walked into that."

They all started talking together, picking up the fragments of ideas and forming them into a cohesive, workable plan. They were adding to her idea and refining it, making it something bigger and more powerful. Huh. Maybe there was something to the whole sharing business. Regardless, that was it. They were going to finish the Hotel once and for all.

"I'm glad you told us your idea," Roman said. "But we still need to figure out how to get out of here."

"I'll take care of that," Emma said.

Chapter 26

Roman hates heights, like, so much.

Roman couldn't imagine what Emma had planned. Blow up the restaurant? Blow up the road? For sure, blow something up. God, he'd been spending too much time with Vain.

Emma looked out the window to the street below. "Mark, the van is in the parking garage across the street, right?"

"Yeah." Mark nodded and shrugged. "I'm not sure how we can get to it though, not if Trick has people waiting in the restaurant. I don't think fighting our way out is a great option."

"We're not leaving by the restaurant. We're going out through the window. I'll create a ramp across the gap between the buildings."

"Can you do that?" asked Vain. "That's got to be five-hundred feet."

"I think I can. I've only done small ones, but I'm sure this will work."

"Vain has already corrupted you," Hush said. "That's insane. Why are all of you so crazy? Now, if you'll listen to me and somehow get me a leaf blower and bleach, we'll be golden."

"Zip it, Hush," Charm said, but smiled to take the heat out of her words. She clapped her hands, once. "Let's get going, people. We're climbing out the window."

Roman groaned to himself. Emma could give Vain a run for her money in the crazy department. She had the same steel in her that propelled Vain, only hidden away, buried closer to the bottom. With Vain, all the veneer had been rubbed away.

There wasn't much time, and regardless, the second story of a building surrounded by armed thugs wasn't a great place for detailed planning. Seconds galloped by. The group worked with a sense of urgency, on the edge of panic, but keeping it together. A few hours remained until the restaurant closed, and they knew Trick wouldn't rush them with a building full of customers. They scrambled in and out of the room, gathering their belongings and stuffing clothes into backpacks and duffel bags. Hush fretted about his employees and how to keep them safe. He decided to call in a bomb threat before they left, reasoning that would get the cops here and clear everyone out. After about an hour, they were ready.

"Let's do this," said Emma. "It's getting dark outside, so they won't be able to spot us."

"Not easily, but they will see us," said Mark. "We need to cross and get to the car as fast as possible. A group of people floating between buildings on an invisible ramp will draw attention."

Emma gathered energy, and it tugged at Roman. When Vain pulled from him, it was like ripping a piece of duct tape off your arm, quick and sharp. Emma's pull had warmth, like an invitation. It was all air and light.

Hush stood in front of the window, staring at the parking garage. "How far does that look?"

"A football field, at least," said Charm. "Maybe two. This will need to be a thick platform."

"It's not about the thickness, it's about how hard I can make it," Emma said.

"That set-up is nuts." Vain looked around the room, but no one paid any attention to her. "Come on. Is nobody going to take that?"

Roman hid a smile beneath his hand. Vain would never change.

The room had floor-to-ceiling windows, providing a panoramic view of the area outside the building. They had thrown back the curtains, giving them a better line of sight to their target.

"Hush, how does this window open?" asked Emma.

"I'm not sure it does," said Hush. "They're built for style, not access."

"We can take the panes out." Mark produced a knife from somewhere under his jacket and pried away at the frame and grating.

Roman looked to the street below, making out people's shapes from the dim light provided by the streetlamps. It was about a sixty-foot drop. Not a guaranteed death, but at least a broken leg, or worse. For about the tenth time, he tried to come up with a better idea. Why had so much of the past week involved heights?

"When the window is off, I'll make the ramp," said Emma. "I'll come across last to make sure it holds."

"Got it." Mark popped the bottom pane out, leaving a four-foot-tall exit.

He maneuvered the window inside and leaned it up against the bar. The wind howled in, and noise from the traffic below leaked into the room. It was farther up than Roman thought.

Emma made her hands into fists, appearing grim and determined. "Everyone, out of the way."

The air crackled with static, making the hairs on the back of Roman's neck stand up. He smelled burning ozone. The floor beneath the window groaned and buckled as the weight of an invisible energy ramp settled onto it.

"It's in place," Emma said through gritted teeth. "This is harder than I anticipated. It's… wobbly. I might not be able to hold this for long."

"Oh, man," Roman said. "Maybe we should think of another way."

As he spoke, Vain scrambled out the window and stood on thin air a few feet beyond the ledge. She looked straight down at the road below. After a few experimental stomps, she took a cautious step forward.

"Seems sturdy." She hopped up and down and Roman had to steady himself against the wall for the rush of dizziness that came over him. "This is so cool," she continued. Her hesitant steps turned into a full-blown run, and in seconds, she had scampered across while everyone watched, their chins hanging to the floor. A solitary woman, running across nothing.

Emma grunted and gritted her teeth. "Hurry. Not one at a time. You all need to go now. All at the same time. Like right now."

The floor below the window cracked and buckled further under the weight. A small chunk of concrete popped off and dropped, soundlessly, to the street below. Hush finished his call to the police.

Mark pushed the twins and Charm through with Blunt mewling the whole way, grasping his brother's shoulder. Charm's mouth was a tight line. Mark followed, not even hesitating when he stepped out into the open air.

"Go. Now, Roman." Sweat glistened on Emma's face and strands of hair stuck to her forehead.

"Can you go first?" he asked. "I don't want to leave you behind."

"No," she replied. "Go."

He nodded and stepped through the window, putting his foot down on nothing. Solid nothing. It was sturdy, like walking on firm ground, but his mind screamed about how wrong that was. He couldn't make his body leave the safety of the apartment. He stood there, one leg inside, one foot on solid air. The ground lurched below him. Tiny red dots of headlights from far below barely provided enough light to penetrate the darkness this far up. Blurry shapes rushed past underneath the streetlights.

Emma put her hand on his shoulder. "Roman, move."

The wind coming from his left was so strong it was almost a push. Clammy perspiration gathered on the back of his neck. The noise from the traffic below seemed both distant and immediate. Vain and the others were tiny specks, barely visible in the comfortable safety of the parking garage.

He couldn't move; not even to step back inside. His entire body locked.

A small groan slipped from his mouth.

"Roman, shut your eyes, okay?" Emma's voice was a warm breath in his ear. "Take my hand and shut your eyes. I'm going to talk the whole time and you can follow me. We'll walk slowly, okay? I'll go first."

Roman nodded and shut his eyes. Emma gathered his hand and wrapped it in hers. She moved around him to take the lead and her body pressed against his as she squeezed by. He noticed the smell of her, a pleasant hint of cinnamon.

He forced the random thoughts out of his head. Concentrate. The bandages around her fingers were soft, and he tried not to squeeze.

"Roman, please don't grip me so hard, okay?" She sounded out of breath.

He hated himself for not being able to do it. He ground his teeth together, his jaw clenching with the effort. "Talk," he said. "Please, talk. I like your voice. Say anything."

"I'll be here through the whole thing. Focus on me." Her words caught on the wind and she pulled him a step forward. One step. Another pull, and he took another step. He was outside the apartment, standing on nothing. Now, the groan turned into a high-pitched whine and he clamped his free hand over his mouth. Tears dripped from the corner of his eyes.

He forced himself to speak. "What are you going to do when this is all over?"

"It seems that once you're activated you can't go back, so I guess I need to become a superhero. It feels like the logical next step. I'll be a mild-mannered bookworm by day and a crime-fighting hero by night."

Step. Step. Step. They had been walking for seconds or minutes or hours. Her voice was strained, but her grip on his hand remained steady. He concentrated on her. Only her.

"Obviously, the most important part of becoming a superhero is the name. I've noticed that most of them are gender specific, like Wonder *Woman* or Super *Man*. If I went that route, I suppose my name should be Energy Gal or She-Force. But why give away my power and gender right in the name? No, I'd fool criminals by calling myself Fighting Monster. They'd be baffled. They'd reasonably think, 'this hero is a monster who fights, which is horrifying,' and they'd base their plans on that. Then I would show up—a woman—and throw them into disarray."

A gust of wind pushed him forward, and he whimpered. He stumbled a little, but Emma's hand balanced him and she continued guiding him towards safety.

"Of course, I'd need a pre-teen sidekick, so I'd steal an orphan, or adopt a child, which is essentially state-sanctioned orphan-stealing. He'd need to be fast because that would complement my energy powers. The criminals would expect someone with a name like Fast Boy or Lightning Orphan, so I'd befuddle them again by calling him Grandfather Punch."

He laughed out loud at that, a quick bark sucked up by the air. "Fighting Monster and Grandfather Punch?"

"We'd be an unstoppable duo, and our main power would be confusing enemies with our poorly chosen superhero names. 'Look!' they'd yell. 'Here comes Fighting Monster.' Another criminal would say, 'but he is a woman,' before arguing about gender pronouns and perhaps learning about the inherent respect contained in 'they'. Grandfather Punch would appear, and they'd say, 'how strange. I expected an elderly man, a tangible reminder of my mortality. Someone with the desiccated visage of an octogenarian, and perhaps punching. Instead, here is a fast child, flush and heady with youth. This disconnect makes it difficult to do the crime we wanted.' While they tried to sort that out, I would swoop in and energy blast them. Done."

It was funny enough to keep him distracted, but his foot clipped something solid and he stumbled forward, dropping Emma's hand. A full scream escaped, and he made no effort to hold it back. Hands were there to stop his fall, and he opened his eyes. He was across. The garage was empty, with a few scattered cars parked throughout. Emma let out an explosive breath and dropped to her knees.

He looked back the way they had come. Jesus Christ.

"Are you okay?" asked Vain. She turned to frown at Emma. "What did you do to him?"

"He needed help." Emma waved her hand. Her head drooped. "It was difficult to maintain that much solid energy for that long."

"I'm fine, Vain." His face flushed a hot red. Everyone was looking at him. "I don't like heights. Or invisible energy pathways, apparently."

"Let's move," said Mark. "The van is this way." He pointed and the group followed, putting some hurry in their steps.

Tires squealed and an engine revved somewhere below. A red SUV peeled around the ramp, followed by another similar car. Both headed straight for the group. They'd been spotted.

"Shit," said Mark, summing up the situation.

They had no time to react. In moments, the first SUV screeched past them and slid to a stop, cutting off their exit. The second did the same behind them. Four Wyatts jumped out of the lead vehicle, all but one brandishing guns. The unarmed one held an open umbrella. One raised his gun at the group and Roman leaped onto Vain, pushing her to the ground.

"Get down!" he yelled. Vain struggled underneath him. Emma had pushed herself up against the side of the concrete barrier, and he was relieved she was safe. The twins and Blunt stood frozen in place.

"I'm taking the ones in front," said Mark. "I can't do all of them. Vain or Emma, you need to solve that problem." He gestured to the other car behind him.

Mark walked to the Wyatts in the first SUV who screamed at him to stop moving and get on his knees. He put his hands up in a gesture of surrender, but then lunged at the umbrella-wielding Wyatt. Something happened that involved fists and punches and quick moves, and the Wyatt was on the ground. Another cradled his broken wrist, gun at his feet. The remaining two closed in on Mark and one grabbed him from behind.

"Get off me," said Vain.

Roman rolled over, and she sprang to her feet.

Behind them, another four Wyatts approached, holding the same formation—the umbrella holder out in front, the ones with guns behind. One took a shot, and the noise was unbelievably loud in the enclosed space. Sharp, acrid gunpowder smoke filled the garage. No rubber bullets this time. The twins and Charm dropped to the ground, all awkward limbs and blurry shapes, and he couldn't tell if they were hit or ducking for safety. Over the din of everyone screaming, the Wyatts were even louder, ordering them to stand still.

"I'm pulling," said Vain.

Cold lethargy enveloped him as Vain sucked the energy from his body. "Vain, the umbrella," he said. "You can't get through it."

"Emma. Do you have anything left?"

Emma shook her head.

Another gunshot rang through the garage. Vain charged at the Wyatts with her head down. When she hit the man with the umbrella, he pushed against her solid wall of invisible energy. For a moment, nothing happened, but Vain yelled and pushed and he moved back a step. She dropped to one knee, her arms still crossed in front of her. Her invisible energy wall kept them back, but she couldn't take them out.

The pull of energy was immense, and Roman was exhausted, but he forced himself to his feet and around the edge of Vain's barrier. All the focus was on her. The Wyatts yelled, pounding at the solid air in front of them. With his remaining strength, he charged at the one with the umbrella from the side, hitting him with a flying tackle. They both tumbled to the ground, throwing wild punches. The umbrella flew to the edge of the garage.

With it removed, Vain sucked out his remaining energy and it was like having the blanket yanked off him on a cold winter morning. His arms became too heavy to hold up and dropped to his sides. The Wyatt used the opportunity to punch him in the face a bunch of times. An excessive amount, Roman thought, as the pounding continued. Blood filled his mouth and spots bounced in front of his eyes.

He heard a series of grunts and the three Wyatts fell to the ground. The one hitting him was thrown back against the concrete wall, slamming into it with a bone-snapping thud before collapsing.

Vain stormed forward, hands clenched into fists, almost crackling with energy. "Motherfucker." She stood over one of the Wyatts, accentuating her words with kicks to his head. "This is for…" Kick. "Being a stupid…" Kick. "Stupid…" Kick. "Asshole."

"Vain, enough." Roman crawled towards her. "Stop."

Vain turned, her eyes wide with rage. "They're Wyatts," she said through clenched teeth. "They're not people. They're things." She provided a last kick, as if to prove her point.

He didn't have the strength to argue further, and it seemed she was all kicked out. His ears rang from the gunshots and he realized the parking garage was quiet. The whole incident had taken less than two minutes.

Mark approached from behind, cursing under his breath. He somehow single-handedly disarmed the other four Wyatts. Aside from his right eye, which was already starting to swell, he showed no outward signs of having been in a fight with four men at once. Against the wall, Blunt, Hush and Charm were getting to their feet, a little unsteady.

"We have to move now," Mark said. "People probably heard the gunshots and called the police. Is everyone okay? Vain? Emma? I'm glad the two of you handled it over there."

"Vain did," said Emma. "I didn't have anything left."

"You took them out by yourself?" Mark smiled at Vain. "All four guys?"

"Well, Roman took out the guy with the umbrella," Vain said. "Those stupid umbrellas are a pain in the ass. Rhianna is full of shit."

"I know this is a terrible time, but if we make it out of this, would you like to get coffee or something?" Mark looked down at her, wringing his hands like a young boy in shorts asking for more allowance. He tucked a wayward strand of hair behind his ear. "I mean, casual, or whatever."

Vain did that thing where she stared without blinking for longer than was necessary or comfortable, but she was chewing her lower lip, too. Well damn. Roman couldn't believe it. She was going to say yes.

"Sure," she finally said. "Coffee sounds nice. That would be great."

"Alright, then," replied Mark. He looked around as if not sure what to do next.

"That was an exceptional moment," Hush said. "I'm glad we could bring the two of you together, it's precisely why I hired a bodyguard at enormous personal expense—on the off chance that Vain returned and needed a date. You've satisfied the conditions of your employment, Mark, so I guess there's nothing left for you to do here." He snapped his fingers. "Oh wait, I thought of one last thing. Can you please get us the hell out of here?"

Mark straightened his collar, blushing to his roots. Roman helped Emma to her feet.

"You alright?" he asked.

"Exhausted."

"Thanks for helping me out, Fighting Monster," he said.

She smiled weakly at him and put her hands up in a boxer's pose. "I'll take them all on."

"What are you two doing?" said Vain. "We have to go." She turned and walked away without waiting to see if they would follow.

Chapter 27

Vain and the group do some planning.

They piled into the van and peeled out of the parking lot. Outside the building, a crowd had gathered, drawn by the gunshots. Vain squinted, looking through the windows into the restaurant. Everyone looked normal. How many of them were Trick's hired goons? How long before they realized the Wyatt attack had failed? Minutes, maybe.

Mark drove recklessly, winding the minivan through the streets of downtown Minneapolis. Beside him, Blunt tapped on his phone, calling out confusing and contradictory directions.

"We have to get to highway thirty-five. Take the next left." Mark put on his indicator and Blunt protested. "No, my left. The other left."

"We're facing the same way, Blunt," said Mark through gritted teeth. "We have the same left."

"Yeah, but I'm looking at the map on my phone, so left is up. You need to turn up, not left."

"I don't know how to turn up. What does that even mean?"

"At the next lights, go up-left but straight!"

"Jesus Christ." From the backseat, Hush yanked the phone from his brother's hand and corrected the directions.

Shortly after, they were on the highway heading for Nevada. They all kept checking out the window, looking for signs of pursuit. Any car that pulled up behind them caused a mild panic, and only Mark kept them calm. After an hour free from any indications of Trick or the Wyatts, they managed to relax.

It was a long drive, and they went in shifts, with Mark, Emma, and Roman doing most of the driving. For whatever reason, Vain was positive that she didn't know how to drive a car, and the twins and Charm seemed uncomfortable about it too. They took turns napping, waking up to worry or ponder out the window. None of them managed any real sleep. The next day was it. Come hell or high water, it would be over in twenty-four hours.

To the extent anyone talked, it was for planning. She grudgingly admitted they improved on some of her original ideas, most of which involved hitting people with tire irons and punching. After the incident in the parking lot, she found herself a huge fan of tire iron-based assaults. She wondered how Pranav was doing or if he was telling people her story. She wondered if anyone would tell her story.

On the outskirts of Nevada, long after dark, they pulled into a motel and piled inside. Hush threw a wad of money at the clerk and booked five rooms. Everyone went to their own spots and Vain slumped onto her bed without even bothering to check what shows were available. She couldn't stop her mind from racing.

Of all the horrible things Arthur had done to her, taking her memory was the worst. She had watched movies about people who were taken prisoner, and they always told a story about their childhood, or their home life, or the loved ones left behind. They would take strength from that, and it would give them courage to get to the end.

Vain had nothing to draw on for hope. No one waited for her outside the Hotel and she had no soft and blurry memories of childhood to fade into; no downy thoughts of better days to gather strength from. Just hard edges, hard choices, and hard times.

She wished for one memory before the Hotel. Just one; even an inkling. That didn't seem unreasonable. She ran her finger over the scar on her elbow, the one that had no stitch marks. Who was she? Had she been loved? Did someone miss her? Did they go to the police, tearfully handing over crumpled pictures to bored officers, taking communion in the hopes their prayers would be answered and their little girl would be returned?

God damn it, what was her real name?

The thoughts piled on, faster and faster, and she pushed away tears with the heel of her hand. Enough of this. If she died tomorrow, all the wishing would amount to nothing, anyway. If she lived, she'd have Roman, and they'd figure out what to do together.

Unless he left her for Emma.

Those two were getting close. Very close. They shared more glances, more 'oh, I'll sit here beside Emma, I like the middle'. He was making Emma laugh now, using his so-stupid-they-were-funny jokes and breezy smile. Those jokes belonged to her, and Emma was stealing them.

Vain never let herself dwell on the future. What would be the point? The future was a dim bulb down a long hallway, difficult to see and perhaps impossible to reach. In the rare instances when she imagined a life free from the Hotel, she'd picture her and Roman making each other laugh, talking about normal things like how jobs involved a lot of spreadsheets, and how bus fare was too expensive, and whose turn was it to pick up a loaf of French bread. They would live together, of course, and he would take a job at a local business, wear a suit, and talk about balance sheets and water coolers. She'd stay at home and watch movies and invent dumb jokes to make him smile. After work they'd eat popcorn, and she would show him her favorite scenes; he would drink coffee and talk about files that were due tomorrow. They'd be happy and safe, and nothing would ever change and it would stay that way, forever.

Well, fine. Roman could do whatever he wanted, and if Roman was happy, she was happy. She would keep telling herself that, over and over, until she believed it. She would ignore the ice sitting in the bottom of her stomach whenever she saw them together and she would remind herself that she loved Roman more than anything in the world and all she wanted was for him to find peace and happiness. And if his happiness took the form of a bookish, redheaded thief who would steal him and leave her with nothing, she'd keep fighting, because what else did she have?

Well past midnight, she settled into an uneasy doze, curled up into a ball and hugging her pillow, not even bothered by the dampness on her cheeks. Probably the humidity, anyway.

The next morning, she woke up exhausted and took a cold shower to perk herself up. All night she'd had dreams about being trapped alone in an empty, dark void and the way out was forever out of reach, no matter how hard she ran.

Sounds of muffled laughter and voices reached her through the door. She checked the clock; it was after ten. People were awake. Time to get going.

The Motel was shaped like an L, with the area between the rooms opening onto a courtyard with tables and umbrellas. The humid air stuck to her clothes, and she smelled the faint moisture from last night's brief rain shower. Emma, Roman, and Charm sat around one of the tables. Roman was sitting across from Emma and both had their hands on the table, not that far apart. Roman gave her all his attention. He said something, and she laughed, covering her mouth with her hand.

She had probably come back from a run. She wore sweats, and her hair was tied back in a ponytail. Was she pretty? Tough to say. Vain got how guys would find her attractive if they had a thing for redheads.

Roman had a large takeout breakfast in front of him and Charm sipped on tea. As she approached the table, she waved hello and plopped herself down.

"Emma was telling us about her last date," said Roman by way of greeting. "She's in love with a guy named Smoove Dick."

"Oh my God, stop." Emma giggled behind her hand.

Even her giggle was pretty, and Vain smoothed down her stupid, crappy hair.

"He was this gross guy I met before I had the seizure that led to all this," Emma said. "He was harmless, although he liked rapping about his genitals."

"Ha," Vain said the actual word. "Genital rap is one of my favorite subgenres."

An awkward pause followed. There was always an awkward pause when Vain opened her mouth. She had been trying to make a joke, like Roman would have. Why was it only funny when he said it?

"To genital rap. No better or worse than normal rap." Roman held up his coffee in a mock salute. Charm smiled and followed suit. Everyone relaxed, and it was better again.

"Where do you think we'll appear when this is over? After we use the Padlock this time? It's the only thing I can't figure out." She had been thinking about that all night.

She raised the question to everyone, but looked right at Charm after saying it. No one knew more about the Hotel than her. Some people whispered she'd been there since the beginning; as long as Arthur himself.

Charm took a sip of her tea and settled into her seat. "I think you'll end up the same place you started."

"How?" Vain asked. "The last time, I was teleported halfway across the country."

"Devices all work the same way, basically. Pour this weird energy of ours into a thing so it does something. But the energy needs to go somewhere. When the Padlock opens, it displaces the energy, leaving it empty. If there's too much, it needs a deposit. We already figured out that Emma was the repository on this world."

"That makes no sense though," said Vain. "If Arthur used this thing to keep himself alive, wouldn't he already have activated hundreds of Emmas?"

"I don't think so," said Charm. "Arthur's elevator can take him anywhere he wants, to any world he wants. So why the Portal? Why does the connection to this specific world remain separate from the places he travels to through the Elevator?"

Vain rested her head in her hands, fascinated. She'd never thought about it. There was the Elevator and there was the Portal. Who cares why there are two? But now that Charm mentioned it, she realized it must mean something.

"I believe this is the only world he's ever found with people like us. People who can become Utilities and Conduits. That's why he treats this world as special and focuses all of his time and Wyatts here. He needs us, this world, to power the Well. That's why he built the Portal. To make sure he would have permanent and easy access."

"If that's true," Charm continued, "that would mean that if he died on another Earth, there wouldn't be any Emma to dump the power into. That type of Emma only exists on this version of Earth. But the energy needs to go somewhere. And where's the one place in all the worlds we know about that can absorb that much energy?"

"The Well," said Roman.

"The Well," agreed Charm. "My guess is that whenever Arthur used the Padlock, it used the Well as a dumping ground. All the leftovers would end up in there."

"We'll end up in the Hotel?" Emma looked horrified. "I thought the whole point of this was to avoid that place."

"Only if there's leftover energy," Vain said.

"Can you provide the math behind magic-energy-to-human-resurrection ratios?" Emma said. "Would that use the standard 'e equals hf' used in determining the energy of a photon?" She sounded annoyed.

Vain shrugged, not sure if Emma was asking seriously or trying to be funny. "We'll be safe. It will be different this time because there are more of us and there won't be energy left over. It will boop us out of danger and we'll be done." Several sets of eyes regarded her. What more did they want? "Bada-bing, bada-boom," she added. There.

Charm snorted, sounding both entertained and exasperated. "As much as it pains me to admit it, she's probably right, though. I don't think it will take us back to the Hotel."

"You don't have to come, Charm," Vain replied. "We need the twins to get us in, but you can stay back and wait."

"Sure. And I'll sit here and twiddle my thumbs, not knowing if any of you are alive or dead. You're the only family I have left. Either we make it together, or what's the point?" She looked down at the table, playing with her hands. After a long silence, she said, "I miss Patience," her voice hiccupping with a small hitch. The blood drained from Vain's face. "I thought I would get better, but I'm not. She was my heart, and my tomorrow, and she's gone. If I don't survive, at least I'll be with her again." A fat, solitary tear ran down her cheek.

"We'll make them pay for Patience, Charm," Vain said. "All of them. Arthur, Trick; every single one of them. I promise."

"You don't get it, Vain. You've never understood. I don't want revenge. I've made peace with what happened, and I've let it go. I want this to be over."

"How can you forgive them?"

"Who said anything about forgiving them? Everyone says you have to forgive people to move on. Forgiveness has nothing to do with it. It's acceptance. The world is a horrible place, and sometimes horrible things happen. The world is also a wonderful place, and sometimes wonderful things happen. I had many years with Patience and loved every one of them. Whether it was at the hands of the Hotel, or by natural causes, eventually our time together would have ended. It happened sooner than I would have liked, but it was going to happen."

Vain didn't know what to say. Charm didn't seem angry, but she was weeping. Emma rubbed her back. Charm sniffled and continued.

"I don't want anyone to suffer, but this thing we're doing needs to be finished. This is a way to stop Arthur from ruining more lives. When it's over, regardless of what happens, Patience will still be gone, and I'll still be alone. I'd rather face that with you guys than on my own."

"We won't leave again, Charm," said Roman. "We'll get through this together."

Vain didn't like how personal the conversation had gotten. If anyone killed Roman, she'd set the world on fire to watch them burn. And if she got caught in the flames? She'd scream at the assholes and kick down the door to hell herself.

Into this awkward outpouring of emotion strode Mark, coming up from behind Charm and plopping himself down on the bench. "I'm sorry, is everyone okay?"

"It's fine, Mark," said Charm. "What did you find?"

Before he spoke, he looked at Vain and raised an eyebrow. Vain nodded, giving him the go-ahead.

"The building is an hour's drive from here. As you get closer, the area is blocked off by chain-link fences and lots of threatening signs. Not that they need them; it's in the middle of nowhere and there's no one around for miles. It's only accessible by back roads. They've razed the ground surrounding it, there's no way to approach that they won't spot from two hundred yards away."

"Is it doable?" asked Vain. "Can we get in?"

"We have to go at night, and we have to go fast. The main road that leads to the building runs through a heavy gate and a guardhouse. If we didn't have the twins, I'd say we scout the perimeter, find a weak point, and try to go in that way. But since we can force people to do what we want..." he shrugged. "The front is easiest, and they won't expect it. From there, it's a short drive to the compound. Assuming no one sounds the alarm, we should be able to get close. Once we're there, the twins can tell everyone to leave."

"Hush said he can do twenty people at once, no problem," Vain said.

"Hush specifically said he can perhaps do at most twenty people if there weren't any distractions and the command was very simple, and he was incredibly lucky and everything went flawlessly," Emma clarified.

"How is that any different from what I said? He tells them to leave the building, we get one of them to give us a pass card or whatever they use, and we find the Portal to the Hotel."

"It's theoretically possible, but in practice? Complete insanity," Mark said. "It all hinges on the twins being able to control who knows how many Wyatts in who knows what circumstances. Speaking of which, where are they?"

"Blunt is pretty shaken up and freaked out by all of this, so Hush is trying to settle him down. They said to leave them alone for a little while."

Mark nodded. "People handle it differently."

They continued eating in companionable silence until Roman said, "Will this be it? Will this work?"

"Of course it'll work." Vain's eyes were locked onto his. "This is the end, Roman. After tonight, we'll be free."

Chapter 28

Roman saves some of the day.

Roman rested his head against the window of the minivan, unable to make out anything beyond vague shapes and endless desert flats. The moon provided some small amount of illumination, but this far out in the scrub of Nevada, seeing for any great distance was impossible. He'd traveled to so many parts of the country since leaving the Hotel, but he didn't think he'd seen any of it. It might be nice to visit a cheesy tourist attraction without worrying about getting jumped by Wyatts. When this was over, maybe he'd go on a road trip.

Assuming he survived.

The thought didn't prompt much reaction in him. Not like it was the first time he'd considered his mortality. Nothing about the life he'd been thrust into with Vain was easy. For the millionth time, he wondered who he had been in his past life. He had a head for numbers, seemed to have a laid-back disposition, and somehow knew how to play guitar. Aside from that, there was nothing. Arthur stole his backstory, and ever since, he'd been making it up as he went along. His identity was inexorably tied to Vain and the purpose he found in keeping her safe. Tonight would go against all of that. Walking into the hands of the men who wanted to kill you was not the best way to keep loved ones out of danger. But it was what they needed to do.

"Everyone ready?" Mark asked.

"Yes," said Hush. "Drive to the gate."

Vain's plan was simplicity and lunacy wrapped into one: blow up the Portal. With the Portal destroyed, Arthur had no access to this world, at least not without finding an alternate path using the elevator. And that could take years. Decades. She wanted to do it from the start, but the how eluded her. For one thing, she couldn't generate an explosion large enough. Two, even if she had an explosion, anything that large would kill her the second she detonated it.

Emma solved problem number one. The Padlock solved problem number two.

Once close to the Portal, Emma would pull all the ambient energy. This time, instead of pouring it back into the Padlock, she'd explode it the same way she had at the gas station, but on a larger scale. A massive scale. It was crazy and suicidal, and everyone admitted it had a fraction of a chance of working.

Vain must have been planning it from the start, but she denied it.

"Lucky then," Emma had said, "that this all worked out."

Vain grinned her teeth-only smile and said, "Luck is a word people use when they don't remember creating the opportunity. I don't forget."

Madness. But there he was, driving up to the guardhouse; with no time left to consider if it was a good idea. He would see it through to the end. He trusted Vain, and he would protect her one last time. Somehow.

Mark stopped the van at the end of the winding gravel road. They came to rest beside a booth that stood in front of a gate and concrete wall. In the booth were two men, ostensibly security guards, although both wore militarized gear and had pistols at their sides. They stepped out, one going to either side of the car. Strangely, they weren't Wyatts. Trick and Arthur must have been using private security to keep people away. Mark rolled down the window.

"Turn around, folks," said the guy on Mark's side. He was a squat ball of muscle, all rectangular. His head was a solid block and his flat-topped hair completed the image. He wore a jacket over his standard-issue security guard outfit.

"I don't know how you ended up here," he continued, "but you're in the wrong place. This is a restricted government area. You need to turn your vehicle around. In about five miles, you'll be back to the main highway." He tapped on the roof twice. *Clink. Clink.*

"You really like us," said Hush, leaning over to the window.

Roman had always wondered how Hush transformed energy into cooperation. It was a complete mystery to him, but as long as it worked, he didn't care about the specifics.

"You're relaxed," Hush continued. "Everything's going to be alright."

A thick lethargy soaked into Roman's bones and a weight pushed against him from somewhere outside the van. His nerves, previously jangling in his brain like a collection of bells, fell silent. The tension poured from his shoulders and he leaned back in his chair. A dumb grin found its way onto his face and he looked over at Emma, who wore a similar expression.

The guard outside turned down the collar of his jacket and the light glinted off something affixed to his chest. A tiny part of his brain screamed at him that something was wrong. "When you are about to storm an armed compound in the middle of nowhere using poorly understood superpowers, you absolutely should be nervous", it said.

He shook his head, once, twice, as if recoiling from a sneeze. What the hell? He looked at Hush and found himself smiling even harder. He liked Hush, a lot. What a great guy.

"Wait", screamed the small voice. "Hush is an asshole. You think he's a complete dick and you don't like the way he treats Vain."

"You are going to do whatever we say." Hush continued speaking to the guard, but his ordinarily smooth voice held a hint of uncertainty. The weight on Roman's shoulders settled in. It was kind of nice. Comforting.

"Get out of the vehicle," said the guard.

Roman fumbled with his seatbelt. He needed to get out of the van. He wrestled with the door, pushing Emma out of the way. Everyone else was doing the same, jostling to get out as fast as they could.

Roman's mind screamed at him. "Stay in the goddamn van, you stupid lunatic". Man, that tiny part of his brain sure was fired up about something, but he couldn't make himself care. He practically leaped out, legs trembling, waiting for the guard to tell him what to do next.

"Everyone, line up against the gate."

Roman thought that was a fantastic idea. He really liked that guy. Were they best friends? Probably! He pressed himself against the gate, shoulder to shoulder with Vain. Everyone else arranged themselves to either side. Blunt stopped to give the guard a handshake and Roman clucked his tongue. He should have thought of that. Meanwhile, the small voice in his head banged on the walls and set fires to the curtains. "Wake up!"

"You two," said the guard, pointing to Hush and Blunt. "Keep up your hypnosis thing. Don't stop."

Hush nodded and said, "You're happy and relaxed and you'll do whatever we say."

Roman grinned foolishly, happy and relaxed, and wondered how he could do whatever Hush said.

"Vain," he said, trying to think through the smog. "Is something wrong?" He poked her arm, and she looked at him, vacant. "Do we love Guard?"

"Guard is awesome," she replied.

Reassured, Roman let his mind fall back asleep. Guard *was* awesome. Vain, as usual, was right. There was nothing to worry about. While one of the guards pointed a gun at them—which was super—the other pulled out a walkie-talkie and turned it on. Roman also thought that was spectacular.

"It's over," the guard said into the walkie-talkie. "They're subdued. Come get them. Who would have thought? A freaking mirror. I owe you ten bucks."

Now that sure seemed like a funny thing for a best friend to say, but it was probably nothing to worry about. The tiny voice in the back of his head tried a different approach. "The guard didn't say anything about not hurting yourself. You should try that. Really mess yourself up. Trust me."

Everyone was making brilliant suggestions today. The guard, Vain, the weird voice in his head.

He bit the inside of his forearm and pulled with all his strength. His teeth tore through the skin, ripping off a chunk. Salty, coppery blood filled his mouth and white-hot pain lanced up his arm.

The agony parted the heavy curtains of his thoughts. He gasped and the weird voice spoke in a tone that allowed for no uncertainty.

"Hush is an asshole, you're acting crazy and the guards are going to kill you."

That time, he completely agreed. Something was wrong. His eyes went to the guard, and the bizarre mirror attached to his chest, under the lapel of his jacket. The mirror was the problem.

The mirror was a Device, reflecting Hush's power back at them.

Before the horrible lethargy subdued him again, he dove at the closest guard. It was unexpected and they both went down in a heap. Roman threw blind punches, hoping that one of them would connect. His arm was on fire.

"It's a trap," he yelled. "They know. Stop them!"

A fist slammed against the side of his head and dancing spots of light filled his vision. He had lost count of how many people had punched him in the face over the past week. The guard pinned him to the ground and continued to throw haymakers. Mark was there in seconds, doing some impressive spin-kick move that hit the guard in the face and sent him flying.

The other guard backed up and pulled out his gun. Aside from Mark, the group was still trying to understand what had happened. Hush was coming out of his haze and started his routine again.

"You're settled, you're relaxed. Drop the gun!" he yelled.

Roman swayed as Hush's power washed over him again. "Stop it," he whispered, but he was too settled and relaxed to put any emphasis into his voice. He looked around for a gun to drop.

"Stay back!" The guard whipped his gun around, trying to cover all of them at once. "I'll kill you, I swear to fucking God!"

Hush took a lurching step forward and tried to grab at the gun, but his movements were too jerky; too robotic. The guard lashed out with a vicious punch to his throat, and Hush doubled over, holding his neck and making horrible barking noises. With Hush down, all traces of lethargy left Roman and his thoughts returned.

The guard brought his gun around to point it at Charm, who looked at him with sad, accepting eyes.

"Patience!" Vain screamed. She dove in front of Charm at the same time the gun fired.

The noise obliterated all thought. Roman didn't know anything could be that loud.

Mark was there in a heartbeat, disarming the guard and throwing him to the ground all in the same move. A final punch knocked him unconscious. Vain lay on top of Charm, panting. Her arm dangled at her side, blood soaking into the ground below. She didn't seem to notice.

"I'm sorry. I'm sorry. I'm sorry," Vain said into Charm's shoulder. "I didn't mean to kill Patience. I'm sorry. I'm sorry."

Roman had never seen Vain like that. She was shaking and sobbing, clutching Charm so hard the whites of her knuckles were visible. Had she been carrying it the whole time? How had he never noticed? He thought back to all the times Vain changed the subject when he talked about leaving the Hotel. All the times she'd claimed she had a headache whenever he brought up the twins and Charm. God, it was so obvious, in retrospect.

He couldn't believe how profoundly he'd failed her. So caught up in his own shit, he didn't recognize her suffering that whole time.

Charm sat up and gathered Vain into a tight hug. She rocked her, making shushing noises and stroking her hair. Tears and snot ran freely down Vain's face, and her entire body hitched with the release of emotion.

"It's okay, Vain. It's okay. You did good. I promise."

"I'm s-sorry," Vain whispered again. "I never wanted them to h-hurt her. I liked her. I liked her so much. I didn't know that would happen."

"I know, sweetie. I know you didn't."

"Did they hurt you?"

"Not this time. You saved me."

They all stood around and kicked up dirt, unsure of what to do. Charm glared at them all and waved them away, obviously demanding privacy. She hugged Vain tighter. Vain's frantic apologies had dropped to silent shudders.

"God, what a mess," Hush said. "What now?"

"Vain needs medical attention," Roman said. "She was shot."

"They knew we were coming," Hush said. "That's it. We're done. It's over."

"Yeah. Let's get out of here. We can regroup back at the motel and figure out our next move."

"We're not going anywhere," Emma said.

Chapter 29

Emma attacks. Again.

Emma debated whether bad luck or bad decisions brought her to that point. Each step that had moved her closer to the present moment seemed logical and sane, like putting together a jigsaw puzzle, only without knowing what the picture on the box looked like.

She could have gone to the police or stayed in Boston. She could have called her Mom or Doreen. A million steps she could have taken, leaps in directions that would have led her off this path. But instead, she readied to storm a secret, guarded facility, led by a five-foot-two lunatic with big eyes and a garbage haircut.

She had too much left to do. Finish school; make her mark on the world; get married; have kids, maybe. Things normal people do. These people she was with had nothing to live for. Their present and past jumbled together, and the Hotel had pushed them to their limits. She experienced a drop of that in the past week, but was she ready to dive all the way in?

This was their only chance, and if they didn't press forward, they might not get another. The guards shot Vain, and they would be walking into a trap. What if more people had Mirrors?

She sat in the dirt, leaned back against the van, and shut her eyes. It never stopped. Without even trying, she let her awareness drift and felt energy, never-ending, creeping into her. She sensed her companions and their flickering pulses.

She strained for Roman, her rock through all of it, with his tousled brown hair her hands itched to smooth back. Steady and present, a wall to lean against. More, she suspected, if she wanted it. If she gave up, would they take him? Would he be gone?

Vain was an engine of perpetual motion; hot, angry, and pulsing even in remorse. An engine of perpetual motion. The Hotel would end her. She knew what the Hotel was, now. She'd seen it firsthand. There was no reasoning with those people, no reassuring logic that would convince them to leave her friends alone. They had guns and limitless Wyatts.

And they had shot Vain. Somehow, that drove the reality of her situation home and she finally believed what Vain told her at the outset.

They won't stop.

She allowed herself ten seconds of self-pity. Exactly ten heartbeats, and into those heartbeats she poured her frustration, the unfairness of her situation, all her tears of rage and helplessness. She gripped her hands together with enough force to drive her nails into her palms.

Ten seconds.

The instant the tenth heartbeat passed, she opened her eyes, clear and focused. She could sit there and sulk or she could get busy solving problems.

A weight left her chest, and she stood up. She would move forward. She didn't want to hurt anyone, but she wouldn't give up. More energy flowed into her, and she made a conscious effort not to draw from her friends. It came from the air, from the scrub brush surrounding her, from distant animals, and even from the men up in the compound.

"We're not leaving." Her voice cut through the chatter of the group. "You are. Mark, get the twins and Charm out of here. We'll go in without you."

"They know you're coming." Mark's eyes flicked towards Vain. "You'll be walking into an ambush."

"Yes," replied Emma. "That will be a problem for them, not us."

"Vain's hurt," Roman protested.

"I'm peachy," Vain said. She'd stood up and disentangled herself from Charm. Her arm hung at her side, blood dripping from her fingertips. Her face was pale, and she swayed on her feet.

"I don't believe you've ever seen an actual peach," Mark said. "You're losing an enormous amount of blood. You need a hospital. This isn't a movie."

"It doesn't hurt at all." She wiped tears from her cheek with her good hand. "The Padlock will heal me."

"What are you going to do?" asked Hush.

Emma turned towards the compound. "What we came to do. End it."

"You can't get in there without us." His protests lacked conviction.

She put a smile onto her face, but it was fake and nothing of it touched her eyes. "I can."

"We can't leave you," said Mark.

"The fewer people there are to protect, the easier this will be," she replied.

A noise came from her left and Emma whipped her head around. Three Wyatts charged over the hill carrying assault rifles.

"Freeze, down, down!" they yelled and opened fire.

Faster than thought, Emma threw an energy shield up like Vain did in the forest. Simultaneously, she formed an energy bubble around the Wyatts heads, cutting off their oxygen.

Everyone else dropped to the ground, but aside from turning her head, Emma never moved. The Wyatts struggled and choked as their air ran out. She concentrated a third time and ripped the guns from their hands. Within moments, they fell over unconscious, and it was over. The group gaped at her, shock written on their faces. She gestured at the Wyatts.

"I don't need you."

The mental shift was visible on Mark's face; he dealt with reality as it was, not as he wanted it to be. He nodded and turned to the twins.

"Can we find out how many others are waiting?" asked Roman.

"Twenty-six Wyatts." Emma closed and opened her hands. "I can read each of them in the building." With each moment, Emma's calm and determination gave way to anger. No, anger didn't cover it; what she felt was fury. How dare they? How dare they come and wreck her life and hurt her friends?

Mark chewed on the inside of his mouth, clearly unhappy to leave them alone; but he had no other options. He turned to Vain, who leaned against the van.

"You owe me a date when this is over." He tried to push some humor into his voice. "Don't forget. Come back safe."

She nodded and stumbled towards Roman. "Are you okay to keep going? I'll need to pull from you a little."

"Am I okay? Vain, you can barely walk."

"Why does everyone keep worrying about me?"

"Do you understand that you've been shot?"

"Here." Mark interrupted the conversation and gave Roman a gun he pulled from underneath his jacket. "You might need this."

"I won't be able to protect them with this," Roman said. "I don't even know how to use it."

Mark laughed, a dry and brittle sound. "These two do not need your protection. This is for you to protect you. You're the one I'm worried about."

Roman regarded the bigger man for a beat and grinned, a tight slash across his usually sedate features. He grabbed the gun with both hands.

"We're leaving them?" Blunt asked.

"It's okay, buddy," said Hush with surprising tenderness. When he spoke to Blunt, the concerned wrinkles smoothed out from his forehead and he looked almost calm. "They know what they're doing. They'll be okay."

"Where will we find you?" asked Roman. "When this is finished?"

"New York," said Hush. "We have backup offices there as a failsafe. There's no way for Trick to know about them."

"Here." Mark handed his phone to Roman. "The numbers are in there. Call when you're finished."

Roman nodded.

Emma thought the chances of them ever making that call were slim, but she couldn't seem to make herself care. Everyone said their goodbyes, with Vain letting Charm give her a final hug. She did not allow anyone else to touch her.

Charm approached Emma and gave her a shaky smile. "End this," she said. "For once and for all. Put this to bed."

Emma nodded, not trusting herself to speak.

Mark piled everyone into the van and backed out of the road. The headlights arced away, leaving darkness behind. A football field away sat the compound, lights from the interior acting as a focal point to move towards.

"I am done running," said Emma. "We are walking into that building, marching to the Portal, and finishing this. If anyone gets in our way, I will stop them."

"You need to keep enough energy to blow everything up," said Vain. "I'm not sure I can fight all of them myself."

'Not sure'. Even having lost half her blood, her arm useless at her side, and barely able to stand, Vain was 'not sure' she'd be able to win a fight against twenty armed men. If Emma weren't so distracted by the power flowing into her, she'd laugh. Vain was like no other person she'd ever met.

"I'll take care of them. I'll gather as I go. I can concentrate most of my pulling to the front. Stay behind and you should be untouched." Without waiting, Emma strode off towards the compound, leaving Vain to catch up.

"We're going to run up to the door and smash it in?" she said to Emma's back.

"Yes. How perfectly Vain, right?"

Emma's voice sounded hollow to her own ears. In front of her, the scrub and grass withered and blackened as she pulled energy from all the living matter in her way. Her hair drifted and hung in the air.

"Can we at least go around the side?" Vain asked

"No. I am finished sneaking and they are finished pursuing. Tonight, I take my life back."

Emma was a sponge, soaking in energy like water. There was so much available and all hers for the taking. She didn't even need people; the air itself held enough. It was both terrifying and exhilarating. As always, her skin stretched like her insides were trying to escape, but this time, she had a better handle on it. She didn't think her fingernails would pop out, but even if they did, she was beyond caring. This tidal wave of power didn't leave room for emotion. A blankness came over her thoughts and she embraced it. Now was not a time for feeling.

"Emma, I can't help you," said Vain. "If I pull, Roman will be defenseless."

"I'll shield us." She poured energy on them. Just like she did in the motel when she practiced levitating items, she covered them in a layer of flexible energy that rested on their bodies like a second skin.

It wasn't uncomfortable, but it felt like wearing one of those x-ray blankets dentists would use. Extra weight added to their movements. Remarkably, she found she could still breathe. Unlike the solid construct she put around the Wyatts, this seemed porous enough to let air through. It was like breathing through a thick pillow; uncomfortable, but not impossible.

"What is this?" Roman looked at his hands in wonder. "It's all over me. How are you doing this?"

"I don't know," said Emma. She hadn't considered doing it until then. His voice was muffled, and she had to strain to hear. "Quiet, now. No more speaking. I will keep us safe."

Vain seemed unhappy, probably because she had to go along with a plan she didn't come up with. Emma was done waiting.

She paused as they approached the building. It was constructed like a giant hangar, squat and functional, with long rows of spotlights that lit up the exterior. The gravel road gave way to pavement and a barbed-wire fence surrounded the whole enclosure. Two fifteen-foot towers overlooked the fences, and as they came to the edge of the circle of light, shapes moved about inside. They would need to walk across fifty feet of contested space.

"When we start, don't stop walking. Don't run away from me because I don't know how far I can protect you. Just walk."

It only took seconds after stepping into the perimeter for spotlights to train on them. They kept pace with their steps, outlining them in a perfect blotter of light. Roman tried to turn in every direction at once, and maneuvered himself between Vain and the towers. Vain clenched her good hand, but whether out of fear or anger, Emma couldn't tell.

There was no warning that time, just bullets; three in rapid succession. It felt like someone poking her in the forehead, the temple, the cheek. Poke, poke, poke. More shots from the tower, and more pokes in the chest, temple, and arm. Roman covered his head and let out a cry of alarm.

"Get out of the tower," she yelled, not caring if they did what she asked. "It's coming down, along with the fence."

More pokes, head, leg, chest. Well, she had warned them. She made a slashing motion with her hand and the base of the towers split in half like a sliced apple. Another gesture and the barbed wire fence in front of them flattened as if crushed by a giant, invisible hand.

The guard towers didn't fall right away. They swayed for a moment and then tilted over, landing with a crash that sounded muffled through her energy cloak. She had not stopped her careful, measured pace forward.

It consumed staggering amounts of energy, but a drop in the bucket against the amount available. She could continue like this indefinitely. There was so much to draw from. She almost giggled, caught in the whirlpool of power.

Now, she was in control. And no one would tell her what to do again.

Chapter 30

Vain and the showdown at the Portal.

Vain survived years in a multi-dimensional, time-displaced Hotel, prisoner to a psychotic lunatic who forced her to pour her power and soul into a bottomless energy well. She had been beaten and healed countless times. Her dearest friend in the world had been targeted and tortured, only to get to her. She had endured through an escape that ended in the death of a companion and nearly killed all of them. Duplicate, murderous thugs had hunted her for a year.

Through the entire experience, she'd held on to her anger; anger at the people who'd done it, anger at the unfairness of it all. She liked it. The rage was a tornado, keeping everything else at bay. With it surrounding her, she'd never experienced fear. Not until now.

Emma terrified her.

She had witnessed Emma grow into her powers, doing things she never believed possible. It seemed almost effortless now, a far cry from that first explosion at the gas station. Emma was the power, and the power was Emma; and it sapped the cheery innocence out of her voice leaving behind only monochrome grey. She was so precise in her actions Vain didn't even feel the tugging lethargy of her pull anymore.

Emma could kill them all without breaking a sweat.

No one knew for sure how powerful Arthur was. People believed he created the Hotel himself. The Hotel, the Well, even the Devices were all rumored to have come from him. How much power would that have taken?

Had she created another Arthur?

Emma stepped through the wreckage of the guard towers, not pausing her horrible, deliberate pace. The ruined metal twisted out of her way, reinforced steel and concrete bending to her will. That wasn't the Emma from the forest, pleading with Vain for help. That was an Emma out of control; so far past the end of her rope the rope wasn't even visible anymore.

Roman's eyes were wide and wild. He held the gun like a phone, gripping it from the side, his finger not even on the trigger. Some of her fear gave way to anger, the same anger that existed whenever Roman was in distress. He needed—he *deserved*—better. When this business was over, she'd find a way to make it right and give him rest.

Their steady pace brought them close to the front of the squat, rectangular building. The whole thing was windowless and utilitarian. Two broad, steel doors off to their left swung open as they approached. Six Wyatts poured out, all armed with assault weaponry. They provided no warning this time, the times for warnings long since passed. They opened fire.

Vain flinched, as did Roman. Hundreds of fingers poked all over her body; tickling, itching at her, but not painful in the slightest. Pressure from the bullets pushed her back, but she braced against it.

Emma stopped. She didn't throw her arms up to block; she didn't cower, she only considered them, head tilted to the side. The Wyatts lined up in two rows, with the first crouched on a single knee and the back row standing.

The barrage of bullets lasted fifteen seconds and when it ended, the silence between the two groups lasted long enough to become awkward. Vain supposed people normally died after a bullet-based introduction, and there was likely no manual for what to do next.

"Um," said one of the Wyatts. "Get on the ground?"

"Stop?" said another.

Emma considered them. "Leave. Or I will kill you."

How was it possible to wash emotion out of a voice like that?

One Wyatt pulled a knife and launched himself at Roman. Apparently, even when confronted by an energy-wielding superwoman with the power to deflect bullets, the man constituted the bigger threat.

He stabbed at Roman, and the knife bounced out of his grip like he had hit a brick wall. He yelled and clutched his hand. Emma frowned and the Wyatt *flew* away like a pebble out of a slingshot. One moment he danced from foot to foot in front of Roman, wringing his injured hand, the next he was gone, a dim speck in the sky above.

"Leave," Emma said again. "I am walking. If you are in my way by the time I get to the doors, you will die." With that, Emma took a step forward.

The five remaining Wyatts scrambled out of the way, running into the darkness. Emma squinted and the steel doors blew inward with a deafening crash.

The entrance opened into a large, single space that looked more like an airport lounge than a room. It had seating spread throughout, a small kitchen area with a stove in the corner, and shelves full of supplies lined the walls. That wasn't only a place to transition, this was a refueling station. This where they came out of the Hotel and got themselves ready to go into the world.

In the middle of the open room a giant door frame towered over everything, fifteen feet tall. There was no door in the frame, only a hazy, purple film. It stood in the middle by itself, its presence unremarkable, but Vain's blood chilled when she looked at it. The Portal to the Hotel. She'd found it. After all this time, she'd found it.

Wyatts were scattered throughout the room, looking alarmed and frantic, all pointing guns at them.

They fired.

The noise was deafening. Vain and Roman both screamed. Bullets whizzed through the air and noxious gun smoke filled the room. Emma only stared, head tilted, a tiny half-smile on her face. Vain's bowels loosened.

The shooting lasted twenty seconds. When it was over, the only sounds were the clackity-clack of guns reloading and spent cartridges falling to the floor.

The Wyatts were agitated beyond control. One ran for a nearby gun rack, seemed to think better of it, and instead ran out the back door. Two huddled against each other, backing away. One dropped to his knees and pleaded with them to stop.

One stupider Wyatt dove at Emma from where he had been crouching in the shadows. Emma didn't turn her head or flinch; she only held up her hand and he froze in mid-air before being launched back twenty feet straight into a pile of chairs against the wall.

Five Wyatts, braver than their peers, charged from the right. Screaming, they rushed in to attack. Emma showed no outward reaction, she didn't even glance at them. Their charge slowed, as if they were trying to run through water. They slowed… and stopped.

Their feet left the floor while they yelled in protest. They swam and flailed, unable to do anything while Emma trapped them in the air.

The moment of silence stretched into eternity. The Wyatts drifted apart, soundlessly, until they floated a good twenty feet away from each other. Their counterparts on the ground pointed and trembled at the power on display.

With brutal force, Emma slammed them together

The unmistakable crack of bone breaking echoed off the walls. Emma separated the men who were now a groaning, crying mess.

Slam. She brought them together again with horrific force. Blood covered one of the Wyatts' faces; he must have connected with a knee or elbow. She separated them again.

Slam. A third concussion and the only sounds left were soft whimpers. They hung limp, unconscious. One Wyatts' leg twisted at an unnatural angle. Emma was crushing them together with the force of multiple car crashes. It was grotesque. She separated them again, five broken puppets suspended in the air. Vain couldn't take her eyes from the growing pool of blood collecting beneath their fractured bodies.

"Emma." Vain's voice was a whisper.

Slam. Emma drove the Wyatts together again, and this time blood splattered against the walls. Vain heard something *tink* onto the floor. A tooth. It was too much. Even for her, that was too much. The five Wyatts were broken bags of flesh and blood.

"Emma." Vain grabbed her arm. "Stop. Please."

Emma turned and Vain flinched. It wasn't Emma. Her soft, open face had contorted into a grotesque parody of the girl Vain drove across the country with. Her eyes were dark and angry, and she bared her clenched teeth. The individual veins in her face crisscrossed her cheeks like red pieces of yarn.

"Please." Vain swallowed, wondering if she was going to die. "Stop."

Emma blinked and some small measure of herself returned. She waved a hand and the pile of jangled limbs and splintered bones dropped to the ground.

The remaining Wyatts cowered, too terrified to even breathe.

"Run," said Emma.

That single word cut through the air, and the Wyatts couldn't move fast enough. They ran in every direction, some out the front, some out the back, some diving into Portal, into the safety of the Hotel, pushing each other out of the way. Within twenty seconds the room was empty.

"This is it?" Her voice was empty.

"Yes," Vain said.

They stood in front of the Portal, staring into the purple void. The center of it swirled in a hypnotic circular motion. A small glowing doorknob positioned at the bottom of the frame seemed out of place.

"Look." Vain reached down. "A doorknob. The Portal isn't the Device, the doorknob is." She tried to move it, but it was rooted firmly in place.

"It's pulling at me," said Emma. She ran her hand over the doorknob, almost with affection. "It's singing. Can you hear it? The singing?"

Vain didn't hear anything. Blood from her arm had soaked her sleeve, and she wiped her hand on her jeans. They needed to end it.

"Roman, you go first, then Emma, then me. Okay?"

She had to make sure Emma went through. Roman nodded and, with a deep breath, strode through the door and vanished. His presence winked out, like turning off a TV. There, then gone. Looking bemused, Emma followed. The darkness in the doorway swallowed her.

Vain surveyed the now-empty room. They were so close, and they had made it so far. She couldn't believe they had made it this far. Half-baked was a generous description of Vain's plans, and if she was honest with herself, she was not super confident the latest one was going to work; but she was so tired of being angry. She needed it to end, and made a silent promise to Roman. "If someone dies today, it will be me". Somehow, she'd keep him safe.

She walked through the door.

*

It was like walking into static, or through a wall of bumblebees. Her skin bubbled with the pricks of a million tiny blips of energy. It seemed like she tripled in size while shrinking down to nothing. The single step took forever and no time at all.

She entered a low, circular room, some thirty feet across, lit by an otherworldly, soft-white glow. They'd passed through this place before, during their frantic escape. The walls and floor were made of rough stone and were warm to the touch. On the other side of the room was the door to the Hotel.

"It's almost alive." Emma ran her fingers over the irregular stone walls. "This place hemorrhages energy. If I pulled for the rest of my life, it wouldn't make a dent. It would be like drinking the ocean through a straw."

"Do you have enough left to explode?" asked Vain.

"Yes. Easily." Emma still wore that detached expression on her face.

"How will blowing this up destroy the Portal?" asked Roman.

"It will." Vain tried to keep her voice confident. Now that she was standing in the center of all that power, she honestly had no idea if it would work. It seemed like trying to destroy a dam with a firecracker.

They reached the center of the room when the door at the opposite end slammed open. Like a blizzard, wind swirled around their bodies and was sucked towards the opening. Roman positioned Vain and Emma behind him and held his gun out.

"Please." The voice coming through the door dripped with mild disgust. "We're well past the point of guns."

Trick stepped through, carrying a massive golf umbrella.

"Jesus Christ," said Vain.

Even behind the brace on his nose, he was sharp and well put together. Stupid, annoyingly good-looking Trick, always showing up where he didn't belong. He opened the umbrella and positioned himself behind it, making himself untouchable to their power.

"How did you beat us here?" she asked.

"I am aware that airplanes exist." He shrugged. "What did you do to my Wyatts? They're incoherent with fear."

"Get out of our way, Trick," Roman said.

He ignored them both and turned his attention to Emma. "I wish we had more time together, Emma." Trick closed the Hotel door behind him and the wind vanished, leaving an eerie silence in the room. "I told Arthur about all the wonderful things you can do, and he very much wants to meet you. I'm sorry you ended up with these two first. It would have been so much different if we worked together."

Emma cocked her head to the side like she was listening to someone speak in her ear. Maybe she was. She said, "You aren't afraid, and I don't know why. You should be."

"Arthur can tell what people are feeling too," he said. "Arthur can do many things. You're only scratching the surface of your power. Let us teach you. Listen, when we had the Wyatts take you, we didn't realize what you were. We would have done it differently had we known. It was our mistake. We thought you were like these two." He gestured at her and Roman. "Empty vessels, waiting to be activated for use. We take them, turn them on and wipe their memory, but that's only for their benefit."

"For our benefit?" Vain said, eyes goggling. "You stole our memories, you stole everything that makes me myself. You stole my name. And you want me to believe you did this for us?"

"Yes. In the early days, we did it differently. We told people our purpose in the Hotel and why they were needed. Many of them stayed with us, but it became painful for them. It's hard to leave your life behind, even when the reason is noble. It was hard for us to watch and hard for them to adjust. So, we came up with this solution. We free you of your memories so you can focus on the present. It's easier for you."

"Easier?" she said. "You made us slaves."

He smiled. "You don't know anything. You don't understand the work we do in the Hotel. We do everything we can to make things as easy for you as possible."

"You beat me almost to death," said Roman, his hand clenched at his side, the other gripping the gun.

"Different people need different encouragement." Trick shrugged. "We've only had to take those drastic measures with Vain. Ultimately, as in life, you decide your destiny. Half our pairs would never leave."

"They're institutionalized," said Vain. "You've broken them."

"Those 'institutionalized' people are what I came to talk to you about. Behind that door, I have amassed the concentrated might of the Hotel. About one hundred pairs of power users are waiting on the other side, ready to obliterate you if you step through. Even

Arthur himself would kneel before that. I don't care how powerful you believe yourself to be Emma, they will end you. This crusade of yours stops now. You cannot be allowed to murder Arthur."

Emma laughed. It was a horrible sound, a mechanical clacking that had no mirth or joy or laughter in it. Even Trick seemed taken aback by the sound.

"Emma, please stop." Vain reached out towards Emma.

"Silly little joke," Emma's laughter trailed off. "You think our plan was to cut the head off the snake? Who cares if the snake exists if he has no home?"

Emma giggled and waved her hand. Tiny detonations pinged off the walls, sending pebbles and bits of rubble to the ground. She snapped, and a chunk of rock fell from the ceiling, narrowly missing Trick.

"What are you doing?" he said.

"Twinkle twinkle, little Trick," Emma sang. "You're stuck here with us now."

The door behind them, the one leading back to their world, slammed shut. Dozens of mini explosions caused debris to fly around the room. Vain yelped as a jagged piece of rock hit her in the head. Hot moisture ran down her face and when she wiped, her hand came away red.

"Boom, boom, boom. We're all trapped in this room."

Emma spun in a circle and the detonations intensified. She was laughing. Vain wasn't sure if any part of Emma remained. Whatever that person was, she was a stranger. Roman reached out a hand to touch her, but she spun away. The air was filled with falling rock.

"Stop it," Trick said. "You're going to destroy the Portal."

"Correct," Emma giggled. She made a throwing motion and an enormous chunk of rock blew off the wall, shaking the floor and causing Vain to lose her balance.

"You're going to destroy the Portal," Trick breathed, realization dawning on his face. "Jesus Christ. No." All traces of smug condescension vanished from his face and he held up his hands in a gesture of pleading. "Vain, Roman. You will destroy the world. You can't let her do this. I can give you what you want if you stop this."

"You don't have anything we want," said Roman.

"You had a life before this. I can give it back to you. It's not too late. I can return your memories, I can put you back in the world."

"Bullshit," said Vain.

"It's not. I can fix all of this for you, make it like nothing ever happened. Vanity. I can give you your name. I can tell you who you are."

Vain licked her lips, wanting him to stop, wanting it to be over. "I know who I am, you piece of shit. My name is Vain. And I'm the last person you'll think about every night from now until the end of your life because I fucking beat you."

"Get out of here, Trick." Roman pointed the gun at him.

Trick held up his hands. "You'll destroy everything. Emma, if you do this, if you go through with this plan, Arthur will never stop. He will be singular in his purpose and his purpose will be to end you."

Emma laughed. "He can't touch me."

"Yes, he can. Vain's plans never work, not the way she intends. And trust me when I say he can do much worse things than coming after you. He can go after your family."

Beside her, Vain heard a crack. Emma had clenched her hands so tightly her knuckles popped. Her lips peeled back to reveal her teeth. The explosions stopped, and she turned her entire focus towards Trick.

"Killing is the least of it," Trick continued. He'd regained some of his composure and was getting the words out in a breathless rush. "He'll reserve killing for your distant acquaintances. For the people you love, it will be much worse. Your friends, your family. He has access to worlds where time doesn't move. Infinite time to take everyone you love and ruin them."

"Stop," Emma said.

"He will turn everyone against you, constantly reminding them *you* are the reason this is happening. Every single waking moment of their lives, consumed by agony, knowing that you are the cause."

"Stop," Emma said louder, and her fists raised to her sides.

Too late, Vain realized what Trick was doing. He was goading her.

"This time we'll find your mother for real and trap her in endless pain. I'll let the Wyatts have her; there are infinite Wyatts and infinite time to use her, over and over and over."

"Stop!" This time Emma yelled and threw her hands in front of her.

The power erupted from her body, aimed squarely at Trick. There was no elegance to it, only raw energy exploding in a torrent. Vain and Roman were both thrown backward and scrambled over each other, each trying to put themselves in the way of danger to protect the other.

Trick ducked behind the giant umbrella, and the power crashed off it with a thunderous clap. The umbrella rocked and smoked, the edges blackening against the release of Emma's strength.

Emma screamed and her body shook with the strain. Vain couldn't see a way to stop it. She was going to burn herself out. Trick's final gambit was so simple, and she had walked right into the trap.

Vain tried to yell over the din, but the outpouring of power consumed her words. The umbrella continued to char and wilt. The sheer magnitude of strength at Emma's command made Vain shaky with fear.

As suddenly as it started, it was over. Emma dropped to the ground, spent. Vain's ears rang in the immediate silence and for moments, no one moved or spoke. She untangled herself from Roman and they both climbed to their feet. Trick's head popped out from behind the umbrella, which was now a charred mass of smoking material and metal on the ground in front of him.

"Christ," he whispered. "What are you? You're more powerful than Arthur. Not even he could do that."

Roman lunged forward and punched him in the face. It was a clean shot, and it took Trick by surprise. He fell to the ground with a thump.

"Enough," said Roman, and threw open the door to the Hotel.

The garden was as she remembered; a lush oasis in the center of a dead rock, lit by jagged lighting from a faded-red sky. In the distance, the Hotel loomed over everything, casting its poisonous glare out over the landscape. It was a cramped, ugly protrusion that jutted from the ground at an improper angle. The colors on the outside had faded to a sickly white and rust-brown eaves lined the building. The number of windows and stories changed every time she blinked. At the top, someone stood on a balcony surrounded by iron fencing.

Arthur.

Could he see her, even from that distance? She fought the instinctual urge to hide, to escape. Like the mouse who sees the hawk in the sky, she saw her own death when she looked at him. The courtyard in front of the Hotel was empty save a smattering of Wyatts who squinted into the void. Trick, as was often the case, had been lying. No one had gathered to stop them.

Roman picked Trick up and heaved him through the opening. He bounced off the harsh rust-colored rock of the courtyard and Roman scrambled to close the door. He shut it with a ponderous slam and sunk down, burying his head in his hands.

Vain rushed over to Emma and rolled her on to her back. She gasped in horror.

Emma was in ruins.

Her eyes leaked blood. Across her skin, her veins had ruptured, leaving terrible, dark purple spider webs across her body. Her fingers were frozen in a rictus of agony, bent at unnatural angles. The noise coming from her lips was grotesque, a kind of gasping-hiccup. When she coughed, bright red blood splashed out on to her shirt.

"We're finished," Vain said. She started to weep. It was over. Her shoulder was in agony and she was out of time. Emma couldn't continue, she was barely conscious, and probably dying. Roman crawled over to them and gasped.

"Oh, Emma." He took her from Vain and cradled her head in his lap.

It broke Vain's heart. "Let's get out of here. We can try something else later. We need to get her to a safe place. A hospital."

"No." Emma's eyes opened, red and hollow, bloody tears streaming down her cheeks. Her voice was hardly more than a croak. "I am stopping this now. Today."

"You can't," said Roman. He stroked her hair.

Vain swallowed through the lump in her throat.

"I can't let this go on." Emma pushed herself away and sat up. Vain didn't know where her strength came from. The whole plan seemed so foolish now.

"Are we…" Roman licked his lips. "Are we going to die?"

"Probably," said Emma. "The power… the power here is too complete. Too total. Too wild." She coughed and spat blood onto the dirt floor. "There won't be anything for the Padlock to revive."

They would die. Vain never considered it, but once Emma said it out loud, the full weight crushed her. She put her head in her hands. Roman arranged himself cross-legged on the cold brick floor, facing her. The three of them, weary and battered, sat in a circle.

Vain was ready. Her life hadn't worked out the way she expected, and she realized, to her surprise, that knowing she would die gave her relief. No more running. She could do it.

Her heart ached for Roman, not for herself. She had sworn to protect him and, instead, she brought him there. There was no other way, though. He smiled at her with real warmth and her heart broke. He didn't blame her for killing him.

"I know you don't like touching, Vain," he said. "But if this is our last moment on earth I wanted to—"

She was crying, the first sob erupting from her like a cork out of a champagne bottle, letting free all the emotions she kept cradled so close to her. She threw herself at him and hugged him with one arm, soaking her wet tears into his neck.

After a startled pause, he hugged her back, his arms circling her tiny frame. It was wonderful. It was safe, and it was warm, and it was wonderful. Why hadn't she ever done that before? She cried into his neck and hugged him as hard as she could.

"I love you, Vain," he said, squeezing her.

"I love you too, Roman. Thank you for being my friend." She wanted to hug him forever, but they needed to move. She drew back and wiped her face. He was crying, too. Beside them, Emma's face was a blank, dull slate.

"I'm starting." Without waiting for an answer, Emma started.

The weight of it smothered her. Emma shivered, a horrible tremor as her body failed, unable to keep up with the strain of pulling that much energy.

"Please," Emma said, with no inflection. "Now. I can't keep this. I have so much energy in me, it needs to go."

"Lie down, Emma," Vain said. There was no way for Emma to grab the Padlock, not with her hands as broken as they were. She lifted Emma's shirt and placed it against her stomach. Roman placed a single finger on the base and Vain touched the lock. They were ready.

Emma closed her eyes, and the air became oppressive and heavy. It took on physical weight, and it came crashing down. Emma was packing the room with energy.

"God." Roman's eyes were wide. "Even I can feel that. How much are you taking?"

"All of it." Tears streamed down Emma's cheeks. "It has to be now."

"I thought of a good closing line," said Vain. "It's the end of the world as we know it. And I feel-"

The world exploded.

Epilogue

What happened next.

Trick was wrong.

They didn't destroy the world, but they broke a large portion of it. The Earthquake that struck Nevada registered 8.4 on the Richter scale, the largest in that State's history. While there was substantial damage to surrounding buildings, surprisingly few people were killed. Seismologists rushed the airwaves to breathlessly recite facts about topography and planetary crusts, attempting to balance between dry science and giddy exuberance from being on the news.

Later, Vain shook her head at the theories about what caused such a large and unexpected quake. Only she knew the truth. Emma dislodged the Hotel, sending it careening through space and time, and, like kicking a pebble down a mountain, it disrupted a few rocks along the way. Simple.

The twins, Mark, and Charm had been driving up highway 93, heading North and East towards New York when the quake hit. It swerved them off the road and Blunt whacked his head hard on the side of the window. Vain felt bad about that but was happy it was the only injury.

This time, she did not transport to Boston, and she experienced no small measure of relief about that. They all ended up in the compound that housed the Portal, some twelve hours after the earthquake hit. The building was still standing, although there were cracks in the walls and plaster dust hung in the air.

Emma was, surprisingly, not dead. The Padlock had done what it was made to do, despite the unprecedented release of energy. It even healed them, fixing the horrific damage done to Emma's body during the final battle. She tried to shake Emma awake, but she only mumbled "sleepy" and swatted Vain's hand away. Aside from being exhausted, Emma seemed healed. Roman, too. After taking some time to recalibrate, they were all able to stand and walk themselves out.

The Portal itself was destroyed, now a broken frame in the middle of a warehouse. The glowing doorknob was nowhere to be seen, although she thought she spotted a doorknob-shaped bulge in Emma's pocket. Vain didn't care; it would be broken beyond repair and if Emma wanted a souvenir, she was welcome to it.

Vain didn't know why they weren't beamed further away. Roman thought it was because there were three of them, and the Padlock ran out of energy to take them any significant distance. It was open and harmless again; back to an ordinary padlock made of ordinary metal, cold to the touch and drained.

In retrospect, they should have told the twins to wait for them, because they soon realized they were stranded in the middle of Nevada with no car. None of them had expected to survive, though. Not really. That was the truth of it. They all genuinely had expected to die, so it's not like they spent a lot of time planning what came after.

Fortunately for them, there were a few of those ugly red SUVs behind the building and they found the keys to one of them. Emma fell asleep almost immediately, lying across both back seats with her hands tucked underneath her head. It fell to Roman to drive. Although Vain was exhausted, she rolled down the window and let the dry Nevada air blow in her hair while she turned her face to the sunlight.

She felt like that day was the first day of her real escape from the Hotel.

"I can't believe that worked," Roman eventually said.

"Charm and I used to talk about what it would take to destroy the Hotel," Vain said. Her mind raced with the actuality of what they'd done, and her words tripped over themselves in an effort to get out. "She thought it was impossible. Even with all the bombs in all the worlds, she didn't think it would work. She thought blowing up the Hotel would be like trying to blow up time or gravity. The Hotel just is. The Portal though… she always thought that could work. I never would have dreamed it without her putting the idea in my head."

"Patience saved us the first time, and Charm saved us the second."

"Emma sure pulled a lot of energy," Vain said, a laughable understatement.

"Yeah."

They both chewed on that sentence for a bit.

"Roman." She bit her bottom lip. "Does Emma scare you? What she can do?"

Roman didn't answer right away; he frowned like he did when he was thinking big thoughts. "What Emma can do scares me, I guess. But Emma doesn't. I can't make myself fear Emma."

"Do you like her?" Vain asked in a small voice. She didn't expect to ask that, and the answer terrified her.

"I think I do," he said. "But it doesn't mean anything for us. Whether I like Emma or not, you and I are still us."

They took five days to drive to New York, taking their time along the way. They arrived a day behind the others. During the drive, Emma didn't say more than two words; she existed in her own bubble of thoughts. Roman tried to joke her out of her somber silence, but nothing seemed to work. On day three, at a rest stop outside Illinois, Emma went to the washroom and Roman confided how concerned he was.

"Nothing is working," he said. "You've seen how she is. She doesn't make eye contact, she doesn't laugh, all she does is stare out the window."

"You have to give her time, Roman. She is dealing with the realization that she's the most powerful human on Earth. Maybe on every Earth. That has to take a little bit to wrap your head around."

"We can help her, if she'd talk to us."

Vain laughed at that. Roman looked annoyed and she rested her hand on his. "Roman, I know you're impatient," she said gently. "But you and I are like babies trying to teach a professional boxer a thing or two about punching. Emma could destroy entire cities if she wanted to. If she decided that Chicago would look better as a smoking crater in the ground, I don't think there's a damn thing either of us could do about it."

"All the more reason to talk about it, then."

"Leave it be, Roman."

For her part, Vain had never felt so unencumbered. The muscles in her shoulder no longer clenched involuntarily when she couldn't see every exit route. She laughed more easily. She talked more. She was free.

Roman, being Roman, saw a new problem to fix in Emma and was increasingly agitated at his inability to do so. Vain was content to let things play out. She had all the time in the world now. Maybe Emma would ultimately be a problem. Maybe one day Emma would need to be stopped, or at least reined in, if she showed any inclination to becoming a new Arthur; but that was future Vain's problem. Present Vain was happy to enjoy the sunlight and see what the day had to offer.

When they arrived in New York, the first thing she did was hug Charm. Apparently, Vain was a hugger, now. She wasn't even ashamed of showing her emotions in front of everyone. Roman put his arm around her and she let him. She experienced a further release of the intolerable pressure that had built on her over the years.

Emma stayed for a bit, and the emotions and tears and reunion seemed to bring her back to herself a little. The day after, she seemed more like the Emma of old; the charmingly awkward girl who babbled too much when she was nervous. She and Roman spent time together by themselves, and the next day Emma announced she was going back to Boston. There were hugs and promises of staying in touch. Emma needed space to put her life back together.

Before she left, they had a moment to talk.

"This never goes away, does it?" Emma asked.

"No. It's a part of you now and you're going to be like this forever."

"What do I do now? Going back to school, getting a job, it all seems so pointless. There are entire other worlds out there."

"I think, for the next year, you don't do anything. You go back to Boston, you get your shit together, and you let this settle in."

Emma didn't respond. They sat in companionable silence.

"I'd like it, I think, if Roman visited me," she said, eventually.

"I know." Vain's heart barely hurt at all to say it. "He'd like to see you too."

"Is this the part where you warn me that if I break his heart, you'll track me down and hurt me?"

"I can protect Roman from a lot of things, but I don't think I can protect him from you. He wouldn't let me, anyway."

"Or, you'll be too busy with Mark?" Emma gave her a slight grin and Vain blushed. Now it was her turn to be silent.

"I'm sorry I did this to you," Vain said. "I didn't know any of this would happen."

Emma nodded. "I can't say I'm glad I met you. Not yet. Maybe I will someday, but now… I need time."

Vain understood.

Without the pressure of Trick and the Wyatts, Mark wasn't needed anymore. He also left, although not before he and Vain had the coffee she promised. It was wonderful and strange. Dating and relationships were so far off her radar, she was goofy and awkward through the whole thing, unsure how to act. Still, he seemed to have a nice time, and he laughed at her dumb jokes. "Give me time", she said, and he promised to do just that.

Eventually, it was her and Roman and Charm and the twins; the remaining five who had started out together as six, some of whom barely liked each other, thrown together by a shared goal. They were her family now.

She didn't worry about the next day. She relished living in the moment, with no pressure, no plans, nothing to run from. At some point, she'd have to worry about the future. She and Roman would need to figure out what having a life meant. Also, there was still a whole bunch of Wyatts trapped on their side of the Portal. Arthur would try to find a way back to their Earth.

But, for that day, for an hour, for each minute, she was happy to let the river of life carry her in its currents. No more struggling to steer the raft, no more caring where she ended up. No more anger.

She was content.

The End.

Acknowledgments

No one writes a book by themselves.

More accurately, everyone writes books by themselves, but they lean on the support and strength from those around them to get them over the finish line. The original idea for this book was about a man that carries two sticks and when he pounds them on the ground, dwarves pop out and go crazy and kill everyone. It was going to be called "Knock, knock: Dwarf Murder" and, in retrospect, that's probably the book I should have written.

Anyway, there's a whole bunch of people who helped me get through this and put up with me as I hammered away at the story and figured out what writing a book is all about.

Of course, Brady, who listened patiently, gave feedback through the whole process and was always there to help with feedback or do early reads of unpolished drafts.

Tons of thanks to Yvette, who mostly wanted to grab a coffee and complain about work, but for a solid year found herself drawn into dumb conversations about whether Vain would rather punch the Wyatts in the dick or in the neck. Thanks.

And of course, thanks to all my beta readers, who gave feedback that shaped the final book – Kinch, Carolyn, Mom, Phil, you guys are all the best.

Special thanks to my editor and friend, Alex Woodroe, without whom this book wouldn't exist. I mean, technically I did write it without her, so it would exist, but not quite in the state it is now. Alex – your unflagging support and cheerleading and suggestions made me a better writer. Thanks you for all your help to make this book the best it could be. You are incredible at what you do. I can't thank you enough.

Manufactured by Amazon.ca
Bolton, ON

20245472R00129